Boystown Heartbreakers

KC Carmichael

Text copyright © 2024 by **KC Carmichael**

Cover Illustration © **Cover Ever After**
Distributed by **Blackstone Publishing**

ISBN: 978-1-998076-02-4
Ebook: 978-1-998076-03-1

FIC027250   FICTION / Romance / Romantic Comedy
FIC027190   FICTION / Romance / LGBTQ+ / Gay
FIC027020   FICTION / Romance / Contemporary

#BoystownHeartbreakers

Follow Rising Action on our socials!
Twitter: @RAPubCollective
Instagram: @risingactionpublishingco
Tiktok: @risingactionpublishingco

To anyone who's ever worked a day behind the chair

BOYSTOWN
Heartbreakers

CHAPTER 1

I n the city of Chicago, walk-in closets are a rarity, and in Boystown, they are purely a myth. It's not uncommon for a single person of means to live in a two-bedroom apartment only to use the smaller of the two spaces as a place to hang their clothes and display their shoes. Bastian doesn't have this problem. He had managed to stumble upon the one great unicorn of Chicago living—a legend that most believe to be as realistic as Bigfoot or a long-term commitment found on Grindr—a studio apartment with a walk-in closet, complete with shelving and two tiers of hanging rods. The enormity of the closet was enough to make Bastian overlook the tiny kitchen and its lack of cabinet space, to let go of his dream of having a legitimate lakefront view, and to look past the fact that his little corner of heaven was located right outside the building's sole elevator. These were worthy sacrifices for having a proper place to hang his clothes.

It wasn't until he moved in that he discovered his favorite detail about the closet. Written on the side of the doorframe, in a place the landlord would indeed never find, was a shared list created by all the previous inhabitants for at least a decade. In five different scripts, the past occupants and now Bastian have kept a running tally of those who have broken their hearts, the men who are no longer worth their time and effort. It's a very long list. One man, Raheem Wallace, appears on this list three times—even Bastian fell victim to him.

But as Bastian steps into his beloved closet to prepare for his date with Ryan Andrews tonight, he runs his fingers down the list of "Boystown Heartbreakers" and scoffs at it. He and Ryan have been going strong for six months now, and it's starting to feel permanent. He's confident that this list ends with Raheem Wallace's last appearance. Ryan is not going to make this list; Bastian is sure of it. He feels it in his heart as he steps out of his shorts and steps into his favorite pair of fashionably ripped, dark grey skinny jeans. He shrugs on a simple, lightweight black cashmere sweater and tucks it into his pants. He then grabs his best pair of patent leather Gucci loafers bought on clearance and slides them onto his feet. With a final spin in front of the mirror and a quick tug of his meticulously styled, caramel curls away from his brow, he's ready, sure that Ryan will devour him faster than the noodles they're about to eat in their preferred corner booth at Joy's.

He snaps a picture of himself in the mirror, filters it to make him look more ethereal, and adds a song track, "I Wanna Be Adored" by the Stone Roses, then hits post to his Instagram story. It's not up for fifteen seconds before his mother calls him, interrupting his ability to watch in real-time as his friends, clients, and lurkers check out his post.

"Hey, Mom," he says as he answers, a sigh in his voice. If he doesn't answer, she'll call him again in another hour. She's eager for any updates he might have on his love life. Not that he minds. His mom's unending support for him and all he does is something to be grateful for. He tucks his phone between his ear and his shoulder, grabs his keys with one hand, and shuts the closet light off with the other. "I'm running out the door. Can I call you later?"

"Sure, love," she says, her voice as bright as always. "I only wanted to tell you that you look very handsome tonight. A total catch. I hope that Ryan appreciates how stunning you are."

"Mom!" Bastian's face burns. "I don't look handsome. Ryan is the handsome one. I'm the funny, steal-the-show one in this relationship."

"While you are funny, Sebastian, you're handsome as well. Ryan better know how lucky he is."

"He does." Bastian steps out of his apartment and locks the door.

"Good. And your father and I are looking forward to finally meeting him this weekend. Six months is far too long for you to date someone I haven't met yet."

"I'm thirty. I don't need your approval on the men I date."

"Maybe not, but it's my right as your mother to make sure your heart is in good hands." Without even being in front of her, it's not hard to imagine she's pursing her lips, waiting for his response.

"Well, it is. You don't need to worry." He huffs and runs down the front steps of his building's entrance hall.

"What about Andres, dear?"

"What about Andres?" he asks, turning to head down the sidewalk.

"Has he met Ryan?"

"Of course he's met Ryan! Andres is my best friend."

"No need to get huffy. I'm simply curious about this man you spend all your time with."

Bastian rolls his eyes. "Look, Mom, I really gotta go. I'll call you tomorrow between clients, alright?"

"Alright, dear. Have fun tonight! Make smart choices."

"Don't I always?" he says. He often doesn't, but his mom certainly doesn't need to know that.

"Yes, you do, dear." She giggles. "Now, have a nice time tonight. Talk to you tomorrow."

"Alright," he says and hangs up the phone, then picks up his pace as he walks down Aldine to get to Broadway and then his date destination.

He weaves his way through the small crowds of people already beginning to form on the sidewalks outside the eateries, bars, and nightclubs as the sun starts to dip out of view to the west. For a Monday, it's quite crowded. Still, considering it's late April and the weather has finally broken with the temperature reaching seventy degrees, Bastian is not surprised to see his fellow Chicagoans milling about outside after a long winter holed up in their apartments. Like him, the inhabitants of Boystown likely missed the sidewalk patios for eating and drinking, the rainbow Art Deco pillars that denote the main thoroughfare's neighborhood lines, and the vibrant personalities hanging out of the apartment windows that overlook it all. He might be a bit of a homebody, but Chicago is a city to enjoy and explore, no matter how long you've lived here, and Bastian has been itching to go out. Perhaps, even though he has to work tomorrow and has a full book of eight clients scheduled to sit in his chair at the salon, he can talk Ryan into stopping at Roscoe's for a drink before they go back to Ryan's for a tumble in his sheets.

The enticing smell of garlic and ginger hangs in the air of the dimly lit restaurant as he enters. Bastian finds Ryan tapping away on his phone and sitting by the window instead of in the back like they usually would. With spring having thawed winter thoroughly today, a seat by the window will be a nice change.

"Hey," he says as he sits. "Sorry, I'm late."

Ryan holds up one finger but doesn't look up from his phone.

"Sorry." Bastian winces and looks around. Ryan is already halfway through his drink, even though Bastian technically wasn't late at all. He only apologized out of courtesy for having kept Ryan waiting. Now it's Bastian's turn to wait. Ryan is preoccupied, his brow furrowed, as he looks down at his phone and continues to type away. Bastian catches their server's attention and signals he'd like a glass of the white wine that Ryan's been drinking.

Finally, Ryan puts his phone down.

"Rough day at work?" Bastian asks, trying to dissipate the tension that is circling in the air around them.

Ryan shrugs and takes a sip of his wine. He looks out the window, his face completely unreadable.

"What can I get for you?" their server asks as she places Bastian's wine glass in front of him on the dark wood table. He's quick to grab it and takes a very large gulp.

"I'll take an order of the Pad Woon Sen," Ryan demands and then chugs what's left of his wine. "And another one of these."

Their server nods, then looks at Bastian expectantly. "And for you?"

"The Bai-Tong Noodles, please," he says, hoping to make up for Ryan's brusqueness.

She smiles at him, tucks her notepad into her apron, and walks away to place their orders.

"What's got your briefs in a bunch?" Bastian asks, unable to hold back his annoyance.

"Nothing. I'm fine."

Bastian takes another sip of his wine. "You're not acting fine."

"It's been a long day, is all." Ryan sighs, then adds, "You know some of us actually work on Mondays. We can't just lounge in our apartments all day."

"Hey, that's not fair," Bastian says, sitting more upright in his seat, his brows furrowing. "This is *my* weekend. I hope you remember that the next time you're sleeping in on a Saturday, and I'm knee-deep in rich women needing their roots touched up."

Ryan rolls his eyes and grabs the glass of wine out of their server's hand as she delivers it. "As if gossiping in the salon all day is stressful."

"And you think you have it hard sitting at your desk all day?" Bastian challenges. He knows damn well that most of Ryan's day at the advertising firm is spent shooting Nerf guns at his cubicle mates.

"Harder than your day dolling people up and reading centaur porn with the girls in the backroom between clients." Ryan smirks, and his eyes lose their hard glint.

"Those novels are titillating." Bastian laughs and is relieved to hear Ryan chuckle with him. It seems the centaur porn novels serve their purpose of providing a much-needed comedic release at this restaurant table as they do in the salon's breakroom. Nothing else cures the headache of having talked a client off the ledge when they freak out after seeing themselves with the bangs they insisted he cut on them for the first time.

"If you say so." Ryan takes another sip of his drink.

"You know, I'd be glad to read them out loud to you after a hard day if you'd like," Bastian offers with a sly grin.

"No thanks." Ryan chuckles again. "I'm not sure centaur porn is gonna do it for me."

"There was that great one with the Kraken, and I have a minotaur one arriving at the salon sometime this week."

"I can't believe you waste your money on those."

"It's a collective purchase. We all chip in a dollar out of our tips. Besides, it's in good fun."

"If the salon's clients only knew that their stylists were so depraved."

"Trust me, honey," Bastian says, fixing Ryan with his best stone-faced stare. "It's the clients that are the shocking ones. You know I got propositioned to go to another swingers' party last week?"

"Which client?" Ryan asks. "That hot lawyer guy?"

"Oh god, no!" Bastian sits forward in his seat, happy they have settled into their usual playful banter. "He's so deep in the closet I'd die of shock if he invited me out for a cup of coffee, let alone that sort of thing. This was from that Susan Williams woman, the one who's married to the WGN exec."

"She knows you're gay, right?"

"Of course she does." Bastian rolls his eyes. "And it wasn't for her that she was inviting me. I guess she's made some hall pass deal with her husband, who's looking to experiment. Needless to say, I'll be avoiding that," he waves his hands wildly, "situation thoroughly."

"Your clients are so weird," Ryan says as their server places their food on the table.

Bastian thanks her and orders them another round of drinks, then turns his attention back to Ryan as he picks up his chopsticks. "Anyway, you don't have to worry, my dear. I only have eyes for you."

Ryan takes a bite and lets out a sigh. He starts jabbing at his food with his sticks. "About that, Bastian."

"About what?"

"About you only having eyes for me."

"Yeah?" Bastian bites at his lower lip again, the air around them shifting to something less comfortable.

"Maybe you shouldn't rule everything out."

"Why shouldn't I? Is this not working for you?"

Ryan takes another bite, then places his chopsticks down and swallows his food with a sip of his wine. "It's just ... this," he gestures between them, "is great and all. But with summer coming, I don't want to be tied down. I want to explore my options."

Bastian pauses, his chopstick-holding hand frozen over his noodles. "Are you breaking up with me?"

Ryan shrugs.

"In front of my noods!"

"Please don't freak out, Bastian. It's nothing personal."

"Nothing personal! You were supposed to meet my parents this weekend!"

"You know how it is." Ryan shrugs again. "In the winter, we pair off and get all domestic and cozy, but when summer comes, well, it's time to shed our clothes and have fun. And I can't have fun if I'm always attached to you."

Bastian places his chopsticks on the table. "Excuse me, but I'm a helluva a good time."

"You are. But I need to have a different good time this summer."

Bastian picks up his drink and swallows what's left in one big gulp. "Fuck you, Ryan." He rises from his seat, causing the legs of his chair to scrape against the wood floor, pulls two twenties out of his wallet that he drops onto the table, then leaves with his head held high. Until he steps out the door and lets his shoulders slump in defeat—yet another heartbreak.

Once back at his apartment, he approaches the doorframe. The pen dangles from the thick string held by a pushpin in the old hardwood frame. He takes it and looks at the names he's put on this list. Once he adds Ryan Andrews, he will officially take the lead as to who's had their heart broken the most. That's a title he doesn't want to hold but seems to be his lot in life. With a sigh, he uncaps the pen, then adds Ryan's name, taking deliberate care to form each letter clearly—yet another disappointment on the ever-growing list of Boystown Heartbreakers.

CHAPTER 2

that the object he adds these. And now, he will actually take the lead actor who's had their heart broken the most? That's rare, he does . . . ways to hold his . . . ms . . . he his fun in life. With a sigh, he . . . the . . . of . . . let's rise . . .

U pon waking the following day, Bastian shuffles from his bed to his kitchen counter. His eyes are bloodshot, and his hair is messy from tossing and turning all night. Once there, he grabs a coffee filter from the cabinet, places it in the cheap thirty-dollar machine, and adds a precisely measured amount of grounds. After adding the water, he sets his coffee pot to brew. He could have slept a little longer. His first client of the day isn't for another two hours, but even while nursing his latest heartbreak, he's unwilling to give up his peaceful morning routine.

Every workday starts the same. He wakes to an alarm set for eight a.m. and gets his coffee going. While that's brewing, he takes a shower. The steaming hot water mingling with the aromatic plum and bergamot scent of his shampoo and conditioner wakes him more fully, or at least helps him open his eyes enough so that he can see himself in the little mirror suction-cupped to the wall of his shower and give himself a close shave. From there, he towels off, moisturizes his face with two serums and a cream, styles his hair, then spritzes himself down with a dry oil spray—half for the way it keeps his skin supple, shiny, and smooth and half because he likes the way it smells. Besides, when one spends their entire day crowding others' personal space, it's best to smell enticing and friendly but not overpowering.

Now wrapped in his robe, he fixes himself a cup of coffee with a decadent splash of almond milk and opens up Spotify on his phone. He selects Joy Division's "Atmosphere" to reflect his dismal mood and lets the app's algorithm take it from there. With his coffee in hand and the appropriate soundtrack playing softly on his tiny Bluetooth speaker, he sits in his overstuffed reading chair by his wide bay window and takes a sip. He sets his coffee on the end table beside a picture of him with his parents and his childhood best friend, Andres Wood, taken the day Bastian was awarded his chair at Salon Azure Blue. He picks it up, his lips lifting into a half smile. He can't believe he's been working there for ten years. Then, grimacing, he remembers that he will have to call his mother and explain that dinner with Ryan this weekend will no longer be necessary. Placing the picture down and grabbing his phone, he opts to text her instead.

> *Good news. Turns out there's no reason for you to meet Ryan at all. We split. I'll call you later.*

He closes the message to his mother, knowing that he will purposefully forget to call her later as he's not in the mood for her advice or coddling. Next, he opens the salon's employee app and checks his client schedule for the day. Fully booked. It's rare that Bastian isn't already booked out three weeks in advance and even rarer if Oliver at the front desk bothered to schedule him a lunch break, which he didn't do for today. Bastian will have to make do with something quick and easy to eat while an assistant is shampooing one of his clients.

He glances back over the list. Luckily, Andres is his two o'clock. If he texts him now, maybe he can sweet-talk him into bringing him lunch from one of his restaurants, preferably Graze, as their menu has the most vegetarian options.

> Hey! Lunch in exchange for an extra-long head message?

Andres, as always, is quick to reply even though he probably should be sleeping. The man works until all hours of the night, yet he never fails to answer Bastian's texts, no matter how whiney.

> Depends. Which head are we talking about?

Bastian practically spits out his coffee with a laugh.

> Whichever one will get you to bring me a black bean burger and fries.

> Food in return for sexual favors. How scandalous of you. What would Ryan say?

14

Bastian frowns.

> Nothing. We broke up.

> His loss. You can do better.

> Thanks. And you're right!

He hits send despite the fact he doesn't believe it.

Contrary to the evidence presented by his behavior on their final date last night, Ryan was the best man Bastian had ever dated. Sure, he wasn't the most attentive of boyfriends and spent most of his time on his phone. And yes, he couldn't cook worth a damn and had an unfortunate aversion to eating ass, but on paper, he looked great. He was mid-thirties, head of his team in the print advertising division of *The Nerdery*, owned a small condo on the lakefront, and drove a brand-new Prius.

> Seriously Bastian. You can do better. I'll see you in a bit.

Bastian rolls his eyes and leaves him on read. Andres has never liked any of Bastian's boyfriends. Not a single one. Bastian didn't expect him to have a kind word about Ryan, but it would be nice if Andres would admit that Bastian wasn't that much of a catch. It's one thing for his mother always to tell him that he deserves better—she's his mother, and that's her job. But his best friend could at least be honest and objective with him. Bastian just turned thirty in March and has nothing to his name except

15

a twelve-hundred-dollar pair of shears and a designer wardrobe purchased mostly on off-season clearance. Sure, he can cook—a skill formed from making inventive struggle meals throughout his late teens and early twenties when apprenticing and building his clientele—but beyond that and being able to provide any potential partner a free haircut whenever they wish, he doesn't have much to bring to the table. Yet, here Andres is, once again reminding him that he can do better.

Bastian blows a puff of air through his lips, then chugs what's left of his coffee before he rises from his reading chair and pours himself a second mug. He takes it into his closet with him to mull over his wardrobe. Outside of Andres, his clients for the day consist of one high-powered female attorney, two trust-fund kids attending Columbia College who always book tandem appointments, and one bartender. Then it's Sharon Clark, head of Chicago Public Schools, who he has to book for an extra hour of time—that he's not compensated for—because she will inevitably find no less than four individual highlights out of place. This is a day to dress for comfort, not flash, so he chooses a pair of simple black trousers that hug his ass nicely and a gray chenille sweater to match his mood. From there, he grabs his low-top Nike blazers, a gift from Andres, who swore up and down that they were the best shoes for standing on your feet all day. He wasn't wrong, and every time Bastian wears them to the salon, he says a little prayer to the hair gods that his boss doesn't notice what they are.

Despite being sleek and stylish for a gym shoe, utterly devoid of the telltale swoosh, simply holding Nike's brand name denoting them as sneakers is enough for them to be put on the no-go list as far as Salon Azure Blue's dress code is concerned. But today, he doesn't care and slips them on as he checks the time on his phone. He better get moving if he's going to catch the next Redline train heading south towards the Loop.

Located in River North, across the street from the Merchandise Mart—a beacon of the Chicago design and fashion world—sits Salon Azure Blue. For most hair stylists, it's *the* goal place to work. The neighborhood is trendy and full of money, and all "L" train lines have a stop within walking distance of the salon's front door. Though it takes up the top two floors of an old but well-maintained three-story Greystone, the salon itself is relatively small. It's only large enough to hold twelve very coveted workstations that the salon's two assistants, Bethany and Lizzie, are gunning for when one becomes available. And Bastian has the absolute best station. From where he sits perched on the third-floor windowsill next to his workstation, he can see Andres Wood circling the block on his motorcycle—an all-black Softail Harley—searching for the perfect place to park where he can shirk the meter. The bike's engine rumbles as it cruises by, sending Bastian's favorite assistant, Bethany, to his side.

"Did I hear Andres?" she asks as if she doesn't know that Andres is Bastian's two o'clock. The whole staff knows. They've been doing a countdown all day, and each of the assistants has attempted to bribe Bastian so they can shampoo the long-haired god of a man.

"Maybe." Bastian winks at her. "Can you beat Lizzie's offer of her chocolate chip cookie?"

"You mean carob chip cookie?" she says with a smirk.

"Ew." Bastian grimaces.

"I have a brownie in my purse you can have."

"Fine, you can shampoo him. But you should know that I've already bartered him for lunch in exchange for an extra-long head massage. So, make it count."

"Don't I always?" she says and checks herself out in Bastian's station's mirror, artfully swooping her fringe and pulling at the hem of her shirt to tighten it up and elongate the V-neck.

"Barking up the wrong tree, girl!" he teases and hops off the windowsill. "Andres has zero interest in dating anyone."

Laura laughs from her station beside Bastian's. She's a sun-kissed blonde with beach waves and Bastian's second closest friend after Andres. "What he means to say," she interjects while parting her client's hair, "is that Andres only has interest in dating *one* specific person."

"For the thousandth time, Laura." Bastian rolls his eyes. "No matter how much you and your fiancé dream about your respective groomsmen—"

"Men of honor," Laura corrects.

"Whatever, 'men of honor,'" he amends as he shoos Bethany away to greet Andres at the front desk and bring him upstairs, "we're not going to date. We're friends. That's it."

"I don't see how that's relevant," Laura says. She makes eye contact with her client through the mirror. "Watch these two idiots with me while I touch up your balayage, will you?"

"Gladly," Laura's client answers, clearly eager for a bit of salon drama as if it's a daytime television show. Which, in some ways, it is. Supplying clients with beautiful hair colors and a silhouette they can recreate at home is only half the job. The other half is putting on a show, one that each client believes they are the only ones privy to. And now Laura, no doubt tired of recapping wedding planning details to her clients for the fifth hour in a row, has passed the job of entertaining her current client over to Bastian. It's fine. Andres and his rugged good looks are enough to distract anyone from their own boring lives for an hour.

"Thanks." Bastian mouths to Laura, who winks in return and goes back to sectioning her client's hair into quarters.

"Can I get you anything to drink?" Bethany asks Andres as she leads him to Bastian's chair.

"Just water, please," Andres says in his baritone voice as he places a paper-handled bag stamped 'Graze' onto Bastian's workstation, then sits.

"Bastian." Marny, who works kitty-corner from him, shuts off her blow dryer and catches his eyes through the mirror. "Do you think you could open the window by you?" She fans herself with her free hand, causing the fringe of her heavily layered shag to flutter. "It suddenly got hot in here."

Bastian narrows his eyes at her, and she has the nerve to stick her tongue out at him. She's a lesbian, not even attracted to Andres, and she's stirring up drama. It works, as all the eyes in the room covertly find some way to check out the tall, broad man who has arrived.

"I've got it," Andres says, reaching over with one hand and opening the window a few inches. A cool spring breeze blows across the room.

"Thank you," Bastian says as he lets Andres's hair out of the messy knot that was securing the long, dark, wavy lengths at the crown of his head. Andres has every stylist's dream head of hair; it's easily shapeable and requires minimal effort to maintain. He ruffles the strands with his fingers and scratches lightly at Andres's scalp. "Am I only trimming you today?"

"Yeah," Andres agrees, relaxing into Bastian's touch. His shoulders soften, and he slouches slightly in the chair. "However much you think it needs, so long as I can still pull it back for work."

"No problem," Bastian says. He keeps his fingers in Andres's hair, idly massaging around the backs of his ears, and turns his attention to Bethany. "He's feeling a bit dry. Use the Hydrate Wash and Rinse on him, please, and comb it through the ends before you rinse out."

"Yes, sir," Bethany says, nodding. Her smile accentuates her high, round cheekbones.

"Hey!" Andres protests. "This wasn't part of the deal we made earlier."

"Sure it is! Food in exchange for a long head massage," Bastian says, pulling his fingers away from Andres's hair. "Bethany gives an amazing scalp massage."

"Then I guess *Bethany* is going to have an equally amazing black bean burger and fries for lunch today." Andres smiles at her, and Bastian is pretty sure he sees her knees temporarily give out.

"You wouldn't dare," Bastian says, bringing a hand to his chest. He knows damn well that Andres would never rescind his lunch, but that's never going to stop him from laying it on thick.

"Fine, I won't give your lunch away," Andres relents with what looks to be a faint blush rising up his bronze cheeks. It's out of place on Andres, who is nearly impossible to ruffle. "But only if you agree to come by Graze tonight after your last client."

Bastian feels the entire room's worth of eyes and ears on him. Marny has even turned her client diagonally to have a direct line of sight on Bastian and Andres. Silence, outside of the 'snip, snip'

21

of Marny's texturizing shears and the salon's "focus flow" playlist, has befallen the room.

"Alright, deal," Bastian says and grabs the bag containing his lunch. "But you're paying for my Uber to get home tonight. There's no quick way by train to get to Boystown from the West Loop."

"I wouldn't have it any other way," Andres says, his tone reassuring as he rises from his seat and follows Bethany out of the room and into the darkened shampoo area, away from all the hubbub.

Bastian follows behind them and catches Laura saying to her client as he walks past, "See what I mean?"

CHAPTER 3

'*See what I mean.*' Bastian internally scoffs for what has to be the one-hundredth time today as Laura's smug voice replays in his brain, apparently living there rent-free. Laura doesn't know what she's talking about. Sure, she may be Bastian's other best friend outside of Andres, but she doesn't understand the complexity of their friendship. They've known each other since they were five, having met on the first day of kindergarten. Bastian, terrified of school and shy, had been convinced he'd never make a friend despite his mother's reassurance. Yet, on the first day of school, Andres offered him a hand as they lined up to be assigned an animal-themed seat on the giant round rug in their classroom. To his delight, he and his new outgoing friend were seated next to each other, where they would sit criss-cross applesauce for the year's entirety of seated lessons.

They've been side by side ever since, experiencing life's triumphs and tragedies together—from Bastian's dad losing his job and no longer being able to afford Bastian's educational track through private schools to the slow and arduous process of watching Andres's younger brother Julian fade away due to childhood leukemia. Their bond as friends is so deep that Bastian supposes it's easy for an outsider like Laura to mistake it for something more than what it is. She's so starry-eyed right now as she plans her wedding to, coincidentally, Andres's business partner, that all she sees is love matches everywhere. Bastian and Andres are just friends, no matter how much Laura and the rest of the salon gossips would like them to be more than that.

"See what I mean," he mutters again as he pulls open the wide front door of Graze, located at the corner of Randolph and Green Street. His grumbling is hushed the moment he steps inside the cavernous space filled with warm wood furniture, greenery, and tabletop candles. For a Tuesday, the restaurant is pretty jam-packed with fashionable hipsters and other trendy twenty-and-thirty-somethings who can drink on a weeknight and still function the next day. Bastian is damn proud to be a part of that demographic still, even if he is not financially on par with the bulk of Graze's patrons. He recognizes some diners as clients of the salon; they only vaguely acknowledge his presence as he walks by. He tries not to let their dismissal ruffle his feathers. It's part of what makes him a good hairstylist, having the ability to be bright-eyed and bushy-tailed with his perfectly coiffed curls despite the circumstances, heartbreaks, or hangovers. The show must go on, no matter how shitty one feels.

Though now that Bastian is at Graze—the second of Andres and Justin's restaurants, the first being a gourmet, five-star French-fusion hot spot called Partager that has an attached coffee shop, Brew, located two blocks west of the salon—he can put a symbolic pause on the Bastian show. The channel has been changed from the Today Show with your host, Bastian Russo, to Late Night with Andres Wood. This is a far more dimly lit studio, with better music and the cacophony of cocktail shakers to set the beat.

"Bastian! Over here!" Andres calls from the front corner of the restaurant's bar. Andres often parks himself there, as it has the best vantage point to see all the goings-on inside. His attention turns back to the server who is batting her eyelashes at him.

Bastian nods his chin in acknowledgment at Andres and walks over to the high-backed wooden barstool that Andres is patting. Once beside him at the bar, Bastian accepts Andres's casual kiss on the cheek before sitting and ignores Laura's voice, screaming in his mind, 'See what I mean!' At least her speculation is occupying the brain space that otherwise would have been reserved for wallowing over Ryan.

"Jess, guests in your section are waiting," Andres reminds the server.

"I know," she says. "I wanted to see if you needed me."

"I do not," he says, and she heads on her way.

"Fraternizing with the staff again, huh?" Bastian asks once they are alone.

"Nah," Andres says and sits back down. "I won't be making that mistake again."

"Sticking strictly to customers now?" Bastian teases.

Andres shakes his head and laughs. "Do you want a drink?"

"Depends." Bastian raises an eyebrow at Andres. "What am I here for? Is this a friends having drinks visit, or are you going to make me tell you every detail about my breakup with Ryan?"

"I'm not going to make you tell me." Andres fidgets with the straw in his glass, swirling the ice, lemon, and lime wedges around. "But, I do know that if you don't tell at least one person the real version instead of the played-for-tips version the salon got all day, you'll be doomed to make the same mistakes again."

"Excuse you!" Bastian says half-heartedly. Andres isn't wrong. The version of events he gave his clients today had Bastian doing the breaking and not the other way around. Much better to showcase himself as strong and independent, which he is, than the poor, heartbroken, lonely soul that clients will twist him into. "And what mistakes are you implying that I made again?"

"Nothing major, really. "

"Nothing major?" Bastian repeats with suspicion while flipping through his mental catalog of what red flags Andres may have seen in Ryan that he warned Bastian about that Bastian likely ignored.

Andres holds up his right hand, all five fingers extended wide. With his left, he starts ticking through them as he lists. "Didn't know how to cook."

"That's not a deal-breaker."

"Listened to country."

"Orville Peck doesn't count as country."

"You know that's not all he listened to," Andres says. "He was from Texas, which is its own red flag."

"Being from Texas is not a red flag!"

"Says the guy who won't date anyone from Ohio."

Bastian, relaxing into their comfortable, playful banter, wrinkles his nose at Andres. "It's Ohio, gross."

"And I suggest you add Texas to that list too."

"Fine." Bastian pauses and brings two fingers to either side of his head. "'Texas' can be on the red flag list now. Are you happy? You've narrowed my dating options down to forty-eight states."

"Forty-eight plus Puerto Rico." Andres points out.

"I don't own enough Air Force Ones to date a Puerto Rican." Bastian flicks his eyes to the white sneakers with a small Puerto Rican flag embroidered on the sides of Andres's feet. A pristine pair of the exact shoes he mentioned.

"These are good work shoes!" Andres protests.

"Sure they are." Bastian laughs and flags the bartender down. "And I'm sure you don't have a pair of crusty, slip-on Vans in your office that you can step into in case you need to join the line in the kitchen if dinner service gets backed up."

Andres gestures back at his well-cared-for shoes. "These are limited edition!"

"You're not helping your case," Bastian says with his chin held high and his shoulders set back as the bartender arrives.

"What can I get you, doll?" she asks, dumping ice from four used glasses into one sink.

"Can I get a Black and Gold, please," he says.

She nods, then looks at Andres and grabs his glass, quickly filling it with more soda water from the gun, then squeezing and dropping new lemon and lime wedges inside.

"He's on me tonight," Andres answers her unspoken question when she places Andres's drink on the coaster in front of him.

"Invite me for a drink, but let me drink alone," Bastian says, tucking his chin towards his shoulder, knowing full well that Andres doesn't like to drink on the job, even when his job sometimes only involves keeping an eye on things from a corner seat at the bar until it's time to count the money. "I see how it is. If I didn't know you so well, I'd be suspicious."

"You couldn't be in safer company," Andres says.

"Exactly," Bastian agrees and internally chides Laura and her *See what I mean* in his head again. Andres is his best friend, and he'd never do anything to harm Bastian, including wanting to date him.

Bastian lifts his drink in cheers to Andres. "To friendship!" he says and clinks their glasses together.

"To friendship," Andres says without Bastian's gusto.

Ignoring Andres's lack of enthusiasm, Bastian takes a slow sip and sighs as he swallows.

"So, are you going to tell me what happened?" Andres asks over the rim of his glass.

"Fine," Bastian relents. "I'll give you the abridged version." He takes another sip of his cocktail and then places it down on the bar. Resting his elbow beside the drink, he lets his fist hold his head up and focuses his gaze on Andres. "It really wasn't anything major. Just ... you know, the usual winter has thawed, and so have my feelings for you bullshit."

"Ahh, yes. The 'I want to keep my options open for summertime fun' conundrum," Andres says. "We've heard that one before."

"Who's this *we*?" Bastian asks. "When has anybody ever used that line on you?"

Andres rightfully shrugs. For all the red flag talk and relationship advice he loves to spout off to Bastian, the man has never actually been in a relationship. Instead, he survives off of a plethora of one-night stands and friends-with-benefits arrangements from men and women alike. He makes it clear from the very start that their canoodling will not develop further than consolation pancakes at Bongo in the morning.

"Okay, touché," Andres says. "But that's not what I meant, and you know it."

"What did you mean?"

"Come on, Bastian." Andres rubs the back of his own neck. "How many of your ex-boyfriends have we sent to a metaphorical Mars so you can pretend that they don't exist after your heart gets broken?"

"All of them." Bastian narrows his eyes at Andres. "Besides, pretending my ex-boyfriends don't exist is self-care."

"Self-care, huh?"

"Yes." Bastian pauses, lifts his head off of his fist, and takes a very smug sip of his drink. "Not all of us can sleep around and have it not mean anything."

Andres looks away. "It'll mean something to me when it's with the right person."

"How would you know? Bed hopping isn't really putting yourself out there."

Andres turns back to look directly at Bastian again. "Hey, this was supposed to be about you, remember?"

"You're right. I'm sorry." Bastian takes a breath. "But I find it hard to believe that you know how I feel. It's not like you've ever been broken up with."

"Bastian," Andres says, his face looking pained. "I don't need a list ten names deep on my closet wall to know what heartbreak feels like."

Bastian's jaw drops. "I've only added seven names!"

"Which officially puts you in the lead now, doesn't it?"

"No." Andres raises one eyebrow. "Fine. It does. But that's not my fault."

"Don't play dumb, Bastian. You're smarter than this—"

"Says the boy who got to go to Fenwick for high school while I rotted away at OPRF." Bastian takes another sip of his drink.

"Had your father not gotten laid off, you could've gone to Fenwick with me. You got in," Andres says. "And not getting to go to Fenwick doesn't mean that you suddenly became any less smart. It's a shame you can't use that brain of yours to navigate the dating scene better."

"I'm a hopeless romantic." Bastian swallows what's left of his drink in one gulp. "What can I say?"

Andres signals the bartender to make another for Bastian. "You got it right with the hopeless part—but you need some help with the romance."

"And I suppose you think you're the one to help me with it," Bastian says, backing away slightly in his seat.

"Why can't I be?" Andres challenges. "I've known you since we were five. I've witnessed every iteration of Bastian that there has ever been for two and a half decades and loved them all equally. Who better for the job?"

"So, what do you want to be? My matchmaker?" Bastian asks as his next drink gets delivered. He quickly takes a sip, not quite sure he's comfortable with where this conversation is going. Especially as Laura's 'See what I mean' rings through his head again. She's always been forthright with her opinion that not only should Bastian and Andres date, but that Andres has been holding out for Bastian this whole time—no matter how hard Bastian has insisted that's not the case. Now, here he sits, his heart rate picking up, wondering if he's been wrong all along.

"I was thinking, maybe it's time for me and you to give dating a go?" Andres looks at Bastian's drink, then grabs it and takes a sip. "Quality control." His explanation is bullshit. They've entered territory they're both uncomfortable with or at least nervous about.

"Us?" Bastian laughs because he can't think of anything else to do, and he most certainly can't admit that Laura was right, for fuck's sake. Nor can he admit to himself that while Andres's offer is tempting and he has always harbored a bit of a crush on the man, risking their friendship has never been an option. Bastian isn't someone who can remain friends with an ex. He never has, and he never will be, and he most certainly can't handle the prospect of ever having to write his best friend's name on the closet list of Boystown Heartbreakers. That would be a heartbreak he'd never recover from. "Why would we give dating a go?"

Andres pulls out his bun, tussles his hair, and scratches at his scalp a bit, then hastily begins to knot it back up as he continues with his absurd idea. "Do you remember when we were twelve?"

"Of course."

"And you were being bullied relentlessly by that Evan Lackney kid."

"Ugh, yeah. And you beat the shit out of him for me," Bastian says, trying to deflect once again before Andres leads him into an even deeper place of vulnerability.

"And afterward," Andres continues right on. "You confessed to me that there was truth behind his teasing. That you were gay and liked boys, but you weren't ready for anybody to know that yet. And you were afraid I was going to hate you, and you were going to lose your best friend—"

"I didn't mean at the time that I wanted to date you."

"No." Andres shakes his head. "You didn't. But we did make an agreement."

"What agreement?" Bastian asks, biting his lip. An inkling of a memory creeps out of the recesses of his mind. He and Andres lying on his bedroom floor late one night, looking up at the multi-colored, plastic, glow-in-the-dark stars affixed to Bastian's ceiling. He can hear Andres's prepubescent voice speaking along with his smooth baritone now.

"You were scared that no one would ever love you if they knew the truth. And I told you that you were wrong. You doubted me, and I made you a promise that if you found yourself unloved in your thirties, I would have to marry you."

"And then we laughed uproariously at the ridiculousness of that statement." Inside Bastian's chest a burst of sentimental affection for his longtime friend blooms.

"Maybe so," Andres says, a hint of a smile playing across his lips. "But I think we might have been onto something."

"You think we should date? Or, more accurately, get married?"

"Maybe not married right away. But yeah, what's wrong with us trying to date and seeing where it goes?"

Bastian holds his hands up and sits more upright. "I can think of about a million things wrong with that."

"Name one."

"To start, what happens to our friendship if we don't work out?" Bastian chews some more at his lip. "We've already established that I can't remain friends with an ex." He tries to laugh. It's not convincing.

"Who says we won't work out? I already know your annoying habits and infuriating quirks, and you know mine."

"Do I ever," Bastian says around another sip of his drink.

"I think it's worth exploring."

"And worth risking our friendship over?"

"We've weathered worse things." Andres takes another small sip of Bastian's drink.

Bastian regards him thoughtfully. Andres is handsome for sure, so it's not as if he's not attracted to him. If he's being honest, Bastian has woken up on more than a handful of occasions with thoughts of Andres lingering in his mind. Andres has always felt like home to Bastian. Dating him, however, could upend their friendship, and then, if they didn't work out, where would that leave Bastian? In worse shape than he is today.

"Think about it, Bastian," Andres says with a gentle pat to Bastian's knee. "We can take things slow. There's no need to jump into anything. Know that the offer is on the table if you should decide to take it. If not, we carry on like we always have, hand in hand, without the kissing."

"Alright," Bastian says, not trusting himself not to screw this whole thing up. "I'll think about it. But I'm not giving you an answer today. And I want another one of these." He gestures at his drink; he needs to numb the feelings lingering inside of him. "And a plate of that potato gnocchi."

"As you wish," Andres says and signals for the bartender to come over yet again—Bastian resolves to give her the best tip possible for dealing with him tonight.

"Can we talk about something else now?" Bastian asks, hoping to salvage his evening with a bit of normalcy.

"Sure," Andres says. "How's your mom and dad?"

"Ugh. They're fine. Mom asks about you constantly."

"Of course she does," Andres says, a smirk playing across his lips that Bastian usually would enjoy. After their previous conversation, he wants to wipe it off his face.

"How are *your* parents?"

35

Andres's shoulders slump, and his chin drops toward his chest. "They're fine," he says and changes the subject. "We're hiring some new people at Brew. Let me know if the baristas can't get your coffee right."

"Will do. You know I love being able to play restaurant critic."

"I do." Andres pats him on the shoulder. "You helped us perfect the black bean burger recipe after all."

"Which I noticed you ordered for yourself." Bastian shimmies his shoulders proudly and takes a sip of his drink. "Any other new restaurant endeavors coming up?"

"Maybe. We'll see. Justin is a little preoccupied with his and Laura's wedding."

"Yeah, she's the same. The only thing she likes talking about more is me."

"Oh no, she didn't accidentally out your heartache to the boss, did she?"

"Thank god, no," Bastian says as their food arrives. "Even if she did, it's not like I'd get any sympathy from him. The only thing he cares about is making sure his little money-making machines, a.k.a. us stylists, keep raking in the dough for him."

"When are you going to quit that job?" Andres asks, then takes a bite of his burger.

"When Laura and I can afford to open up a place of our own."

"You know Justin and I can help you two with that."

Bastian frowns and takes a bite of his gnocchi, the taste of which has the perfect balance of garlic and cream. "I don't want your help."

"But Laura will be getting Justin's."

"It's different." Bastian cuts off Andres before he can argue. "And you know it."

"Fine," Andres says. He nudges Bastian's shoulder with his own. "How's your gnocchi?"

"Infuriatingly perfect." Bastian sighs as he swallows, then continues his meal in relative silence, trying not to let everything they discussed tonight ruin his free meal.

"Just like you," Andres says, jostling Bastian's shoulder again, causing Bastian to smile despite himself.

At the end of the night, Bastian and Andres step out of Graze.

"I'll get an Uber," Bastian says, attempting to brush Andres off as he loops an arm around Bastian's waist.

"Oh no," Andres says and holds Bastian a little firmer. His body is warm, sturdy and oh so easy for Bastian to relax into. Too easy. Bastian tries to pull away again—he can't let himself thoroughly enjoy it, or he'll wind up doing something stupid, like giving into his best friend's ridiculous idea of them dating. "I'm not putting you in a stranger's car while you're this drunk."

37

Bastian stiffens up and stands straighter. "I'm not drunk—I'm tipsy."

"Regardless. You're too *tipsy* to get into a stranger's car." He keeps a sure grip on Bastian and begins to lead them north, away from the restaurant and towards Andres's Fulton Market condo. "You're coming home with me."

"You wish," Bastian teases, trying to pull out of Andres's hold again.

"I do wish, but not for the reasons you're thinking," Andres says and holds him closer. "Now come on, it's not too much further."

"Stop making such a fuss," Bastian says as he trips.

Andres catches him quickly. "Stop being difficult, Bastian."

"I'm not difficult."

"You are too," Andres says, his laughter tickling Bastian's ear as Andres pulls him in again.

Bastian stops fighting and lets himself be held up by Andres as they walk. After all, it is quite cozy inside his hold, despite the fact that Bastian wishes it wasn't.

It doesn't take long to get to Andres's place. Before he knows it, he is being ushered past the doorman into the exquisitely decorated lobby of the luxury building. Bastian is practically falling asleep with his head resting on Andres's shoulder as they ride the elevator to the twelfth floor. He stumbles down the hall to Andres's unit's door and into his bedroom.

Andres deposits Bastian onto his bed, and then rummages through his drawers before he lays out some clothes for Bastian to sleep in. "Here, put these on," he says and turns away.

Bastian furrows his brow before he begins changing. "For someone so adamant that we date, you're awfully bashful over there."

"You haven't agreed to date me yet," Andres says, still not looking at Bastian.

"That hasn't stopped us from changing in front of each other before."

"Touché. But you set a boundary, and I'm not crossing it until you give me the okay."

Bastian rolls his eyes as he pulls off his top and replaces it with Andres's too-big T-shirt. "The boundary is that I'll knee you in the balls if you try and get fresh with me."

"Noted," Andres says.

"You can turn around. I'm done now," Bastian says after pulling on Andres's shorts.

As Andres turns he almost looks shy, but the expression is washed away as he steps over to Bastian and lays him down on the bed, pulling the blanket up to Bastian's chin. "Good night, Bastian."

"Good night, Andres," Bastian mumbles, falling asleep before Andres even turns off the lights.

CHAPTER 4

U pon waking the following day, Bastian is sure of exactly two things. One, he is not dating Andres. And two, despite that, he has woken up in Andres's very large bed. A cursory feel around the luxurious sheets with his hands and feet alerts him that Andres's "side" is cold and unrumpled, with no signs of him having slept there. *Odd*, Bastian thinks. For someone so adamant last night that they should try dating, you'd think he'd have jumped on the opportunity for a drunken roll in the sheets.

Yet, while Andres may have a reputation for being a bed hopper, he is a stickler for clearly communicated consent. That alone should be reason enough for Bastian to take Andres's offer of dating him seriously. He'd be in excellent hands, adequately taken care of, and respected. But who is Bastian to take such things from his friend? Surely there is someone out there who is better and more deserving of Andres's affection? Someone within his league, social standing, and income bracket. All of which Bastian considers himself woefully inadequate. Andres hasn't opened himself up yet to find that person who can check all these boxes.

Bastian can't blame him. For as large as Andres's heart is, he is very guarded with where he places his trust. The fact that Bastian had managed to slip through his defenses at such a young age is not lost on him. But again, those defenses at five were not fully formed yet; Andres was a much more open, vibrant, and optimistic person before his brother Julian passed. There are glimmers of the old Andres on occasion, but only when he is truly comfortable, and more often than not, those times are specific to Bastian. He's witnessed it on many occasions, Andres shedding his outer protective layer like a tailored suit once he is out of view of the rest of the world. That alone could go on the list of reasons why dating is a terrible idea. Why would they risk the familiarity they have with each other over something as unrealistic, especially based on both their relationship track records? It's reckless. It's bound to end in disaster. It's a wholly ridiculous idea that Bastian is not at all entertaining.

Rolling over in the bed, he reaches for his phone and is momentarily distracted by a framed photo on the bedside table of Andres, Julian, and himself as gangly, awkward kids. Andres is the most prominent in the picture, standing center with his arms around Bastian and Julian on the stone porch of their family's Frank Lloyd Wright original home. Though Andres is center, it's Julian who captures Bastian's attention. Like Andres, he was blessed with an abundance of dark, loose, curly hair any stylist would give anything to get their hands into. Andres had always gone for a longer look, but Julian had kept his cropped short and meticulously styled, even at a young age, before he lost it all. He was such a funny kid. Careful and thoughtful, every step deliberate and planned, the complete opposite of Andres, who simply barged in and took charge, confidently knowing that he knew best, even when he wasn't. Even in this photo, the stark difference between the two brothers is evident. Andres is all smiles, his sweeping arms holding what's dear to him close. Julian is stiff, poised, and well put together in miniature designer duds. And Bastian, looking somewhat out of place in his slightly ill-fitting clothes, looks slyly at Andres, as if his friend is the most magnanimous person to ever walk the earth. Though this was clearly taken before everything changed for Andres, it's no wonder it's on his bedside table. But even more curious is why he would want to gamble his connection with Bastian over something as potentially dangerous as dating him? He's already lost a brother; why risk losing his closest friend?

Bastian grabs his phone from the bedside table and unplugs it from the charger. Checking the time, eight-thirty, he groans in annoyance. An hour and a half is not nearly enough time for him to make it from the West Loop back up to Boystown, shower, change, and back down to River North to make it to work on time for his first client. Even foregoing public transportation and using an Uber, or better yet, having Andres zip through traffic on his motorcycle to help Bastian get from point A to point B and then point C, would be a very tight squeeze on an unforgiving timeline.

"Knock, knock," Andres says, accompanying his words with an actual knock on the bedroom door. A waft of freshly brewed coffee is ushered in with the breeze of the door opening, along with Andres clad in a plain white tee and gray sweatpants; he looks infuriatingly sexy. "Thought you might need a little pick me up."

"Thanks," Bastian says, sitting upright and taking the proffered mug from his friend. He takes a sip and tries to ignore that it has been made precisely to his liking. "Don't suppose this can teleport me back up north to my apartment, can it?"

"Sorry, I haven't perfected that technology yet. But I have put a set of clean towels in the bathroom for you, and you can borrow anything in my closet if you'd like a change of clothes."

Bastian takes another sip of his coffee. "You don't want that. I have three men's cuts today."

"So?"

"Those tiny, freshly shorn clippings get stuck in everything. I will not subject you to that itching and the inevitable hair splinters."

"I'll take them to the dry cleaner," Andres says. "And yours as well. They reek like the whiskey you spilled down the front of them."

Bastian grimaces upon remembering that he was lucky enough to have found that Gucci sweater on clearance. "If it's not too much trouble, then yes. Could I please borrow something from your closet? Assuming I can find anything that fits. Why are you so much bigger than me?"

"I'm a few inches taller than you. That's hardly an issue. Besides, nobody knows how to pull an outfit together better than you do."

Bastian smirks and fluffs his sleep mussed curls. "You do have a point there."

"So humble," Andres says with a shake of his head. He turns and starts to walk out the door. "Get yourself cleaned up, and I'll make us some breakfast."

With Andres's back now turned to him, Bastian's eyes betray him as they flick up and down his friend's backside, feasting on the barely concealed, taut, and toned muscles of a longtime swimmer. Andres's broad shoulders are stretching the fabric of his T-shirt, the hem of which isn't even trying to be long enough to hang over Andres's impressive and ample ass. The man looks like he's smuggling cantaloupes in his pants. It's simply unfair. Bastian shakes his head and rubs at his eyes. Once again, he is *not* entertaining the idea of dating him. But a boy can still look. He sneaks another peek.

Twenty or so minutes later, already feeling worlds better after taking a hot shower in Andres's marble walk-in, Bastian reemerges from the bedroom. He's dressed in a pair of Andres's skinny jeans, which aren't so skinny on Bastian, and a long, white, dress shirt cuffed to right below his elbows. It's not the best he's ever looked, but once he steps into his shoes, he'll look the part of every under-fed fashion model in the magazines laid out around the salon.

He does a little spin in the kitchen for Andres and accepts an-other mug full of perfectly prepared coffee. "How do I look?"

Andres eyes him up and down, a pinkish glow rising on his face as if he'd picked out Bastian's ensemble himself. "You look good. Fresh as a daisy."

"I think you and I both know I'm no daisy." Bastian takes a sip of his coffee and tries to peer around Andres at the stove to see what he is making. "Whatcha got there?"

"Veggie and tofu scramble with some carrot bacon, and English muffins with my blueberry compote. Does this suit your delicate palate?"

"It'll do." Bastian's mouth is watering at the sight and smell of the garlic and chipotle pepper that the tofu was cooked with.

Andres laughs and shakes his head at him. "Go sit down, would ya? This is ready."

"Yes, Daddy," Bastian says.

"You're incorrigible. You know that, right?" He places two plates of food down on the table, then grabs the English muffins from the toaster. "Eat up. I'll give you a ride to work if you'd like when we're done."

"Don't you want to go back to bed?" Bastian asks. "Just because I have to go to work, that's no reason for you to be up. I mean, outside of making me breakfast, of course." He takes a bite of his food. "Fuck, this is good." He moans as he chews.

Andres winks and takes a bite of his own breakfast. "It's no trouble, Bastian. Really, I'm happy to do it."

"Alright then," Bastian says, checking the time on his phone. Thirty minutes until he has to be at work. "As long as you don't mind. It really would be a big help."

"Well, well, well. Look who it is." Laura tut-tuts at Bastian, looking at him from the sides of her eyes as she cleans out her Mason Pearson Denman brush with a wide-tooth comb while Bastian makes his way to his station beside her. Her voice is incredibly smug, and Bastian can see one perfectly arched eyebrow raised in the reflection of her station mirror. "Arriving barely on time with fresh-off-the-back-of-a-motorcycle windblown curls."

Bastian opens his station's product drawer, then grabs his container of pomade and begins to reset his curls into their proper place. "I don't know what you're insinuating."

"Did you or did you not arrive here on the back of Andres Wood's motorcycle?" She pauses, and Bastian feels her looking him up and down, silently making note of his ensemble before she adds with emphasis. "Wearing his designer clothes!"

"Pfft." Bastian scoffs, still avoiding her eyes. He gives a final twist to one of his curls, then smooths the too-long shirt. "These are my clothes."

"Sure, they are," she says, and Bastian can feel her stare reach straight into his soul. "And I see you're not denying the ride here on the back of a certain someone's motorcycle."

"There's no ride to deny," Bastian says, now creating a crisper and cleaner cuff to his rolled-up sleeves. He'd purposefully gotten off at the corner instead of having Andres drop him off at the front door, claiming it was easier for Andres to do that than to go the extra two blocks east he'd need in order to hit the one-way street the salon sits on. It had absolutely nothing to do with Bastian wanting to avoid this kind of interrogation.

"Bethany," Laura calls out, prompting the young assistant to poke her head out from the shampoo area where she's stocking the back bar with freshly laundered towels for the day.

"Yes, Laura?" Bethany asks.

"Can you please recall what you saw this morning while you were grabbing my dirty chai from Brew?" Laura grabs the branded paper cup off her station counter and takes a pointed sip, eying Bastian over the brim.

Oh shit. They rode right past Andres and Justin's coffee shop connected to their restaurant, Partager, down the street from the salon. Of course, Bethany was down there fetching Laura's coffee at the time.

Bethany gives Bastian a sheepish smile. "I saw Bastian on the back of Andres's motorcycle."

"Fine," Bastian admits. He can still play innocent-ish, which he is. Nothing happened, and he most certainly is not dating Andres anyway. "Andres did give me a ride to work today. We had breakfast this morning. Like *friends* do sometimes. It was nothing."

"Bethany," Laura says in a tone that implies she knows something Bastian doesn't. "When you saw Bastian holding onto Andres on the back of his bike, did he look like Andres's friend or his boyfriend?"

Bethany looks at Bastian apologetically. He can practically hear her pleading for mercy from him as she answers Laura's question. "He looked like Andres's boyfriend."

"How?" Bastian asks, giving them both a cold, hard stare.

Laura seemingly finally cuts Bethany a break and fills in the details for her. "Arms wrapped around Andres's waist, thighs hugging the outside of his hips, your chin hooked over his shoulder, lips hovering near his ears. Sounds pretty intimate to me."

"Sounds like the only safe way to ride on the back of somebody's motorcycle." Bastian laughs, pulling his shears out of their case and giving them a quick wipe with a cloth before he sets them on a towel. "Honestly, Laura, we're just friends."

"Andres and Justin are just friends as well, and I've never seen Justin so much as hold onto Andres's shoulders, let alone wrap his arms around his waist when Andres gives him a quick lift somewhere."

"That's because, unlike your fiancé, I'm not afraid of people correctly assuming that I'm gay for holding on for dear life on the back of that death trap," Bastian says.

"Alright. I'll give you that." Laura laughs. "God, straight boys are weird, huh?"

"Yes! They are weird. Very weird. And I don't appreciate being held to their peculiar way of doing things. Andres gave me a ride to work after breakfast. That's it. There's nothing more to it."

"Uh-huh," Laura says and steps over to him. She brings a perfectly manicured finger to his cheek. She presses it into the flesh hard enough that Bastian is worried she may create a permanent dimple. "If there's nothing more to it, then why are you blushing?"

"Oh, fuck off."

"Bastian," the sing-song voice of Lizzie, the salon's other assistant, says as she enters the room. "Graham has arrived. Shall I bring him up?"

"Yes, please, Lizzie," Bastian says. Never has he been so happy to see Lizzie in the six months that she's worked here, having started the apprentice program shortly after Bethany. Despite her seemingly sweet nature, she's proving to be quite the competitive force in giving Bethany a real run for her money as to who will be awarded a coveted Salon Azure Blue chair next. Typically, Bastian prefers to have Bethany work in their section to help him as needed, but seeing as she ratted him out today, he's feeling uncommonly favorable to Lizzie. "And could you please be on hand today?" he asks. "It's going to be a bit hectic."

"Sure thing," Lizzie trills, adding in a dreamy tone as she walks out of the room to get Bastian's client, "I hardly ever get to work up here."

"Really, Bastian?" Laura huffs as Bethany's shoulders slump, and she heads back to her duty of folding towels.

Bastian doesn't respond. He gives himself one last once-over in the mirror, self-conscious in the clothes that aren't his, and strides to the breakroom to grab a bottle of water for his station. His phone vibrates in his pocket.

It's a picture of Andres, back in his sweatpants and T-shirt, lounging in his bed.

> So much nicer than the couch.

Bastian huffs out a laugh as he types.

> You could've slept in the bed, you know? We have shared before—many times.

> And risk bodily harm. You threatened to knee me in the balls if I tried anything funny.

Bastian grimaces at his vague memory of last night.

> Not my fault you didn't think you could follow the rules.

> What can I say? You are irresistible.

> And you aren't as charming as you think.

Despite his proclamation, Bastian feels his cheeks beginning to glow. He shakes his head.

> My client is here. I gotta go.

> Aren't you going to wish me goodnight?

> It's 10 am!

> So?

> Fine. Sweet Dreams, Andres.

> Sweet workday, Bastian.

Bastian, smiling, pockets his phone.

"Isn't your client here?" Mitchel, Bastian's boss, says from inside the office connected to the breakroom.

With his head turned, Bastian rolls his eyes so his boss can't see. "Yes. And I'm on my way right now."

Mitchel pokes his head out the door, his hair slightly messy, his clothes rumpled, and his nose pink from likely too much gin the night before. He looks Bastian up and down. "Nice clothes. Looks like I'm paying you too much."

Bastian puts on a tight smile. "What can I say? I treated myself," he says, then takes a deep breath, turns on his heel, and reopens the door to step out of the breakroom and back onto the salon floor. It's showtime, and he must put his best face forward for the day, leaving behind the flagrant judgment his boss just placed on him and any lingering thoughts about Andres lounging around in his gray sweatpants.

Bastian's workday was anything but sweet, and by the time he's putting his workstation back in order for the night—locking up his shears, cleaning out his brushes, and reorganizing his product drawer—he cannot wait to run down the two flights of stairs and out the front door of the salon to get home and finally put his feet up. He's so done with today, having had to explain to a freshly single girl that he can't glue her hair back on because she now regrets the bangs she insisted she needed, which he warned her she didn't actually want. This was after having to deal with another woman who didn't want to understand that he can't take her artificially jet-black hair and make it platinum blonde in one sitting, resulting in her storming out of the salon and Bastian missing out on two hours' worth of money. At least he got to start reading the new backroom monster porn for the rest of the staff who were either on a break or had a hole in their books during those two hours. On top of all of that, the prickly remnants of hair trimmings from the three men's cuts he had today are sticking in and poking through every layer of fabric of his—well, Andres's—clothes and causing him to itch all over.

He's about to pull out his phone to order an Uber, far too over today to deal with taking public transportation, when the distinct sound of a particular motorcycle engine idling in front of the salon makes him pause. His lips turn up at their corners. If Andres is here, maybe he can talk him into giving him a ride home. He pockets his phone and slips a twenty out of his roll of tips for the day to Lizzie for her assistance as he heads out of the door.

"Hey there, good looking!" Andres exclaims with an exaggerated and playful wink from his seat, straddling the idling motorcycle.

"Who? Me?" Bastian plays along, looking shocked and bringing a hand to his chest. Truthfully, he's quite happy to see Andres, even if last night's development has caused a bit of a shift in the terms of their friendship.

Andres nods at him. "Lemme holla at you."

Bastian rolls his eyes and lets out a full belly laugh. "You're ridiculous. Nobody's holla-ing at anybody."

Andres lights up like a star and pats the backseat of his bike. "Hop on. I'll give you a ride home."

"Oh, I don't know," Bastian says, holding his hands behind his back and stepping over to stand beside Andres, eyeing the backseat of the bike. He briefly wonders if indulging Andres in this flirtation is a good idea, even if he is having fun. Is this leading him on? "It looks dangerous, and my mother always said to stay away from boys like you."

"Bullshit," Andres proclaims. "Your mother loves me."

"Does she?" Bastian questions. He twists up his face in thought. "Hmm ... Maybe it was my father who told me you were no good."

"Nope. Not him, either. I have it in good authority that he fully approves of me."

"Then I guess it must be my girlfriends who warned me about you."

Laura's voice rings from above them, "He's lying to you, Andres! We're on your side!"

He looks up to see Laura and Marny practically hanging from their waists out of the salon's third-floor window. He glares and flicks them both the bird.

Andres pats the back of his bike again. "Hop on."

Bastian, now with an audience he doesn't want to please, plays even harder to get. "But it's cold."

Andres flips open the flimsy saddle bag on the side of his bike and pulls out a lump of fabric that he holds out to Bastian. "Then it's good I brought you one of my hoodies."

Bastian eyes the hoodie, torn. On the one hand, he wants to grab it and accept the ride home. On the other, taking the hoodie and accepting the ride feels like a date instead of the regular ride home Andres would occasionally surprise Bastian with.

Andres holds the hoodie out more forcefully for Bastian. "Do you want the ride or not, Bastian? It's that simple."

"Fine," Bastian says as he grabs the hoodie and shrugs it on. A series of wolf whistles and a call of, "Put it on!" rings out from above.

"There. Was that so hard?" Andres asks as Bastian climbs onto the bike and situates himself snuggly behind Andres.

"Yes," Bastian says into Andres's ear. "It was."

"You can't ever make anything easy, can you?" Andres kicks back the kickstand and puts the bike into gear. "Including anything easier on yourself."

"There's no need to insult me," Bastian says.

"I'm not!" Andres says. "Your obstinance, for whatever reason, is part of your charm."

"Or maybe you can't take a hint."

"Or maybe *you* know what's good for you but are too afraid to grab hold of it."

"And I suppose you think you're what's good for me?" Bastian asks and ignores the part of his gut that agrees with Andres, the part that is saying, 'See, this is nice. It changes hardly anything.' Except Bastian knows that's not true. Dating Andres would change *everything*. And Bastian isn't someone who likes change all that much.

"You could do worse," Andres jokes. "Fuck, you have done worse."

"Says you."

"Says the ever-growing list of dating disasters on your closet wall."

"Pfft, that list is a culmination of myself and at least four other tragic gays who lived in the apartment in the years before me. If I were you, I'd shut up before you find yourself on that list."

Andres engages the clutch, then takes his right hand off the throttle and mimes zipping his lip before bringing his hand back and hitting the gas. They remain silent, Andres weaving in and out of traffic while Bastian watches the comings and goings of his beloved city, its many neighborhoods, and its inhabitants from the best view in the metaphorical house. From the back of the motorcycle, he can see it all. The streetlights are shining, and the soft, navy blue of the darkening sky is peeking between the buildings which morph from three flats to mid-rises to skyscrapers all on one block and then back again. He holds his breath when Andres makes the turn onto Lake Shore Drive and breaks his zipped lip, speaking again, telling Bastian, "Hold on tight." And hold on, he does.

With the roar of the engine rumbling beneath him, his body pressed firmly against his best friend, Chicago's most desirable real estate to his left, and the vast lake extending farther than the eye can see to his right, Bastian exhales fully. He hooks his chin over Andres's shoulder and adjusts his hands at Andres's sternum to give him an even tighter squeeze, all the frustrations of the day floating away behind him with the motorcycle's exhaust. Andres takes his hand off the clutch and brings it to where Bastian's hands are resting, giving them a little pat before holding them in his own. From his seat right now, Bastian can almost forget about the risks. Forget about his past disasters. Forget about the list he so desperately wants to end with Ryan Andrews' name and not Andres Wood's.

With his mind clear of fears and worst-case scenarios, Bastian wants to tell Andres to keep going instead of taking the Belmont off-ramp heading into Boystown. But who knows what other plans Andres has? Surely, he needs to be at work or something. Andres's schedule is even more demanding than Bastian's. Running restaurants is more than a full-time job, especially when one takes a very hands-on approach, as Andres does. But who is Bastian to dictate his night? Andres has already gone out of his way to drive Bastian all the way home to Boystown.

"Thank you for the ride," Bastian says as Andres takes a right onto Halsted, and the bright, rainbow Art Deco street pylons of Boystown come into view.

"You're welcome," Andres says as he begins slowing the motorcycle down to safely navigate the street. It's full of vibrant people enjoying the crisp spring weather, happy to no longer be cooped up by winter.

Something in Bastian doesn't want this night to be over now that Andres is rounding the corner onto his street. It propels him to ask, "Are you working tonight?"

"Technically, I'm working right now. But Alex has it under control. He said he didn't mind if I went to run an errand."

"Oh, so I'm an errand now, am I?"

"That's not what I meant, and you know it." Andres chuckles.

"So I guess you gotta go, huh?" Bastian asks. "I can't repay you with a meal cooked by me?"

"I'll take a raincheck," Andres says as he stops the bike in front of Bastian's apartment.

"Alright," Bastian agrees, giving Andres one last squeeze around the middle before he dismounts the bike. "You tell me when, and I'll whip up something special."

"Okay, I'll let you know when my schedule allows."

"Alright," Bastian says again, this time a little more awkwardly, not sure where to go from here. He begins to walk backward and away. "Thanks again for the ride."

"Anytime, Bastian. I'm happy to be of service."

Bastian's cheeks burn traitorously. Has his skin always behaved this way, or is this a new phenomenon? He doesn't know. All he does know is that he's suddenly hot and flustered, and he needs it to stop. He starts to pull at the length of the sleeves of the hoodie right as Andres is about to put the bike back into gear. "Wait!" he calls out, letting go of the sleeves to begin tugging on the sweatshirt hem. "You forgot your hoodie!"

"Keep it!" Andres yells, hitting the gas. "You're gonna need it again anyway."

Bastian stands, bewildered, in his building's alcove and watches as Andres speeds around the corner and out of sight. He ignores the slight fluttering in his belly and decides that it's merely hunger pangs after a long day on his feet. Because he is not, in any way, entertaining the idea of dating Andres Wood.

CHAPTER 5

Since Bastian isn't dating anyone, he sees no reason why he can't reactivate his Grindr account. Or so he reasons, though he's uneasy about the whole Andres thing and where the mere suggestion of them dating leaves their friendship. Regardless, it's Sunday, his day off, and there's nothing wrong with having a little look-see at what or who's available to a guy like Bastian these days. After all, he is a catch for people of his social standing. His mom and his best friend have told him as much. Granted, his mom isn't trying to date him.

However, he is starting to wonder if his mom is conspiring with Andres. She'd sent him a text containing a picture of him and Andres as children, dressed as the founding fathers for some dumb first-grade play, her accompanying message saying, *If only the founding fathers could've foretold this.* That wasn't even the first one she sent. It was only the first one today. Yesterday, during the typical Saturday salon craziness, he received back-to-back messages from her. One with a picture of him and Andres dressed as pirates for Halloween when they were eight and another of them at eighteen in much less billowy and ruffled suits than their pirate costumes, standing posed like a traditional couple before hopping into a limo to attend Bastian's senior prom; Andres had agreed to go with him as a pity date.

His sixth sense, honed to near psychic levels from having to deal with people so intimately behind the salon chair, is telling him that it's not innocent, motherly reminiscing. This is starting to feel like a setup, albeit less obvious than the clients who pull the, "Oh my god, you have to meet my co-worker! He's so cute and fun! You'll love him!" attempts he's grown used to ducking. Why everyone assumes that being gay is enough to make two people compatible is an annoyance Bastian is done trying to figure out. Not to mention, who do these clients think they're kidding? Members of their social club are not going to be happy dating someone who's only a hairstylist. He can imagine the looks on these so-called dating options' faces if they were to ever see his tiny, Boystown studio apartment. Now, every time a client tries to set him up with a friend, brother, cousin, or co-worker, he politely declines, telling them that it would be a shame for him to lose them in the client/friend custody agreement should things go sour. It doesn't always work, but an idle threat of losing him as their hair and ego fixer does deter the bulk of them.

His mother is a different case and far more challenging to rebuff with a simple 'no thanks.' Having raised Bastian, she's far more innovative in how to plant ideas into his heart than the average client who sits in his chair. She knows where his soft spots are—proof of such appearing as a thumbnail floating in a notification at the top of his phone screen right now.

It's of Julian—alive but looking rather sickly, a complete contrast to the photo beside Andres's bed—standing between Bastian and Andres at Julian's thirteenth and last birthday party. She's playing dirty.

Bastian flicks the notification bubble off the top of his screen and resumes casually scrolling through the Grindr grid of who is in his area. He's bound to find somebody on here worth having a drink or two and a salacious rendezvous with later on this afternoon. Or, at the very least, someone who can distract him from his traitorous thoughts of Andres in his gray sweatpants. Those thoughts had kept him up well past midnight when all he wanted to do was get a solid night's sleep after a long, hard week of massaging people's vanities. Even if nothing comes immediately from his perusing, there's comfort in the scroll through prospective hookups.

A comfort that is being interrupted yet again by his mother as his phone vibrates in his hand. Annoyed by her interruption, he sighs heavily and answers it, bringing his phone to his ear. "Hi, Mom."

"Oh, hello, dear. Did you get the picture I sent? I came across it, and I had to share it with you. Pass it along to Andres, would you, darling; I know how much he misses his brother." She rambles this all off in one breath before she gives Bastian a chance to answer.

"Yeah, I got it. Thanks for sending it. Though, I might not pass it on to Andres. He tends to get a bit melancholy in all things pertaining to Julian." He adds just a hint of scolding to his tone.

"I know he does," she says. "Poor, sweet soul. He's always taken too much on and held it all in. It warmed my heart to see the three of you together, is all. Can you believe it's been almost fifteen years now?"

Bastian's heart is heavy. "It feels like yesterday sometimes."

"It really does," she says. "I should call Juanita. It's been forever and a day since I've spoken to her. How is she?"

"Honestly, I'm not sure." Bastian's laugh is feeble. "They're kind of an off-limits subject with Andres. You probably talk to them more often than he does."

"Maybe. They've been through a lot. I do what I can."

Bastian lets that linger. His mom has always been this way, continually meddling and trying to hold everyone together at all costs. He's not about to tell her that it's a futile effort. From what he's garnered from Andres's rare mentions of his parents, it seems as though Juanita and Walter Wood have let fifteen years of accumulated grief hold them back from any sort of meaningful existence. They float through their days like ghosts in their Oak

Park mansion. Their crippling grief at the loss of their youngest son drove a wedge between them and their oldest, resulting in what essentially has become the loss of two children.

"Which, speaking of," she says, and Bastian is yet again wondering if his mom is attempting to meddle in the affairs of his heart, "why don't you come out for dinner tonight? Just because you and that Ryan broke up doesn't get you out of our dinner plans. See if Andres wants to join us."

Bastian huffs. "Andres is working tonight, Mom," he says. "And honestly, it's been a long week. I just want to lounge in my reading chair with a book and maybe some Netflix." *Or better yet, a possible Grindr connection for drinks and a fuck*, but he keeps that part to himself.

"Alright, dear," she says, sounding more disappointed than Bastian thinks is necessary. "But you'll come out next Sunday, right? It's been too long since I've seen my favorite son."

"Your only son."

"Biological, maybe, but Andres is giving you and your grumpy pants self a run for your money."

"Andres is your son now?"

"Andres has always been my son," she says. "Someone had to keep an eye on him while his parents were overwhelmed with caring for Julian. And he's always been such a good boy. Why you two haven't gotten together, I'll never know."

Bastian lets out a long-suffering sigh.

"Oh, stop," she scolds. "You've always been so hard-headed, refusing to see what's in front of you."

"I see what's in front of me now."

"And what's that, dear?"

"The disconnect button if you don't change the subject."

She laughs. "You seem cranky anyway. Enjoy your book. I'll see you next Sunday. No excuses."

"Fine," Bastian agrees.

"And, Sebastian?"

"Yes, Mom?"

"I love you."

"I love you too." He feels more than slightly guilty for his tone on this call. "I'll see you next Sunday."

"And bring Andres." He hears her say as he hits End Call and goes back to Grindr, aggressively hitting the fire button on options he'd usually scroll past to increase his chances of finding someone to foot the bill for his cocktails this evening.

His mother isn't technically to blame for the bad date that Bastian is on, but he's blaming her anyway from where he's sitting at the high-top table nestled in the corner of Roscoe's.

In theory, Daniel Kim isn't horrible. He's good-looking with his lean muscles, dark brown eyes, and strong jaw, but he's tremendously dull. Plus, he'd failed to mention in his bio that he's originally from Ohio, an egregious sin that Bastian isn't willing to look past, even when his only motivation for this date is as a distraction.

"This is nice," Daniel says and makes a presumptuous grab for Bastian's hand.

Bastian takes a sip of his Blood Orange Bliss and eyes Daniel's hand over his, then flicks his eyes back up to meet Daniel's. His lack of spoken words seems to have worked, as Daniel slowly slides his hand away and slumps in his seat.

"Sorry." He mouths silently, and Bastian almost feels guilty.

He changes the subject before that guilt persuades him to do anything else. "You're a personal trainer. How's that working for you?"

"Pretty good," Daniel says with a cocky grin and even has the gall to raise his right arm to shoulder height and make a fist, flexing his bicep, which stretches the sleeve of his shirt. Bastian will grant him that it is an impressive bicep. "Business has picked up since I transferred to that gym on Broadway."

"Where were you before?" Bastian asks, not interested.

"Up in Evanston. Too many rich housewives up there. They were more interested in yoga and spin class than they were in actually putting in work for their bodies," Daniel says.

Bastian, for however annoyed he is at his mother, gets indignant on her and every other woman's behalf. "Huh." Bastian huffs. "You know, my mother swears by yoga, as do most of the women I work with. They say it's highly beneficial."

"Oh, it is," Daniel says with a dismissive wave of his hand. "But it will never get anyone to achieve their fullest potential with what their body can do. I mean, sure, they can do the splits, but can they lift a box of books when moving?"

"They could do what I do," Bastian says and takes another sip of his drink.

"And what's that?" Daniel says and reaches to squeeze Bastian's narrow arm.

"Call one of their local muscle gay friends for help." Bastian eyes Daniel up and down with his eyebrow raised, trying to silently imply that's about all Daniel would ever be good for in his life.

Daniel lets out a booming laugh. "Come have a complimentary training session with me, and I'll get you lifting your own books."

"I can lift my *own* books just fine," Bastian says, leaving out the fact that Andres had been the one to move his six boxes of books the last time Bastian had switched apartments. To his credit, he could've moved them himself, but Andres had emphatically insisted that he would take care of them. And who was Bastian to argue with such a chivalrous gesture? Those boxes truly were quite heavy.

"I'm sure you can. One at a time," Daniel says.

"Excuse you!" Bastian exclaims. "I may not be a gym rat like you, but I am perfectly capable of doing some heavy lifting."

"So what do you lift?" Daniel asks, leaning forward.

"My blow dryer," Bastian says and fixes him with a stern look. "Eight to ten times a day."

"That's not weightlifting—"

"Oh really? I'd like to see you after a day of blow-drying waist-length hair while standing on your feet for ten hours. It's more physically intensive work than you do in a week." It's at this moment that Bastian changes his mind. Daniel is, in fact, very horrible. Not only boring but boorish as well. *Risking everything with Andres is a better option than this.* He rises from his seat at the table and swallows down the rest of his drink in one gulp.

"Hey!" Daniel protests. "Where are you going? I thought we were having a good time?"

"If this is your idea of a good time, you are sorely in need of a life coach."

Daniel looks stung and surprised that Bastian is as sharp with his tongue as he is with his cutting shears. "Aren't you going to at least pay for your portion of the tab?"

"No," Bastian says, grabbing his phone from the table. "Consider this your monthly asshole tax." He turns on his heel and walks through the crowded bar and out the door.

Once outside, he gives himself a quick shake like a dog ridding itself of unwanted water. "Asshole," he says under his breath right as his phone vibrates the rapid pulse of a text message.

> Where you at?

Andres's timing is uncanny.

> *Storming out of Roscoe's, currently. Where are you?*

Bastian types as he does indeed storm away from Roscoe's, heading home.

> *Work.*

> *It must be a slow night if you're texting me.*

From what Bastian knows, Sunday nights are reasonably tame in the restaurant world. It tends to be full of folks who opt to avoid the brunch crowd and want to sit and relax and have a laid-back meal without a ridiculously long wait. That being said, it's still a night that surely should keep Andres busy with more important things than texting Bastian.

His phone buzzes again, and a photo of Andres with his feet on his office desk at Graze pops up on the screen.

> *I'm taking a much needed break from putting out fires all day.*

> *Hopefully not any real fires.*

Bastian types back.

> *Funny you should say that...*

Andres's message and the three blinking dots following seem ominous. It takes a minute, but another photo comes through.

This one of the vast, usually pristine kitchen at Graze and two line cooks looking slightly harried, if not a little pleased with themselves, as they hold fire-scorched towels in front of an industrial-size griddle covered in what Bastian is guessing is baking soda.

> *Things got a little hot at the end of brunch service.*

Bastian flips back up to the picture of Andres and, this time notices that he has some soot on his white dress shirt and a smudge across his forehead.

> *Are you alright?*

> *I am now.*

> *Did you have to close the restaurant down?*

> *Nah. Front of the house wasn't even bothered.*

> *Well, that's good.*

Relief hits Bastian, notably for Andres's safety and not because the restaurant was able to function business as usual. He's been privy to more than his fair share of nightmare kitchen stories from Andres, who has spent his entire adult life working all aspects of the high-end service industry. When he doesn't get another message from Andres right away, Bastian furrows his brow and makes the turn onto his street. He checks the time: nine-thirty.

> Are you getting off any time soon?

> Doubtful. I still need to fill out the incident report, and the assistant manager sliced her finger open on a paring knife behind the bar.

> Oof.

Bastian types out as he cringes.

> But, I was hoping to take you up on your offer to make me dinner. Are you free tomorrow?

Outside of his usual Monday trip to the grocery store, Bastian is very free tomorrow.

> I have a hot date, actually.

> That hot date better be with me, or I'm revoking all rides to the beach on my motorcycle this summer.

Bastian gasps.

> You wouldn't!

> Oh, you better believe I would.

> Alright. You caught me. The date IS with you. Any special requests?

Bastian pulls out his keys and unlocks the door to his building as he waits for Andres's reply.

> Beggars can't be choosers. Besides, every-
> thing you make is ten times better than what
> we serve in our restaurants.

Lies.

The food at Andres and Justin's restaurants is Michelin-rated. The only reason Bastian can even eat it is because Andres insists he eats for free.

Hamburger Helper, it is then!

> You're going to make things difficult, aren't
> you?

Yes.

Bastian types, then unlocks and opens his apartment door.

> How about this? Let's have a pizza night. I'll
> take care of the toppings for us if you concen-
> trate on making the crust.

Are you saying you want to top my bottom?

Bastian can't resist the joke.

> That's precisely what I'm saying. Do we have a deal?

> I do love a good topping.

Bastian types, continuing the joke, despite the fact that anyone would constitute this type of brazen outward flirtation as playing with fire.

> So you've told me but have yet to accept my offer for help with that.

> Touche. Consider this me saying yes to your topping.

Bastian types with both thumbs, his phone held tight to his chest as he kicks his shoes off.

> Really?

> YES! I want the full experience! Mushrooms, red onions, green pepper, garlic, and spinach!

> Are we still talking about pizza?

Bastian feigns innocence.

> Of course! What else could we possibly be talking about?

> *You're incorrigible. Do you know that?*

You tell me that almost every day.

> *See you tomorrow for your full topping. Have a good night!*

I'll be sure to clean out my pan.

Bastian, now officially in a much better mood, pockets his phone, then picks up his shoes and walks to his closet. He places them onto their shelf and then grabs the pen affixed by a string to the doorframe next to the infamous list. What's one more name, he figures, then writes, *Daniel Kim. Not a heartbreaker, just a complete waste of time.*

Bastian is checking the rise on his pizza dough in the oven when he hears Andres' motorcycle pull up outside of his building. Checking the time, he's surprised to see that Andres is fifteen minutes earlier than their agreed-upon time of six-thirty. Traffic must have been light. Without looking out his large bay window, Bastian hits and holds the buzzer for a long ten count to let Andres into his building, then opens his apartment door and uses the deadbolt to keep the door propped open. From there, he goes back to his kitchen counter and begins to uncork one of the bottles of wine he mulled over for a solid fifteen minutes, weighing out what he could afford that wouldn't be embarrassing to serve to Andres. He'd eventually settled on two bottles of moderately priced Malbec over the cheaper Pinot Noir for their evening.

"You have no sense of self-preservation," Andres says as he enters and places a Whole Foods tote bag onto Bastian's small wooden table set for two.

"Says the man who rides a motorcycle from the moment the snow thaws until the snow starts again." Bastian hands Andres a glass of wine and then holds his up to cheers his friend.

Andres clinks his glass. "You buzzed me into your building without even waiting for me to ring the bell, then left your apartment door propped open like I was here to fulfill some fantasy of yours you negotiated on Grindr."

"Wait, that's not why you're here?" Bastian asks, feigning disappointment.

"Sorry, but my wishes for you and me go way beyond a Grindr hookup." Andres gives Bastian a wink before he turns his attention back to his grocery bag. He begins pulling out an assortment of glossy fresh peppers, onions, and plump mushrooms.

"Pfft." Bastian scoffs. "You're the professional at one-night stands. If anything, I'm fulfilling your fantasy."

"More than you'll ever know, my dear Bastian," Andres says, tossing a pepper at him that Bastian catches and begins rinsing under the kitchen tap. "I've always dreamed of making pizza, drinking wine, and having a truly wholesome evening with someone."

"I should put the leather away then?"

"Definitely." Andres nods. "This is a purely wholesome date."

"This is two friends having dinner," Bastian corrects him, his tone switching to serious, and hating the fact that now he has to make this kind of distinction when before they could comfortably banter and tease like it was no big deal. Unless it was always like this, and Bastian has been missing the signs.

"So stubborn." Andres rolls his eyes and swiftly makes the two strides it takes to get to the sink, then kisses Bastian loudly on the cheek. Much to Bastian's annoyance, he feels his face begin to heat up. Andres hums happily and presses his finger to Bastian's pink skin. "There's hope for me yet."

Now it's Bastian's turn to roll his eyes, mostly out of annoyance at himself and his turncoat's cheeks. It's ridiculous that he's blushing like a schoolgirl with a crush. He takes a sip of his wine, then resumes rinsing the vegetables that Andres keeps handing him. "You're the least hopeless person I've ever met. Half this city would throw themselves at your feet for a pair of your dirty underwear."

"You really think half?" Andres asks. "If I charged for them, I could retire early. Buy us a condo someplace warm. Keep you tanned and freckled year-round."

"You could buy yourself another condo now," Bastian retorts, suddenly feeling very self-conscious of his tiny rental. "No need to sell your used wears."

"Ahh, but I didn't say for myself. I said for you and me," Andres says. "And let's face it; you don't come cheap, baby."

"The term isn't 'Sugar Baby' for nothing," Bastian says as he shuts off the tap a little more aggressively than necessary. "And despite your beliefs, I actually do not crave a condo in the land of perpetual summer. I like it here."

"So do I." Andres looks directly at Bastian over the rim of his wine glass as he takes a sip. He holds Bastian's gaze, his eyes soulful and warm.

Bastian wants to look away, but he can't seem to. Something about the way Andres is regarding him keeps his gaze glued to where it is. He bites at his lower lip, trapping it between his teeth. He and Andres know each other inside and out, for good and bad, hopes and dreams, and their history; though it brings Bastian an intense amount of comfort, it scares him immensely. If he makes this leap that Andres has made it clear that he would like him to, he risks losing all of this. And he wouldn't be able to bounce back from the loss. Andres could. He has other friends, like his business partner Justin and their chef Alex, and Simone, their head bartender. Plus, though he never mentions them, there are always his friends he made at Fenwick. Those private school boys tend to stick together and form legacy connections for their children.

Hell, that's how Andres and Justin met in the first place. With Bastian no longer attached to him like dead weight once high school started, Andres was able to thrive and meet new fancy friends whose parents could afford the prestigious private school tuition. Not that Andres ever made him feel that way. He always had time for Bastian. Even when he eventually went to study business on the North Shore at Northwestern and Bastian rotted away at the cheapest cosmetology school closest to his parents' house, Andres always made room for Bastian in his life. He even came to Bastian's ceremonial final swipe of his school timecard, denoting the completion of his fifteen hundred hours of beauty school hell. They went and partied that night, utilizing Andres's good looks and Bastian's fake ID to get into the largest Boystown bar, Sidetrack, for an evening of gay debauchery.

Bastian was nineteen and broke but full of so much hope, convinced that now that his education was over, his life would finally begin. After chance gave him a practical interview, he'd been offered an apprenticeship at Salon Azure Blue, an opportunity to learn and be molded by Chicago's top stylists. It finally happened that at nineteen, doors were opening for Bastian. Andres was beside him the whole time: showing up fifteen minutes early to be Bastian's model for class, letting Bastian cut and color his hair into myriad shapes, styles, and hues. And as when Bastian graduated from cosmetology school, Andres was there when he finished his apprenticeship. At that event, he arrived holding a bouquet of morning glories, amaryllis, and asters, and even though he didn't need a haircut, Andres booked himself into Bastian's first available appointment as a professional hairstylist, cementing himself forever as Bastian's first official paying client.

Andres clapped his hands, effectively breaking Bastian from his thought-filled stupor. "Where's the dough?" he asks.

Bastian shakes his head. "In the oven," he says and finally looks away from Andres. He takes a deep breath, his mind flashing to the list on his closet wall, particularly the section of the list that is his. He has a horrible track record for dating, and he'll be damned if he's going to take the risk and end up adding Andres's name to that list when Bastian inevitably ends up fucking up any chance of success between them.

There's too much at stake. Too many years. Too many memories. Too much happiness to be soured by being arrogant enough to think he can find and hold onto romantic love with Andres. He quickly chugs the wine that's left in his glass, then pours himself another one and tops off Andres's. With another sip, he tries to swallow his disappointment in himself and his life's worth of failures in all things but styling other people's hair.

After dinner, Bastian refills Andres's wine glass with what's left in the bottle, then holds up another one, shaking it in question.

"Yeah." Andres nods. "May as well. I'm gonna need an Uber home anyway. There's no way I'm riding my bike tonight."

"Don't be ridiculous," Bastian says as he pulls up the cork with a soft, hollow pop. After pouring himself another glass, he grabs the whole bottle and takes it with him to the window seat on the ledge of his apartment's bay window, where he and Andres have moved to, watching the comings and goings of Aldine Street under the twilight sky with New Order's album *Power, Corruption & Lies* playing softly in the background. He tosses Andres a pillow to lean against. "Spend the night here. You can ride home in the morning."

Andres's eyes flicker to the lone bed briefly, then settle on Bastian, making Bastian suddenly aware of how small his bed is compared to Andres's. "You're only insisting because you want me to give you a ride to work in the morning."

"You caught me." Bastian smirks. It's silly for Andres to waste his money on not one but two Uber rides when he'd need to come back to retrieve his motorcycle anyway. Besides, they've shared a bed before, more times than Bastian has ever shared one with anyone.

"Okay," Andres agrees and takes a sip of his wine. "But I'll sleep in the chair."

"You'll sleep in the bed! Why are you being so weird?"

Andres shrugs and looks away from Bastian. "I'm not the one being weird."

Bastian rolls his eyes and lets out an exaggerated breath. "See, Andres, this is precisely why you and I can't date. There's too much history of polite friendship between us. We can't even negotiate a simple sleepover without running into issues now."

"It does require some adjustments, that's for sure," Andres says. "I don't want to blur the lines."

"Too late for that." Bastian laughs. "The lines were blurred when you brought up the idea of us dating."

"Okay, touché." Andres looks back at him. "I could've done that better. It's just ... I like you, Bastian. I always have."

"Of course you like me. We've been friends for twenty-five years. I'd hate to think we've gone this long, and you've been secretly hating me."

"If anybody secretly hates anybody, it's you hating me," Andres says. "Or maybe I've underestimated your ability to play hard to get."

"Or maybe you've never had anyone play hard to get with you before, and it's making you uncomfortable to not immediately get what you want," Bastian suggests and looks Andres up and down. He doesn't mean for it to sound cruel or judgmental. It's an honest observation he's always made regarding Andres. Certain privileges are bestowed upon people born not only rich but handsome as well. Sure, Andres works hard in his career, harder than most people Bastian knows, but never at getting what he wants in other matters. Those types of desires are handed to him on a silver platter.

"I already have what I want," Andres says, fixing Bastian with the softest of gazes. Andres has always been a big softie, a bit of a teddy bear—albeit a tall and well-chiseled one.

"Is that so?" Bastian questions, holding Andres's gaze and feeling his cheeks flush yet again. He makes a note to blame the wine if Andres points it out for a second time.

"Of course, it's so," Andres says with complete surety. "Whether we make a go of this or not, I'm still keeping you in my life. Nothing will change that."

He says that now, but what will happen if an experimental coupling between us goes horribly wrong? Bastian will lose everything important to him.

"You say that." Bastian sighs and moves his gaze from Andres' to look out the window. "But I don't see that with me. I'm not someone who handles break-ups well. I think you already know that."

"I'll give you that." He toes gently at Bastian from across the window seat. "Besides, it's not like I really want to join your exes on Mars anyway."

"Nor do I ever want to have a reason to send you there." Bastian presses his forehead to the window, his mind quickly playing back at least fifteen years of heartbreak, starting with Jackson, his first boyfriend, who crushed his heart in freshman year by refusing to hold Bastian's hand in public. Apparently, Bastian's hand was only good for hand jobs hidden under the bleachers at football games.

Andres toes at Bastian again, the insistency causing Bastian to look back at him. "Besides, who's been there for you after you waved goodbye to all those idiots who didn't appreciate how amazing you are?"

"You have," Bastian mumbles.

"Fuck, how many of those assholes did I punch before their metaphorical bus took off?" Andres asks, his voice still kind. If anyone else were to be talking about Bastian's past like this, Bastian—not someone who likes to make reminiscing a group project—would've shown them the door by now. But coming from Andres, there's a warmth that's ushered in with the usually bitter memories.

"Countless." Bastian finally laughs, locking eyes with Andres. He twists his mouth in thought, and his eyes flicker to Andres's full lips. "And that's why I can't date you. Who's gonna punch you before your journey out of my life and off of this planet?"

"No one," Andres says, completely serious. "Because I'd never hurt you. And I think you know that."

Bastian raises an eyebrow at his friend. He does know that Andres would never hurt him. It's more that deep down, underneath all of his joking and deflecting, Bastian is afraid that he will be the one to hurt Andres. And that is something he'd never be able to live with himself for doing. "I know," he says softly. "But things get messy when it comes to dating."

Andres shifts in his seat, crisscrossing his long legs, and leans forward toward Bastian. "It doesn't have to."

"But it will."

"And if it does, we'll clean it up."

"You've never so much as cleaned up your own bedroom," Bastian quips.

"Maybe not." Andres reaches to brush Bastian's curls that have fallen forward, the fringe hanging in Bastian's eyeline, back and away. "But I've cleaned you up, and the messes others have left you in, more times than I can count."

This is true. Andres has always been the one to pull Bastian back up onto his feet.

Andres brings both hands to rest on Bastian's shoulders, effectively holding Bastian's full attention. "Look, I don't want to pressure you. And I'm not going to try to talk you into something you're not interested in, but I think it's something you should consider. And I also think you know I'm right."

With his eyes on Andres's collarbones, Bastian shrugs. "I'll concede that, in theory, you're not wrong. But I will not go as far as to say that you are right."

"I'm gonna take that as a win," Andres says, bringing one hand away from Bastian's shoulder to stifle a yawn. With the weight of

Andres's hand suddenly gone, that shoulder feels empty compared to the other.

"Tired?" Bastian asks.

"Exhausted." Andres rubs at his face with his free hand.

"Since you're staying, should we put on a movie or something and move this to the bed?"

"Yeah." Andres nods. "That would be nice."

Bastian drops his right ear to Andres's left hand, which is still resting on Bastian's shoulder. "I'll get this cleaned up," he says. "All your spare stuff is still in the middle drawer of the vanity in the bathroom if you need it. If not, pick something on Netflix. I'm happy with anything."

"Schitt's Creek," Andres suggests, his hand rubbing at Bastian's shoulder.

"Good choice. Lord knows I need to check in with Stevie, my spirit character."

"Nah, you're too good-looking not to be Alexis."

"I'm too cynical to be Alexis."

"How about we compromise with David, then?"

"Okay, that I can do." Bastian nods, his gaze lingering on Andres, admiring the bronze tone of his skin.

Andres leans a little further forward, and Bastian steadies himself, sure that Andres is about to kiss him. He's surprised at how much he welcomes that idea after their tense conversation. And he's more crestfallen than he thought possible when Andres doesn't kiss him but rises from his seat and heads to get ready for bed.

CHAPTER 6

Bastian wakes well-rested and comfortable, even if his double bed is a little cramped. Sighing, he snuggles closer to the warm body pressed up behind him, not even minding that it's Andres instead of someone more suitable. More suitable isn't the correct term. Andres is more than suitable. He's technically ideal. But Bastian doesn't do ideal. He does emotionally unavailable air signs and reckless fire signs—he smartly avoids domineering and hard-headed earth signs—and he most certainly does not do sweet yet strong, sensitive water signs, which Andres is. They're too much alike, with too many opportunities for brooding and bouts of melancholy soundtracked by The Smiths. Not that Bastian doesn't do that enough on his own.

These concerns are forgotten as Andres holds him a little tighter and lets out a sleepy sigh of his own, his breath bristling the errant curls at Bastian's neckline. It's not the first time Bastian has woken up like this, enveloped in Andres's arms. As kids, they slept side by side quite frequently, from their first sleepover as five-year-olds to the many nights, sometimes full weeks, Andres would stay with Bastian's family when his own family spent multiple nights in a row at the hospital with Andres's brother Julian. This act of waking up together is so easy, so familiar, so comfortable and second nature, that Bastian isn't even bothered by the way Andres's very apparent boner is poking him. He'd be tempted to tease his friend once he opens his eyes, but that could open him up to his own bout of ridicule, or worse, an invitation for some mutual release in the form of hand stuff once Andres notices that Bastian has a hard-on to match.

"Good morning," Andres mumbles from behind him, lips grazing over the vertebrae of Bastian's neck. Neither makes any effort to move. If anything, they sink deeper into the bed and beneath the blankets together. "What time do you have to be at work today?"

"Ten, probably," Bastian says and lazily reaches for his phone. He's thwarted by Andres pulling him tighter to his chest. "Andres," Bastian says with a laugh. "I need my phone to check my schedule. And the time, for that matter."

"Sun's still low," Andres says, his voice muffled from the back of Bastian's neck. "We have plenty of time."

He's not wrong. Bastian's phone hasn't begun trilling with its usual eight a.m. alarm yet, and if Andres is still planning on giving him a ride to work today, they have even more time to have a luxuriating lie-in together. He grabs his phone and checks it anyway, in the off chance that his first client canceled and he can allow himself an even lazier morning—no such luck. Pouting, he places his phone down on the mattress and snuggles in closer to Andres, wiggling his backside against him.

"Don't start something you're not going to finish," Andres says with a slight growl in his voice, his hand sliding to Bastian's narrow hip bone.

Bastian wiggles a little bit more. Playfully, he teases, "Is this really how you want our first time to go?"

"If this is you agreeing with me that we will *have* a first time, I don't care how it goes."

"And here I thought you were supposed to be the romantic one of the two of us," Bastian says, grabbing Andres's hand from his hip and holding it to rest over his heart. "A morning quickie doesn't seem like the grand gesture of a budding relationship."

"Are you saying you want to start a relationship?" Andres asks, a hint of hope kicking up at the end of the question.

"No!" Bastian exclaims.

"Rubbing your ass on me is a funny way of saying no," Andres grumbles.

"What I'm saying is, this is nice." His heart is beginning to race like it did the first time he got on the back of Andres's motorcycle. He was terrified, convinced that he was going to die. Instead, all he ended up with was some extremely tangled curls. In theory, a roll in the sheets with Andres this morning would end with the same result. Like that first ride on the motorcycle, Bastian—not that he'll admit it out loud—is terrified. He rotates himself in Andres's arms, careful to keep some space between the two of them. "I'm saying that you're not wrong. But I'm also not ready to make this leap with you yet."

The sleepy smile that lights up Andres's face at Bastian's words is meltingly beautiful, and Bastian internally curses himself for even daring to dip his toes into these uncharted waters. He shivers slightly as Andres brings his hand up to his curls and brushes them away from his forehead, much like he had the night before. "We can go as slow with this as you want," Andres says. "No pressure. No expectations. No rush towards anything."

"And if it doesn't work out?"

"Then it doesn't work out," Andres says. "And we go back to friendship as usual."

Bastian narrows his eyes at Andres skeptically. "How can you say it like it's that simple?"

"Because it is," Andres says, brushing Bastian's curls with his fingertips again, and adds, "and because I know I'm right about this. How many times do we have to have this conversation?"

"As many times as I need, at my pace, at my speed, remember?"

Andres closes his eyes and takes a breath. "You're right. Your pace, your speed. We can discuss the what ifs however many times you need because my answer is always going to be the same."

"You're admitting that there is no going back?"

"I'm admitting that no matter how much you attempt to push me away, and no matter how hard you try to self-sabotage, you and I have been on this path from the beginning."

"Are you trying to suggest that we're soulmates or some shit?" Bastian asks with a roll of his eyes, even if it pains him. For all his wistful dreaming of having a man proclaim Bastian as his soulmate, not once had he ever dared to imagine that it would be Andres to finally suggest it to him.

"Are you trying to deny that we're not?"

"I mean, platonic, maybe. But soulmate soulmates? You're far too practical of a man to believe in that."

"Am I?" Andres laughs.

"Yes!" Bastian says. "You have to be. Because there is nothing about me that is soulmate material."

Andres narrows his eyes at him. "You know, for someone who spends his days building up other people's self-confidence, you'd think you'd see the value in yourself a little better."

"I value myself."

"Not nearly enough." Andres nudges Bastian to lie on his back, then slots himself between Bastian's parted legs, though he uses his arms to keep himself from pressing down onto Bastian. For all his verbal protests to the contrary, something deep and carnal inside Bastian is practically crying out for Andres to close this gap between them from hips to lips and everything in between.

Instead, all he gets is a quick kiss on his forehead. "But I'll show you exactly how perfect you are."

"I'm far from perfect." Bastian sighs. "You and I both know that."

This earns him another kiss on his forehead. "You're biased. Let me be the judge of that from here on out," Andres says, then rolls off of Bastian and out of bed. "Go shower. I'll brew us some coffee."

Bastian whines at the loss of Andres above him and the thought of getting out of bed.

"Fine, I'll make us some breakfast too," Andres says, opening Bastian's refrigerator and rummaging within it.

Bastian rolls on his side and watches Andres move about his tiny kitchen. He knows where to look for the coffee, where to find the pots and pans he needs, and how to move around Bastian's life as if they're already woven together. It's the domestic bliss he wanted with Ryan. Though Ryan never made an ounce of effort towards having this kind of comfortability in Bastian's life. What Andres is doing more or less resembles Bastian's role in all of his previous relationships, the one that works to make things work. The one that puts in all the effort. It's odd and disorienting, and Bastian feels far from worthy of it. In a flash, he's out of bed and off to the shower, where he can hide underneath the steaming hot water and let it rinse his anxieties away from him.

92

Once showered, fed, and dressed with Andres's hoodie thrown over his work clothes to keep him warm on the back of the bike, Bastian and Andres make their way outside. He doesn't even protest as Andres grabs his hand for the walk to his bike parked in front of Bastian's building. He only lets go when Andres straddles the bike and roars it to life, leaving Bastian to watch from the curb, where he waits for Andres to give him the go-ahead to hop on.

"You ready?" Andres asks, patting the seat behind him as he always does.

Bastian nods, feeling unnecessarily shy, as he places his hands on Andres's shoulders, then steps onto the footpeg. Once seated, he wraps his arms around Andres's waist and hooks his chin over Andres's shoulder.

"Lake Shore Drive or side streets?" Andres asks him.

"Side streets, please. I don't want the wind destroying my hair."

"As if you don't have an arsenal of ladies armed with blow dryers and hair products to sort you out when you walk through the door," Andres jokes. "Besides, there's nothing sexier than a head of mussed-up curls."

"Maybe to you." Bastian laughs, warming slightly at the thought of Andres finding his disheveled curls sexy. More proof, however, that anything developing between them is not something they can turn back from once getting started, no matter how much Andres tries to convince him they can.

"Definitely to me. Why else do you think I've been giving you all these rides to and from work?"

"This is only the third time," Bastian deadpans.

"Only the third time this year," Andres corrects and puts the bike into gear. "Now, hold on tight. We're moving."

Bastian does as he's told and settles into his seat to watch the world go by instead of worrying about this new direction life seems to be taking him. It's funny how Bastian always finds a sense of peace from the back of a motorcycle. He can't do anything back here except hold on tight. It's a lesson in trust—an example of what happens when you let someone else take the reins for a little while. It used to scare Bastian, but now, he looks forward to these rides and in allowing Andres to hold his physical well-being in his hands. It shouldn't be that much of a leap to trust Andres with his heart as well, and yet, it feels like an impossible canyon to cross. Maybe the trick is, like with riding the bike, he can hand his heart over in little twenty-minute increments. After all, no one goes on a days-long road trip for their first motorcycle ride. They have to be eased in, practice a bit, and then hit the open road with the wind and all its elements whipping them in the face as they speed to their destination. Andres said that they could take this at whatever speed Bastian needed, that they could go at his pace if he chose to give them a try. Maybe he won't be disappointed if Bastian wants to take the slow backroads, the residential side streets, and not the 90/94 expressway.

"I've gotta work tonight," Andres says as he brings the bike to a stop in front of the salon. "But I should be free on Thursday if you want to get together."

"Alright," Bastian agrees, unclasping his hands from around Andres's torso and pushing his sunglasses up onto the top of his head before he rises and dismounts off the back of the motorcycle. "Oh, and my mom wants the both of us to come out for Sunday dinner. Are you free?"

"For your mom, absolutely." Andres nods and smiles. "I'll make sure I'm off on time."

"Okay, I'll let her know." Bastian dips down and checks his reflection in the bike's side mirror, finger combing his curls back into their proper place. "Thanks for the ride."

"You're welcome," Andres says as Bastian stands. He takes his hands off the handlebars and holds the motorcycle steady with the strength in his thighs as he takes Bastian's face between his palms. "You look perfect," he assures, then places the softest of kisses onto Bastian's lips before letting go and putting the bike back into gear. He shouts over his shoulder as he rides away, "See you Thursday!"

"Yeah, see you Thursday," Bastian says to himself, his fingers brushing his lips as all the blood drains from his face. All he wants is to be back on that motorcycle with him. His eyes widen. *Okay, maybe I am dating Andres Wood.* He turns and walks through the salon's front door, his heart beating faster than he ever thought possible.

·❤·❤·❤·❤·❤·

Bastian shuts his station drawer a little too aggressively after grabbing his cutting comb and shears. "Laura, for the last time, I'm not dating Andres!" He may have admitted it to himself earlier, and his lips may still continue to feel the ghost of Andres's kiss, but he's not sure what it all entails or if it's ready for public salon consumption yet.

Laura stares at him from over her client's head as she continues to work and weave in perfectly placed highlights through their part line.

"I'm not!"

More staring, this time with a sculpted eyebrow raised.

"Fine, believe what you want. But you're wrong," Bastian says, turning back to his mirror to see his client's reflection and placing her head just so, making sure it is centered forward before he begins sectioning and cutting. He rolls his eyes dramatically at his client, making her laugh.

"Is he still denying that he and Andres are boyfriends?" Marny interjects from across the room when she shuts her blow dryer off.

"Yes," Laura says with a long-suffering sigh. "The boy is in complete denial."

"The boy is still standing right here," Bastian says, exasperated and combing a meticulous part from the crown of his client's head down to her right ear before he twists the wet hair and clips it out of his way. He looks at his client in the mirror. "Can you believe these two?"

She tilts her head to the side thoughtfully, and Bastian corrects her, tipping it back upright.

"I thought your boyfriend's name was Ryan?" she asks.

"Oh, Ryan's old news," Laura interjects. "Bastian kicked him to the curb last week." She winks at Bastian. He winks back, grateful she knows to keep up that lie when it comes to clients. "And he promptly replaced him with Andres."

"Your best friend, Andres?" Bastian's client asks.

"Best friend and total hottie!" Marny yells from the other side of the room.

"Oh, shut it, you," Bastian says, looking over his shoulder. He turns back to his client, making eye contact through the mirror. With her hair now sectioned off, he raises her chair higher to begin cutting the perimeter and length of her new style. "Don't listen to them. They don't know what they're talking about."

"The hell we don't," Laura says, dipping her applicator brush back into the lightener before applying it to her client's hair. "He can deny it all he wants, but this is the third day in a week that a certain sexy someone named Andres has rattled the salon windows with his motorcycle, either dropping Bastian off or picking him up."

"Accepting a ride from my best friend does not mean we're dating," Bastian sing-songs as he begins to snip at the ends of his client's hair.

"One, I thought *I* was your best friend—"

"You're my work wife," Bastian corrects.

"Whatever. And two, while you are correct that accepting three rides from someone does not make them your boyfriend, wearing his clothes all three times does," she says.

The whole room goes quiet, and everyone turns to look at Bastian. His cheeks burn under their gazes. "It's cold on the back of that bike!" he exclaims. "Excuse me for accepting the offer of his hoodie."

"Did he offer it to you before or after you woke up in the same bed together?"

"I live in a studio apartment," Bastian says. "There's only room for one bed."

"Oh my god!" Marny brings her hands, complete with shears and a comb, to her cheeks. "There was only one bed!"

"I'm not going to feel sorry for you when you accidentally jab yourself in your eye with those." Bastian indicates to the shears, then turns back to his laughing client with another roll of his eyes. "Honestly."

"Wait," Laura's client says from somewhere underneath her head of full foils. "Is this the same Andres that your fiancé is business partners with?"

"It is, indeed," Laura says, weaving through another parting.

"Small world," Laura's client says.

"Not that small." Bastian shrugs as he brings down another parted-off section of his client's hair to cut. "I introduced Laura to Justin."

"Yes," Laura confirms. "Bastian and Andres have been friends since they were kids. And Bastian and I met in beauty school. Andres and Justin met in high school. Bastian introduced us all."

"Bastian went to high school with Justin as well, then?" Laura's client asks as if this is some sort of impossibility.

"No," Bastian says, annoyed by her tone. "I rotted away at public school while Andres moved on to better things at private school."

"Yeah, he *really* moved on," Laura teases, and the room laughs again. "Moved right on to silently pining away for our darling Bastian over here."

"Please." Bastian scoffs. "Hopping from bed to bed is hardly pining."

"He says as if he hasn't done the same thing," Laura teases. She turns her client to face their mirror and flips her foils back away from her forehead so her client can see again. "This boy," she points at Bastian with her tail comb, "over here is a real heartbreaker."

"And if he breaks Andres's heart, I'm gonna burn him with my one-inch curling iron," Marny threatens, not even looking at him, focusing on checking her client's cut for symmetry.

"That makes two of us," Laura agrees, shooting Marny a look through the mirrors before looking back at her client. "Andres is such a catch. Bastian has no idea how lucky he is."

"Excuse you, but I know exactly how lucky I am," Bastian says, lowering his client's chair to get a better angle to work on her layers. "As you previously mentioned, I've been best friends with Andres since we were kids. I know better than anybody here how amazing he is."

"Then what's the issue?" Laura holds up her right hand and, punctuating each point by extending her fingers, says, "One, he's gorgeous. Two, he's rich. Three, he's almost too sweet. And four, he's *crazy* about you!'"

"Sounds like there isn't a problem at all," Marny says.

"Sounds like the perfect situation," Laura's client adds.

"Sounds like my dream man," Marny's client chips in.

"Sounds like someone is scared he's going to fuck this up," Bastian's client says wisely.

"Hey." Bastian steps back and holds his hand to his chest. "I thought you were on my side?"

"I am," she says. "And I think you should date him."

"Guys like Andres don't stay available forever," Laura says. "We all only want the best for you. And he's the best."

"Better than your fiancé?" Bastian challenges.

"Absolutely." Laura laughs. "You've met Justin. He's a complete himbo. A lovable himbo, but a himbo nonetheless." The whole room laughs along with her. She leans against the shared counter between his and her stations and crosses her arms. "Look, all we're saying, Bastian, is that if it walks like a duck and talks like a duck, it's a duck. You're dating Andres Wood."

"I am not."

"Bastian." Lizzie appears out of nowhere as if she's a magical salon fairy here to take the focus off Bastian's love life. Bastian couldn't be more grateful for her presence, relieved at the change of subject her arrival brings.

"Yes, Lizzie," he says warmly.

"Andres sent over lunch for you. Do you want it in the break-room, or should I put it in the fridge?"

Bastian hangs his head, his cheeks flushing with color, as all the ladies in the room explode into uproarious laughter.

"The breakroom will be fine," he says. "I'll eat after this client."

Sitting in the breakroom, Bastian opens the bag of delivered food. It's predictably perfect—a black bean burger and fries made the way he likes, and there's even a small arugula and tomato salad for a quick pick-me-up if he needs it later, which he will. He grabs a fry and pops it into his mouth, then picks up the centaur porn with his other hand to read to Marny, who's across from him at the table eating her own lunch.

"The gap between them closed," Bastian reads aloud, his voice sultry and teasing. "And Elsabeth couldn't decide where to place her hands. Does she explore his broad pecs?"

"She should definitely explore those pecs!" Marny yells out.

"... or should she explore his shoulders?" Bastian places the book down and looks at Marny curiously. "Which set of shoulders, I wonder? Do centaurs have shoulders?"

"Of course they have shoulders." Marny laughs, wiping tears from her eyes.

"No, I know." Bastian laughs. "But like do they have two sets of shoulders or two sets of hips. What's the anatomy here?"

"Does it matter?" Marny chokes out.

"I guess not," he says, then picks the book back up. "She chooses to run her hands over his flank—"

Bastian is interrupted by Mitchel, who is striding through the breakroom and heading into the office. He quickly slides the book out of sight and into his lap, then takes a bite of his food as he and Marny share a knowing look. Backroom fun is over.

"Bastian," Mitchel says. "I pay you to cut hair, not read books."

"Technically, I'm on break, so you aren't actually paying me right now," Bastian quips.

Mitchel turns his attention to Marny. "And what about you? Are you on a break as well? Isn't there a color order that needs to be put away?"

"Don't we have Lizzie and Bethany here to do that?" Marny asks without making eye contact with him as she takes the final bite of her sandwich.

"Why have them do it when you two are back here reading books?"

"Again, we're eating lunch," Bastian says and resists the urge to suggest to Mitchel that he go do it. "But don't worry. I'll make sure the order gets put away once I'm done."

"Be sure that you do," Mitchel says, then steps into his office to do whatever it is that he came here to do that isn't putting away the color order.

Marny rolls her eyes. "Funs over," she says, then gets up and leaves the breakroom.

The door hasn't shut completely before Laura rushes in. Normally, she's so well put together, so the dark circles under her eyes and less-than-perfect bun are odd. If Bastian wasn't annoyed with her being the ringleader in his earlier public tribunal, he'd be quick to ask her what's wrong.

"You gonna eat all that?" Laura asks as she steals a French fry and sits at the breakroom table across from him.

"As a matter of fact, I am." Bastian huffs and slides the food further from her reach.

"Okay, you're mad," Laura says. "I went a little too far out there. I'm sorry."

"You're fine." Bastian takes a bite of his food and thoughtfully chews. She is fine. She wasn't teasing him in any way that she hadn't in the past or that he hadn't when she first started dating Justin. It's just—it feels different when it's about Andres. It feels more personal and less performative. More like a truth coming to light instead of thinly veiled reality to keep some semblance of privacy between hairstylist and client. It's outside the usual dog and pony show required to keep their clients entertained for the hours and money spent in their chairs. It's one thing to come up with a funny spin on how he and Ryan had broken up. It will be a much larger task to explain any heartbreak associated with Andres's disappearance.

"It doesn't feel like I'm fine," she says, this time silently asking with her eyes and her fingers if she can have another fry. Bastian, unable to stay upset with Laura for long, slides the paper a little closer to her as an answer. She grabs one and nods her thanks. "And it also feels like there's more to this story. Like you're not telling me something."

"I've told you all there is to tell. Andres and I are friends, and he's expressed interest in being more than friends."

Her foot nudges him under the table. "And you don't share that interest?"

He takes another bite of his burger.

"So, you do share that interest?"

"I didn't say that!" Bastian says as he swallows.

"You didn't *not* say that," she counters. "Which leads me to believe that you do."

"It's not that I don't," Bastian says, the memory of this morning's kiss dancing across his lips again. "It's more, I never even considered it to be an option."

"Now it is an option. All you have to do is reach out and take it. It's not that hard."

"It actually is quite hard. Andres isn't some random fling, some guy I swiped right on Tinder, or some dude my best friend introduced me to randomly at a restaurant opening," Bastian says pointedly, referring to how he had introduced Laura to Justin. "If this goes sideways, there's more at stake than if you and Justin hadn't worked out."

"How so?"

"To start, if you and Justin hadn't worked out, all you were losing was free meals at their restaurants."

"Pfft." Laura laughs. "I lost that even with us working out. When was the last time Justin sent me lunch?"

Bastian thinks about this. He honestly can't remember a single instance. "True, and we need to have a talk with him about that. You deserve lunch."

"More than you can ever imagine." She sighs, then quickly bristles. "But this isn't about me. This is about you." She points at him and then grabs another of his fries.

"We could make it about you," he teases and cuts what's left of his burger in half with the little compostable knife that Andres included with his meal. He passes it to her, and she smiles at him gratefully. "In fact, I'd much prefer it."

"Oh no, you're not getting off this easy." She takes a bite of the food and drops her head back as she chews. "This is so good. Bless your boyfriend for the sustenance."

"He's not my boyfriend!"

"Sorry," she apologizes. "Bless your best friend for the sustenance."

"Much better." Bastian picks up his phone. He grabs a fry and holds it to his mouth, then snaps a picture of himself. He quickly posts it to Instagram, captioning it, *When the bestie sends you lunch.*

"He's not dating him, but he sends thirst traps to him," Laura says to no one in particular.

"This was hardly a thirst trap. And I didn't send it to him. I posted it on Insta."

"The way you were dangling that fry around your lips was more than a little bit suggestive. Also, why would you post that and not send it to him as a thank-you text? How else are we supposed to get fed around here?" She takes another bite of her food and then quietly adds, "Lord knows Mitchel believes we don't need to eat during a ten-hour day."

Then, as if he heard her, Mitchel's voice rings out from the office. "Laura, shouldn't you be out on the floor preparing for your next client instead of gossiping?"

Laura closes her eyes and takes a deep breath through her nose, her lips pressed tightly together. "She hasn't arrived yet," she explains, her voice stiff with faux cheerfulness.

"You alright?" Bastian asks, his voice barely above a whisper. It's not like Laura to openly complain about the way things are run around here or for her to get snippy around the powers that be. She generally goes with the flow and acts as the model stylist—shows up and runs on time, never says no to squeezing one more person in, works every Sunday wedding that gets booked despite it being her day off. She's a salon owner's wet dream. And it won't come as a surprise to anyone when she finally gets bumped up to Senior Stylist this summer. It's a long time coming and should've been hers last year, but instead, Mitchel chose Bastian. He'd earned it for sure. He's competent and extremely talented when it comes to his craft, but Laura works harder, and it wasn't the first time she had to get in line behind Bastian, who always gets a boost for being a man in this industry largely made up of women.

"I'm fine," she says as Bethany peeks into the breakroom to inform her that her client has arrived. "Thanks, Beth." She wolfs down what's left of the food Bastian had shared with her, then looks at him pleadingly one more time. "Listen, I actually do need to talk to you about something. Justin is working late on Thursday night. Can we have dinner after work?"

"Sure thing," Bastian says. She hardly ever asks him for anything, especially since she and Justin got together. His heart sinks as he realizes that he'll have to cancel plans with Andres to make that happen.

"Laura, your client is waiting," Mitchel reminds her.

"I know!" she says crisply, then looks back at Bastian. "Thanks," she says and walks out of the breakroom and back onto the salon floor with a forced smile on her face that makes Bastian suspicious of what is going on with her. Maybe they are finally getting a little closer to leaving here than he had thought.

He grabs his phone again and texts Andres.

> Something has come up with Laura. I have to cancel for Thursday.

> That's alright.

Andres texts back almost immediately and then sends a follow-up.

> I'll see you Sunday, then?

> Yeah. Sunday sounds good.

> I could come by after work on Saturday if you want. Spend the night, and then we can go out to see your parents together.

Bastian considers this. Logistically, it makes sense. He was going to ask Andres to give him a ride anyway so he could avoid having to take the Red Line to catch the Green Line out to Oak Park. And again, it's not like they've never spent the night together, case in point being last night, but it still feels different, and Bastian's heart rate picks up at the prospect.

> *Sounds good.*

He sends, then quickly types out another message.

> *Sorry again about Thursday.*

And then another.

> *And thanks again for lunch. It really hit the spot.*

A few seconds pass as he finishes eating and watching the tiny expectant dots of Andres writing a text flash continuously on his screen.

> *No problem. See you Saturday.*

CHAPTER 7

S hrugging off his spring jacket and hanging it on the back of his chair, Bastian looks around the vast and utterly unintimate space of Osteria, an Italian restaurant located a short walk northeast of the salon. He furrows his brow in confusion as to why Laura had picked here of all places, especially when one considers that they'll have to pay for their meal instead of only having to tip at one of Justin and Andres's restaurants. Add to that, it's deafening, and she mentioned that she needed to talk to him. This hardly seems like the best place for chatting.

"Alright, Laura. Hit me with it!" Bastian says, straining his voice and unfolding his napkin to place it across his lap. He leans forward in his chair.

"Let's order first," she says and greedily reaches into the breadbasket.

"I thought this was urgent?"

"It is ... ish," she says sheepishly as their server arrives.

The server's fake smile spreads unevenly across his lips. The poor guy looks like he's not a day over nineteen and that the craziness that comes with working at a restaurant a few walkable blocks away from the Mag Mile has run him ragged. Bastian sees his younger self in the kid and vows to leave a decent tip, as well as maybe one of Andres's business cards to get this kid away from the burnout machine that comes with working at a tourist restaurant. "Good evening, folks. Can I start you off with something to drink?"

"Yes, please," Bastian says without having even looked at the drink menu. "We'll split a bottle of prosecco. Whatever you have is fine. Thanks!"

Laura holds up her hand. "I'm not drinking tonight."

Bastian raises an eyebrow at her, then turns back to the server. "Never mind the bottle. A glass for me will be fine."

"And I'm ready to order!" Laura blurts out. Shocked, Bastian turns and looks at her again, quizzically. "I'll have the tagliatelle, Bolognese sauce, please. And more bread. Oh, and some cheese and olive oil if you could. And a sprite."

"Okay," the waiter says, writing her order down. He looks to Bastian. "And you, sir."

Bastian glances at the menu, finds the first thing he can without meat, and orders it. "The ravioli, please." He grabs Laura's menu out of her hand and stacks it with his own, then passes it to their server with a quiet, "Thank you." Bastian turns his attention back to Laura, the strangeness of the moment weighing him. "Alright, what the fuck is going on?"

She looks at him with big, pleading, nervous eyes. "I'm pregnant," she says, then hangs her head.

"Holy shit," Bastian says. "What the fuck did you go and do that for?" He doesn't mean to sound judgmental, but this doesn't coincide with her plans—*their* plans, for that matter, as they've been planting the seeds of ideas and dreams of branching off and opening their own salon for the last few months. However, the consensus has always been the same. "We'll talk about it after the wedding," which is now approximately six months away, planned for late October at the tail end of wedding season.

"It's not like I planned it. It just happened."

"And what does Justin say?"

Her shoulders drop, making her look even sadder. "He's over the moon. You know Justin; he was made to be a dad."

"Don't sell yourself short," Bastian says, offering her a small smile. "You'll make a great mom if that's what you choose."

"Do you think so?" she asks as their server drops off more bread and Bastian's glass of wine.

"Of course I do," he says emphatically, and he really does. Laura is warm and patient but also incredibly playful and funny. Any child would be lucky to call her Mom. But clearly, there is something underneath the surface here. He takes a sip of his drink and eyes her over the rim of the glass. "But you know that. So, let's break this down."

"Please do," she says and rubs at her temples, creating flyaway wings and disheveling her always-perfect hair.

"Alright." He frowns and takes a slow sip of his wine. "What about work?" He does not envy her position and genuinely wishes he could offer her a drink right now.

"I don't know." She sighs. "I couldn't have picked a worse time to get pregnant. My clients are going to murder me. They're already pissed that my honeymoon is scheduled so close to Thanksgiving. They're most certainly not going to be happy about me going on maternity leave throughout the entire holiday season."

"Neither will Mitchel," Bastian points out.

"Nope." Laura laughs. "Definitely not him. I guess I can say goodbye to Senior Stylist."

"Not necessarily." That's a lie. Bastian knows full well that this is not a good sign for her career.

Laura gives him her best stone-faced glare.

"Okay, you're right. I was trying to be nice, but I see you want brutally honest Bastian tonight." He takes another sip of his wine and then breaks himself off a piece of bread before she eats it all. "You can definitely say goodbye to Senior Stylist. And your clients are going to flip their shit. They'll act all happy at first, of course, but then lose it the moment you need to cut back on hours. And you'll be lucky if you get half of them back, let alone your chair, when you return from maternity leave. It's not fair, Laura, and it fucking sucks. But them's the breaks."

"Thank you," she says and looks like she means it.

"Lemme guess, you needed me to tell you straight up how it's gonna go because Justin is infuriatingly telling you that everything is going to be fine."

"Yes." She laughs, though it's tinged with bitterness.

"And he's assuring you that all of your dreams are going to come true and that you can have it all. Because he can, in fact, provide it all. But that's not what you want. You've been self-sufficient for ages. Even when we were living in that squalid one-bedroom apartment together the first year we got our chairs."

"See, you get it," she says. "And it's not that I don't want the best life I can have with Justin and," she gestures down at herself, "our soon-to-be child. It's just ... this changes everything so abruptly."

This, Bastian has to laugh at. "So you do understand my hesitancy towards abrupt change."

"Of course I do." She laughs back at him. "But me having a baby and you dating Andres are two completely different ballparks."

"I really don't think they are," Bastian says and downs what's left in his glass as their server drops off their food. He catches the server's eye and points to his drink. "I'll have another one of these."

"Bastian, my entire life is going to change," she says as she takes a bite, contentedly nodding her approval of the food as she chews.

"And you think mine isn't?" he asks, affronted. "You know you're not the only one who is uncomfortable with change."

"I know," she says by way of apology. "I didn't mean to offend. And I do know that me having a baby affects you too."

"I'm not worried about that." He takes a bite of his food. Sure, he's a little bummed that this will likely change his work situation. He'll have to make up for her absence by taking on some of her clients and working longer hours, and that any plans—even if they were not completely fleshed out—they may have shared to open their own salon are now back-burnered, if not now thrown in the trash entirely. Despite that, he is happy for her and whatever she chooses. He opts to try and change the subject. "So, I guess we'll be returning that size two BHLDN wedding dress then."

"Oh no," she says, shaking her head. "I love that dress. Part of what I wanted to talk to you about was that I wanted to put a rush on my wedding. I'll talk to Justin about moving up the date."

"We're going proper shotgun then?" Bastian teases. "How scandalous."

"Yes, that is the idea." She smirks. "So, after I talk to Justin, I'm going to need your help, and he'll need Andres's to pull this off."

"Whatever you need, we can manage," Bastian says.

"Thank you." She takes a deep breath and smooths the sides of her hair. "I can always count on you to get it."

"Wait, they're changing the wedding date?" Andres asks, his voice slightly muffled from the sound of water hitting him and the tiled walls of Bastian's shower and tub. He jumped in there the moment he arrived at Bastian's place after a long Saturday night shift at Graze. Bastian has to strain to hear him from where he's seated upright in bed, his hair still mussed and his eyes still heavily lidded from the catnap he took awaiting Andres's arrival.

"That's what she's hoping for," Bastian says around a yawn. "They don't have a new date yet, but I imagine she's shooting for July or August at the latest. Anything past that and her dress won't be able to be properly altered to fit flatteringly."

"Why don't they just elope?" Andres asks and shuts the water off.

"You know how they are," Bastian says, his head facing forward but his eyes straining to the side to look into the bathroom, where Andres will no doubt be stepping out of the shower soon. No harm ever came from a little peek. "All pomp and circumstance when it comes to these things."

"Pretty sure pomp and circumstance go out the window in this case." Andres laughs as one of his incredibly long, muscular, and suitably dark, fuzzy-haired legs steps out from behind the shower curtain. The rest of him remains frustratingly obscured by the partially closed bathroom door. Bastian can hear Andres open the vanity cabinet, followed by the sound of fabric being pulled from its depths as Andres grabs a towel.

"You try telling her or Justin that," Bastian says and leans forward in his bed, hoping to get a better view.

Andres pokes his head around the corner, a smirk on his face. "Like what you see?" he teases.

"I see nothing," Bastian says. "And I was only leaning forward so you could hear me better."

"Sure you were," Andres says and steps out of the bathroom with a towel draped around his waist, his freshly washed hair dripping rivulets of water down his well-sculpted chest. Bastian reaches for his water glass on the bedside table and takes a drink. He watches as Andres steps into a pair of boxer briefs and slides them up his legs underneath the cover of the towel. He removes the towel from around his waist and uses it to dry his hair. Now, catching Bastian's eyes, he says, "Thanks again for letting me use the shower."

"No problem," Bastian says. "I wasn't about to allow you into my bed smelling like an industrial kitchen. When was the last time you cleaned your fryers?"

"Every day," Andres says. "What kind of a two-bit operation do you think I run?"

"One that makes you reek like French fries."

"You like the smell of French fries."

"Of course I do. Everyone does. But not on their Egyptian cotton sheets." Bastian takes another sip of his water, trying not to let his eyes linger on the way Andres's abs move with each scrunch

117

of the towel into his hair. He tries to keep his eyes from traveling lower, very aware that Andres is standing next to his bed wearing next to nothing.

"I know. I'm only teasing," Andres says. "You act like I don't shower the minute I get home from work every day anyway. You're constantly scolding me that my scalp is dry."

"It's not as dry as it used to be now that I have you using something that doesn't also clean your balls."

Andres hangs his towel over the bathroom door. "And I shall thank you daily for this, even if it is five times as expensive."

"Try ten times." Bastian lifts his chin towards Andres. "You get yours for cost."

"Damn. Remind me to thank you properly the next time I need a re-up."

"Pfft." Bastian scoffs. "You act like you couldn't afford the actual cost. And besides, you more than make it up to me with lunch deliveries. That's how this whole barter system works."

"Oh, so we're bartering now?" Andres questions as he slips into Bastian's bed.

"Haven't we always been?"

"I mean, I guess." Andres looks at Bastian innocently. It's an off-putting look for someone who consistently looks nothing short of confident, and Bastian feels as if he's been caught in a trap. "If lunch gets me hair products, what do I need to do in exchange for a goodnight kiss?"

Definitely a trap. "I will not barter you for kisses."

"Damn." Andres hums. He slides an arm around Bastian's waist and pulls them both further under the covers. He places a kiss on Bastian's shoulder. "What about a blowjob?"

"Excuse me!" Bastian says, affronted, though truthfully a little curious about the proposition, remembering the kiss Andres laid on him at the beginning of the week. "I'm no easy conquest. You're going to have to do a lot more than bring me lunch to get a blowjob out of me."

"I was talking about one for you," Andres says with a laugh and pulls Bastian closer to his chest. "You're cute when you're outraged. You know that, right?"

"And you're appalling," he says, but the words don't feel right on his tongue.

"Oh, you have no idea," Andres teases, his lips hovering around Bastian's ear. He places a little kiss on the shell. "I guess these little kisses to your freckles will have to do for now." And he kisses Bastian again, this time at the junction where Bastian's jaw meets his neck right below his ear.

"You are insufferable." Bastian lets out a loud sigh, half out of annoyance and half out of arousal.

"Hmmm ..." Andres's hum reverberates up Bastian's spine. He places another kiss on Bastian's neck as if his lips alone can still Bastian's shiver of anticipation. "Good night, Bastian," he says, his lips brushing Bastian's skin.

"Good night?" Bastian questions and tries to turn himself around in Andres's embrace. "Is that it?"

"For now," Andres says sleepily, his arms squeezing Bastian a little bit more. "But maybe when you wake up, you'll be more interested in giving me that kiss."

♥ ・ ♥ ・ ♥ ・ ♥ ・ ♥

Upon waking the next morning, Bastian lets out a deep breath. He'd slept in frustrating, thought-filled fits—both sexual and emotional—and it's all thanks to this smug, though admittedly handsome, best friend of his that has been passed out cold for the last seven hours at his side. At some point in the night, Andres had loosened his hold, and Bastian was able to turn to face him, which is how he wakes right now. His eyes are only half open, but that doesn't ruin the view. If anything, it makes the image of Andres peacefully sleeping that much more vivid. His thick dark waves lay strewn across the pillow, his long lashes cast shadows on his cheeks, which frame his perfectly angular and long sloped nose, his jaw is sharp and shadowed from both needing a shave and the late morning sunlight shining through Bastian's apartment window, and his lips are slightly parted, maddeningly kissable.

Bastian admits to himself that he really does want to kiss those lips again. That he wants to feel Andres's scratchy stubble rub against his face or, even more telling, between his thighs in the way that Andres had suggested before he fell asleep, leaving Bastian half-hard at the idea. He should've kissed him goodnight instead of making things more difficult to his own detriment.

The thing is, Bastian has wanted to say yes to Andres for quite some time, or more accurately, he wanted to say yes some time ago but had previously given up on his hopes that Andres would ever see him in such a way. His attraction to Andres at a young age, the stirring in his belly that felt so unfamiliar and unknown, had helped Bastian realize early that he was gay. Being the smart boy that Bastian was, he knew to squash that down, that eleven-year-old boys don't think about kissing their best friend. So, he had stopped himself from imagining the possibility until Andres had awoken it again years later by proclaiming to Bastian that he was bi. Even then, though he'd missed out on the elite private school education and was attending cosmetology school instead of college like Andres was, Bastian had the foresight to know that two best friends were better off as friends. Even though Andres's proclamation had awakened Bastian's childhood desire to kiss his best friend again, he swallowed it down and hasn't even let himself indulge in a fantasy wank about the scenario.

Now, here Andres lies, being stupidly kissable even in his sleep, and that little piece of Bastian that he has kept dormant for so long is aching to come out and scream about it. *Kiss him, dammit!* that deep yearning keeps yelling. *Get over your bullshit and kiss him!*

The problem with that, though, is that Bastian's bullshit isn't bullshit. There's so much good history between them, and so much bad history in Bastian's love life, that his not wanting to cross-contaminate one with the other shouldn't be an issue. But yet, it is. Because all he wants to do is kiss those stupid, slight-ly-chapped-from-sleep lips. Maybe he can take this leap? Maybe he can finally give in to what it is that Andres is asking for? Maybe he can finally admit to himself again after all these years that he wants this? So what if he'll never be good enough for Andres? So what if he'll never really fit in with Andres's social crowd? Andres seems to be under the impression that Bastian is not leagues below him and his standing in this world. So why not go for it if the smug bastard always insists on being right about everything involving Bastian anyway? Why not, if it means he can get another kiss from Andres's lips along with Andres's promise for so much more.

"Good morning," the lips in question mumble.

"Good morning," Bastian answers, and he hates how dreamy his voice sounds even to his own ears. And he hates even more how his heart beats a little faster in his chest when he sees the soft smile that pulls at Andres's lips as he blinks his eyes awake.

"Did you sleep well?" Andres asks, rubbing his face with his hand.

"I did," Bastian lies.

"Me too." Andres lets out a yawn. "Had lovely dreams about kissing you awake this morning, but it seems you have beaten me to it."

"I don't believe that was part of the barter," Bastian says.

Andres hums, long and low and unmistakably hungry. He reaches with his arm and pulls Bastian flush to his chest. "You do understand the terms of the barter then?"

"Yeah." Bastian laughs. "You suck me off, and I kiss you in return. Sounds like a pretty good deal to me."

"You seem to have the advantage here," Andres says, giving his hips a little nudge forward, his morning wood magnetically finding Bastian's to press up against, and Bastian feels the defensive walls he's built around his feelings and desires crumbling.

"A man must know how to work all situations to his advantage," Bastian says as his traitorous hips jut forward, searching for more contact and pressure from Andres.

"Very true." Andres begins to grind slowly and rhythmically against Bastian. He places his hand on Bastian's ass, squeezes, and lifts him a touch higher and somehow closer. He dips his head slightly, bringing his lips to hover over Bastian's, and Bastian wants to crane his neck to meet him the rest of the way. Huskily, Andres says, "Maybe I can get the kiss first, just this once."

"I'll give you whatever you want as long as you don't stop moving like that," Bastian gasps out, wanting so desperately to reach between them to push the fabric of their briefs out of the way and to slip his dexterous fingers around their mutual morning arousal.

Andres closes the gap and kisses him. His lips move slowly but forcefully and part enough to slip his tongue out to lick at Bastian's bottom lip before he sucks it into his mouth, taking all of Bastian's self-control with it. Bastian lets his hand find its way between them, his fingers dragging across Andres's skin and exploring the ridges of his well-defined abdomen the best that they can with the limited space. He tugs at the elastic waistband of Andres's briefs, pausing to allow Andres the opportunity to stop him before it becomes too late to take it back.

Andres only makes it worse. He slides the hand that's been holding Bastian's ass in place under the waistband of Bastian's briefs and onto his flesh. His broad palm and large fingers grip Bastian possessively, and Bastian wants to give himself entirely over to him. Together, they clumsily remove each other's briefs, their hips stilling and their hands and feet working to rid themselves of the loathsome fabric. Andres pauses their kiss and presses his forehead against Bastian's, seemingly catching his breath but also maybe giving Bastian another out that Bastian isn't about to take. Bastian reaches between them and grabs both of their lengths in his hand, his grip loose enough for them to move, and Andres waits only a second longer to do so.

Pressing his lips back against Bastian's, Andres takes control, his hips moving back and forth, up and down, causing their erections to glide together inside Bastian's grip. It doesn't take long before they are coming together in the space between them, coating Bastian's hand and the skin around their cocks as fast as two schoolboys getting their first feel of what sex can be. By the time their hips still for good, Bastian and Andres are laughing around each other's lips joyously, like this is the stupidest thing they've ever done.

CHAPTER 8

After their sexual exploits this morning, the ride to Bastian's parents' house on Andres's motorcycle has taken on an intimate feel. Bastian is suddenly very aware of all the places they are touching, even if it is through multiple layers of clothing. His chest is pressed against Andres's back, his chin is hooked over his shoulder, his arms are wrapped around Andres's torso, and his thighs cage Andres's hips. Objectively, the only way they could be closer is if they were back in Bastian's bed, their bodies writhing together, the mere thought of which has Bastian's heart racing and his lips pulling up into a boyish grin that he quickly shakes off.

"Cold?" Andres asks with concern in his voice as they soar under the Green Line "L" tracks that run above Lake Street.

"No," Bastian says into Andres's ear. "Only the shivers."

"Hmmm." Andres hums knowingly and engages the clutch, then takes his right hand off the throttle and places it onto Bastian's thigh, giving him a gentle and reassuring squeeze as they coast towards a stop light.

Bastian grips him a little tighter around the waist and closes his eyes. He can already see his mother's face at the sight of them arriving in this very intimate position, and he's not in the mood for having to explain it to her. He suddenly wishes they'd taken Andres's BMW, which is usually reserved for winter instead.

Andres seems to read Bastian's thoughts. "I'm assuming you don't want to tell your parents about our morning."

Bastian laughs out loud. "Do *you* want to tell my parents, specifically my mother, about us having sex?"

"God no!" Andres laughs. "What I meant was us hooking up—"

"Not helping," Bastian says as a flutter ripples through his stomach.

When the light turns green, Andres lets go of Bastian's thigh. He puts the bike back into gear and lightly twists the throttle. "That's not what I meant, and you know it, smartass."

"I know. And you're right. I don't want them to know about us. Not yet, at least. Is that alright?"

"It's fine," Andres says. "I've told you from the start that we can do this at your speed. I'm relieved that your speed involves us mutually getting off now."

"You say that like the happenings of this morning are going to be a regular occurrence."

"If I have any say in it," Andres pauses and brings his hand back to Bastian's thigh, and dammit, if it doesn't make Bastian's cock twitch ever so slightly, "then yes, we will be doing that again. Often."

"Only that?" Bastian asks.

"Don't start something you're not gonna finish. I will find a way to sneak you into your childhood bedroom and nail you on that rickety twin bed frame."

"Wouldn't that be a surprise twist for the Joy Division posters still hanging on my walls to witness," Bastian says with a smile in his voice and more stirring in his pants at the thought of them trying to remain fast and quiet on his childhood bed.

"Anyway, don't worry. We'll tell them when you're ready. I will be on my best behavior today."

Andres's best behavior turns out to be less than impressive. Although, Bastian is no saint either. It's like neither can stop themselves from touching the other, leaning too close, winking when they think no one is looking, or laughing quietly at everything hovering unspoken between them. It doesn't help that they are in cramped quarters inside Bastian's childhood home, a quaint bungalow with small rooms filled with too much furniture, most of which are as old as Bastian.

Andres even manages to sneak Bastian upstairs to Bastian's childhood bedroom as he promised on the bike. "Don't worry," he says, Bastian's face cradled between his palms. "I only wanted to kiss you."

Now, with having officially broken the seal on life as something more than friends, Bastian cannot deny this request. He cranes his neck and meets Andres's lips, unable to contain the smile that pulls at his cheeks at how unmistakably right this all feels.

"You needed that too, huh?" Andres stares deep into Bastian's eyes, unblinking. He gives him one more quick kiss, then spins away and takes in Bastian's room with the rickety bed and mismatched chest of drawers shoved into the corner. The paint on the walls has faded with age and the wear of supporting vintage Cure and Joy Division posters, pictures of the boys from *Gossip Girl* torn from the pages of *People* magazine, and film stills from Velvet Goldmine. "To think it took us twenty-five years to finally share a kiss in this room."

"Any other rooms in this house you want to christen?"

"I thought I was supposed to be on my best behavior today," Andres says, smirking as he gives Bastian a playful yet firm pat on his ass.

Bastian hates the way it excites him. He can't control himself as he counters in an attempt to get back his equilibrium, "Perhaps we can debauch *your* parents' house next."

Andres eyes Bastian, the playful smirk gone. "Don't be a brat, Bastian. You know I've always felt more at home here than there."

"I know," Bastian says and kisses Andres once more. This time, he brings a hand to the hem of Andres's Off-White pullover, his fingertips dragging across the dips and ridges of his abdomen. "But don't ask me to not be a brat. That is kind of my thing, after all."

A smile returns to Andres's face. "You're right," he says, pulling away from Bastian and smoothing his clothes. "Besides, I wouldn't have you any other way."

"Boys!" Bastian's mom calls from the bottom of the stairs. "Are you coming down? Dinner's ready."

Andres leans in close to Bastian. "You sure you don't want to tell her about us?"

"Absolutely not!" Bastian says louder than he should.

"Then why did you bother coming over?" Bastian's mom yells back. "Get down here, boys! I haven't seen you in ages, and you immediately hide in your bedroom like you're teenagers again."

Andres gives Bastian a quick wink and then steps out of the room, leaving Bastian to follow after him, much as Bastian always did when they were children.

"Sorry, Mrs. Russo," Andres says as he makes his way down the stairs.

"None of this Mrs. Russo stuff," Annemarie says, swinging the dish towel in her petite hands to drape it over her narrow shoulder. She looks up at them as they descend the stairs, and a kind and content smile lights up her freckled face before she heads back into the kitchen where dinner is waiting. "Andres, dear, you know better."

"Sorry, Mom," he says. But Bastian can't help but notice the way Andres's shoulders slump ever so slightly at the words, and he suddenly wonders when Andres has last spoken to his own mother. That's a topic Bastian is not about to broach, so, instead, it's his turn to give Andres a playful smack on his ass as he rushes to squeeze past him in the hallway, quickly making his way to the kitchen table and grabbing a seat on the small bench under the window.

Andres sits beside him, and Bastian nudges his knee against Andres's thigh.

"So, you finally decided to rejoin us," Bastian's dad, Dominic, an older and more rugged version of Bastian, says as he pours wine into stemless glasses for each of them from his seat across the small rectangular table. Bastian checks the label on the bottle and bites at his lip when he recognizes it as something from the bottom shelves of the grocery store.

"Sorry," Bastian says, keeping his thigh pressed against Andres's. "Andres wanted to see something in my room."

Dominic's eyes flick over them before he nods and hands Andres a glass. Andres takes it and immediately has a sip, hums politely, and then holds it up to Dominic in approval. Dominic hands the next glass to Bastian. "You missed the end of a sorry game. Bulls lost to the Pistons, one-nineteen to ninety-one."

"Oof," Andres says and grimaces. "There go any of our playoff hopes for this year, huh?"

"I think our hopes for the playoffs were lost before the season even started."

Bastian's mom places a large tray of eggplant parmesan on the table and takes a seat. "Eat up!" she says, and Bastian starts dishing up the food, beginning with a plate for her. She smiles at him and then looks at Andres. "Does your father still have season tickets?" she asks. "Would be fun for the four of you to all go to a game."

"Fun for those three, I think you mean," Bastian titters. "Not me."

Andres takes another sip of his wine before he answers. "I believe he does, though I think he tends to give them to clients. However, if you wanted to attend a game next season, I'm sure I could get us some great seats."

"Could you, dear?" Annemarie asks. "I think I might even like to go to a game." She looks around the table at all three of them. "You boys probably don't remember, but we took the two of you and Julian to a game the year the Bulls won the championship."

Dominic laughs. "You'll have to be a little more specific on the year," he teases. "There were six championships back in their heyday."

"I do remember that," Andres says, a sad smile running across his lips. He takes a deep breath, grabs the serving spoon from Bastian, and fixes himself a plate. "This looks good."

"Oh, do you think so?" Annemarie asks. "I know it's nothing compared to what you serve at your restaurants."

"I'll take a home-cooked meal over restaurant food any day," he says and takes a bite, nodding in approval as he chews. The rest of the table follows his lead.

"Wonderful, honey," Dominic says, reaching to give Bastian's mom a gentle squeeze on her upper arm. She smiles proudly at the praise.

It warms Bastian's heart to see them so content with the simplest things. His mom has been making her family's eggplant parmesan this exact way for ages despite the recipe having never been written down. It used to be enough for him too and he sighs as he takes another bite, wondering when it was that he started feeling that he and his life were not enough.

Something nudges Bastian's foot under the table and brings him back to reality. He glances down, expecting to see his parents' Shih Tzu, Randy. He's surprised to see it's Andres's foot instead. His socked toes are smooth around Bastian's ankle bone. It catches Bastian off guard, and he clears his throat and then coughs into his napkin.

"You alright there, Bastian?" Andres asks, cool as can be.

"I'm fine," Bastian chokes out.

"Are you sure, honey?" Annemarie asks, concern thick in her voice and apparent on her face. "You've been flushed all day. You're not getting sick, are you?"

"You know, maybe I am," Bastian says, tilting his head to the side and knitting his eyebrows together, playing it up. "I've hardly had time to rest all week."

"Darling, you should've said. We could've rescheduled this."

"Yeah, we could've rescheduled this," Dominic says, though his face and tone suggest he knows Bastian is full of shit.

"You work so hard," Annemarie says, reaching across the table to place the back of her hand against Bastian's cheek. "And you do feel warm."

Andres's foot travels up Bastian's calf and then back down around the outside of his shin. It causes his cheeks to flush more, and he chances a quick warning at Andres beside him, who immediately stills his foot. Bastian looks back at his mother.

"I wasn't going to miss coming out here for the second weekend in a row," he says, and this time, he's the one to catch Andres off guard, feigning dropping his napkin back onto his lap and covertly placing his hand onto Andres's upper thigh, near his crotch, and squeezing him. "And I'm not sure if I'm going to have much free time coming up." He keeps his eyes focused softly on his mother while his hand continues to fondle Andres, who's doing a poor job of not squirming under Bastian's ministrations.

"Wedding season starting early this year?" Annemarie asks. "I know how that always eats into your weekends."

"It is," Bastian says, giving Andres's now hardening erection one last squeeze because if he doesn't start eating his food again, it'll look suspicious.

"And then there's Laura and Justin," Andres chimes in, taking a sip of water.

"What about Laura and Justin?" she asks.

"Oh!" Bastian grins like he's about to spill the hottest of tea and looks around the table. "They've had themselves a little," he pauses and holds his hands on either side of his head to do quotations for emphasis, "'accident.' So their wedding date will be moved up by a few months to accommodate."

"That's so exciting," Annemarie says. "Everybody loves a baby."

"Do they?" Bastian asks.

"Yes!" She swats at him.

"What does this mean for you then?" Dominic asks. "I thought the two of you were looking into opening up your own salon."

"Well ..." Bastian takes a drink of his wine. "We were. But, ahh ... this will put that on hold, I imagine."

"Why?" Andres asks.

"It's a lot of work. And since Justin was going to help fund it from her end, I imagine he has new, more important places for his money to go now."

"You know I can always help," Andres says with a shrug and another bite of his food.

"It's fine," Bastian says, slumping his shoulders. "It was always a pipe dream anyway. Besides, the thought of owning my own salon sounds horrific."

"I think you'd be good at it," Andres says.

"It would beat you giving more than half of what you bring into the house to other people, that's for sure," Dominic says. He's never really understood how the salon business, product fees, and commissions work, no matter how many times Bastian has tried to explain it to him. He's a union man, used to construction rules and not the subtleties of salon politics and the industry's dog-eat-dog nature.

"You could change all the things that drive you crazy about Salon Double Blue," Andres says. "I bet we could carve out a nice little space for you above one of our restaurants."

"That's a wonderful idea!" Annemarie says. "Wouldn't that be nice, Sebastian? The two of you working together."

"Me and him?" Bastian jabs his thumb in Andres's direction. "We are not working together." Bastian has only relented to the idea of the two of them sleeping together this morning. Running a business is absolutely not happening.

"Agreed." Andres laughs. "It's only a thought that if we come across another restaurant space soon, maybe we can carve out a section for you and Laura to build something in. Big or small, whatever you like."

"I'll think about it," Bastian says, hoping to change the subject and wondering why everyone around him is so hellbent on trying to insert Andres even more prominently into his life.

After dinner and a series of quick goodbyes, Bastian finds himself clinging to Andres as they soar through the city streets back up to Boystown.

"Do you want to get a drink?" Andres asks, the wind of the night obscuring his voice slightly. "Or would you rather go straight home?"

"Home, please," Bastian says into his ear. While a drink would be nice, he has wine at his place. After all the covert touches and hidden flirting they engaged in at dinner, Bastian wants to get Andres alone and explore the physicality of this new territory more thoroughly.

"Good," Andres says and hits the throttle, rounding the final turn onto Bastian's street. He hastily parks the bike and practically carries Bastian off with him when he dismounts. Bastian goes willingly, thoroughly enjoying having Andres take charge. It's something Ryan never did. He was more of the laze around and wait for Bastian to make a move, or more infuriatingly, bring him dinner type.

The door to Bastian's apartment is barely shut behind them before Andres has Bastian pushed up against it. His hands are cradling Bastian's cheeks again, and his larger frame is practically trying to make Bastian a part of the old hardwood. Bastian doesn't mind at all. It's been forever and a day since he's been manhandled with this much passion.

"Do you want to stay the night again?" Bastian asks while Andres slides his hands roughly down his body, settling his fingers onto Bastian's belt buckle.

"That was my hope," Andres says, a slightly hungry growl in his voice as if he hadn't just been fed a full meal. He removes Bastian's belt, sliding it through the loops in one swift pull that ends with a crack and a snap of the belt as it comes free, the buckle clattering loudly on the floor when it hits the ground. Andres drops to his knees beside it, yanking Bastian's trousers down with him.

"Keep following this track, and I'll never let you leave." Bastian sighs, his hands moving to Andres's hair, pulling it out of its knot and weaving his fingers through the strands.

Andres looks up at him. His eyes are dark and mischievous but full of adoration and want just the same. "I should leave you like this," Andres says. "A little payback for you copping a feel at the dinner table."

"Don't you dare," Bastian says. "What is it you always say? Don't start something you're not going to finish?"

"Oh, I'm finishing you, that's for sure," Andres says, and Bastian gets the impression he doesn't mean getting him off only tonight.

"Has that been your intention all along? To finish me?"

"From the very start," he says solemnly and slips Bastian's briefs down around his thighs before he engulfs Bastian's shaft with his mouth.

"Fuck," Bastian moans, the back of his head thumping on the door, his fingers gripping Andres's hair as if it is the only thing keeping him upright.

Andres works him over in earnest, lavishing him with increased intensity, and Bastian feels as if he's about to blow at any moment. His hips start to thrust forward, pushing himself more into Andres's mouth. He gives three rapid thrusts, and then—Andres has pulled away. He looks up at Bastian and licks his lips, his hands running up and down Bastian's thighs.

"Don't stop," Bastian whines. "I was right there."

"I know." Andres smirks devilishly at him.

"You're not going to leave me like this, are you?"

"What? Unsatisfied? Wanting? Horny as hell?" he asks each question casually as if he isn't kneeling in front of Bastian's dick.

"Yes!" Bastian says, his fingers still in Andres's hair, trying to guide him back to the task at hand, or mouth in this case. "Quit being a tease and finish what you started."

"Now look who's lecturing whom about being a tease," Andres says and swats at Bastian's thigh. He rises to his feet, freeing himself from Bastian's grasp, and rests his forehead against Bastian's. He mercifully brings his hand back to Bastian's erection, loosely pumping it with his fist, and Bastian internally vows to do whatever it takes to keep him from letting go.

"Bed?" Bastian whispers out.

"I thought you'd never ask."

CHAPTER 9

B astian's phone vibrates in his pants pocket as he works on a client's hair. He internally curses. It could be anyone, most likely Laura letting him know how her doctor's appointment went today. But there is always the chance that it's Andres. And that slight chance has Bastian's heart racing as he combs another parting into his client's wet hair to begin cutting the next section.

Luckily for him, his client is engrossed in a magazine, and she's paying him not even the slightest bit of attention. This rare hour-long appointment of silence is one that Bastian never takes for granted. Sure, he loves to chat with and entertain his clients or listen to them talk about what's going on with their lives, but there is something so calming about the occasional client that likes to sit and shut the fuck up. Bastian can take what's left of this hour to recharge his near-empty battery. To breathe without having to speak on the exhale. To get in the rhythm of the simple repetitive actions of a solid, well-executed haircut. There's comfort in each

141

of these methodical partings. It's like a moving meditation when he's afforded the opportunity to take it by a client who comes here for a moment's peace instead of a moment of excitement.

He gets lost in each snip of the hair, his mind replaying the feel of Andres's lips on his own, the way his dick felt in his hand or his mouth, and the other way around. He thinks about having woken up with Andres beside him two days in a row and how empty his bed has felt in the following four days. He has at least one more night to spend by himself, and then, maybe, Andres will be knocking at his door to start the weekend off right after the restaurants close on Saturday. This gamble with their friendship is incredibly risky, though it feels familiar and like something that should've been explored earlier. It also feels frighteningly forbidden, as if, at any moment, the Universe's penchant for equilibrium will smite his decision to dare to taste what Andres is dangling right in front of him.

He thinks back to when they were kids, innocent and unknowing. He would come home from school every day and tell his mother all the wonderful things that he and his new friend had done, and she'd listen to him go on for hours at a time about how amazing Andres was. He'd tell her he was brilliant and funny. He's good at basketball and soccer and would always pick Bastian first to be on his team, even though Bastian was trash at sports. Andres lived in a big house with intricate windows that people from all over the world would take pictures of from the sidewalk. It wasn't until years later, after seeing it in a magazine, that Bastian realized that his best friend lived in a historically protected Frank Lloyd Wright original home. Though it is a Chicago area landmark, the house had always felt so empty and cold inside, haunted well before Julian passed away.

As they got older, Bastian would still talk about his friend. Andres was practically a God in Bastian's eyes. He'd even slept for ages with a photograph of him slid into the underside of his pillowcase. He only stopped after his mother had once indulged in a cleaning service for their home before a party for his eighth-grade graduation. He hadn't realized that part of their duty was to clean everyone's sheets, and when he returned home from school that day to a freshly made bed, there was no trace of a picture of Andres within the folds. From that moment on, pictures of Andres were better left in drawers, between the pages of books, or in a petite frame on his bedside table. Or in its modern form, on the home screen of his phone that is buzzing in his pocket once more.

With the cut finished, Bastian grabs his blow dryer. He tugs a bit more roughly than usual with his round brush in his haste to get her finished so he can check his phone and reply to whoever it is in the few short minutes he has before his next client arrives.

He doesn't even bother trying to push product on his client to purchase as he takes her to the reception area to get checked out. He simply thanks her and quickly heads back up the stairs and into the color dispensary where he can get some privacy to check his texts. There are two, like he knew there would be—one from Andres, which he opens first.

> Can I swing by your place tomorrow night after work?

Which of course he can, and Bastian texts him back as such. And the second text is from Laura.

> Well, it's official now. I'm pregnant. Due the middle of November.

Saturdays at the salon are always a bit of a scramble. Whether it's clients who are running late for their appointment because they overbooked themselves for the day or over-partied the night before, stylists who are trying to squeeze in as many people as they can to fill their pockets with cash tips for the weekend, or in today's case, a bridal party complete with a bride, eight bridesmaids, the mother of the bride, and the mother of the groom all needing to get dolled up for the big day. It's a lot, and Bastian is exhausted, but thankfully, he's almost made it through his final day of work for the week now that the bridal party is out of the way.

"What's the count at, Bastian?" Bethany asks him as they pass each other in the doorway that separates the salon from the break-room.

"One more client between me and my weekend," Bastian says with a faux smile on his face. He started with seven. This countdown has become a Saturday ritual for all the stylists, ticking down the day by how many clients they have left before they can have their freedom back. Bless whoever the daredevil is who books a stylist's last appointment on a Saturday. They better be someone enjoyable and easy-going as well as a good tipper. Bastian prays to the hair gods that whoever this new person is on his books is someone who is not looking for anything complicated. But given his luck today, it's unlikely.

"Hi, I'm Bastian," he says, extending his hand to the woman in his chair. She's young, probably no older than twenty—safe to assume she's not a good tipper—but her dark brown hair is chin-length, so at least it won't be another exhausting blow-dry like the six he's already had to perform today.

"Willow," she says with an air of indifference and loosely slides her palm into his hand, essentially making it feel like he's shaking hands with a dead fish. And people call men like him limp-wristed. At least he knows how to shake another person's hand properly.

He keeps his smile on his face, steps behind her, places his hands in her hair, and makes eye contact through the mirror. "What are we doing today?" he asks, tousling her hair and getting a feel for its texture.

She focuses on him through the mirror, her previous indifference now gone. "The inspiration for my hair is the phoenix," she proclaims with a flourish of her hand. As if this tells Bastian any-thing other than the next hour of his life is going to be a headache.

"Phoenix, like the bird?" he asks, hoping she's joking.

"Yes, exactly that. So you are familiar?"

"Yes," he says with a friendly laugh, though inside, he is feeling anything but friendly. What she's asking for—even as abstract of an idea as it is—isn't possible in the hour time slot that she is booked for. To start, from having his hands in her hair, not even looking at it closely, he can tell that it is already color-treated. For him to achieve anything resembling Phoenix-like colors in her hair will be a two, possibly three-step process. Add to that, although it is already a shortish cut, a pixie cut is more suitable for what she is asking and will have to be mapped out long before coloring it even takes place. So sure, she won't need a full-body exhaust-ing blow-dry like Bastian's previous clients of the day with hair halfway down their backs, but she will need two.

At this point in his week, Bastian is wondering what it is he's done that has made the hair gods curse him. He thought he was a relatively good person. This seems like a cruel joke to play on someone who really wants to go home and lounge around in his apartment half-naked as he waits for Andres to come by after work.

"I want something vibrant and edgy," she says. "Something eye-catching with lots of reds and yellows and oranges. I want my hair to look like I rose from the ashes."

"Bad break-up?" Bastian asks before he can stop himself from asking.

She looks at him, stunned, and Bastian doesn't care. He's been at this for quite some time now, and he knows better than anyone what a post-break-up melt-down looks like in his chair.

"No," she denies. "I've wanted to do this forever."

That may be so, but he's not about to walk into this trap willingly on a Saturday. She's likely to freak out at the sharp color palette difference the vibrant, warm flame-like colors will have against her too-pink skin tone. Something more pastel would suit her better. But Bastian neither has that kind of time or patience nor does he feel like playing therapist and ego builder to a new adult who probably has her mother's credit card on hand to pay for this. This is the type of thing he wishes Oliver at the reception desk would ask when new people make an appointment:

-What's your hair texture?

-Is it color-treated?

-What's the length?

-Are you looking for a big change?

-Did you recently go through a traumatic life event?

The answer to that last question is really all anyone needs to know. With dreams of getting this weekend started and his ass at home with a glass of wine and a proper meal, Bastian talks her into only going for a pixie cut today. With a stroke of genius, he sets her up to be a color model next week for Bethany or Lizzie and saves himself from the headache of trying to pull off a rough transition of color for, at the most, a ten-dollar tip. This isn't the type of client he wants at this point in his career anyway. She's better suited for someone trying to build their book.

By the time he has her finished up and out the door, it's already fifteen minutes past six and fifteen minutes past the time he was scheduled to leave. The countdown is over, and he can finally go home and get some much-needed rest before Andres arrives.

"Bastian!" Laura yells after him as he descends the steps towards the salon's exit. "Wait for me!"

He pauses, turns, looks over his shoulder, and makes a show of checking the time on his watch. He loves Laura dearly, but honestly, he's done socializing for the day. His apartment is calling him.

"Sorry," she says as she catches up to him. "I know you like to scoot out of here quick."

"It will forever vex me as to why you do not."

"I'm not in as big of a hurry as you always seem to be," she says. "Besides, you better get used to it because in another few months, I won't be moving quickly at all."

"How much time do we have until doomsday?" he asks, opening the door and holding it open for her to exit first.

"Due November fifteenth. But I'm assuming I'll be at full waddle by mid-September."

Once out the door, he turns to walk east towards the nearest Red Line stop despite it not being the direction Laura needs to go to head home. He reasons that he's only taking her a little out of her way. It should be fine. "When are you telling Mitchel?"

"As soon as Justin and I iron out a new wedding date," she says. "May as well give him all the news at once."

"That's probably the best route. Let me know if you need anything when the time comes."

"There's something you can do for me already," she says.

He pauses his strides. "What's that?"

"Tell Andres. Justin already thinks Andres works too much, and he's worried that he'll take it all on instead of asking for help."

"Bold of you to assume I haven't already told Andres." Bastian laughs.

"You didn't?" Laura grumbles, her brow furrowing.

"I sure as hell did!" Bastian says. "You think I'd keep that kind of gossip away from my best friend?"

"Boyfriend, you mean?"

"No, I meant what I said," Bastian says, but the smile lifting his cheeks is saying otherwise.

"Whatever." She rolls her eyes at him, and a smirk that says she's caught him pulls at her lips. "I can't believe you already told Andres."

"You should've thought about that before you told me first," Bastian says. "There are no secrets between a gay man and his best friend." *Slash lover.* If only ending this conversation with Laura will get Andres to his place faster.

"Okay, you've got me there," Laura says. "Can you talk to him later, though, and maybe," she swats at him playfully, "give him a reason not to take everything on. You know how he gets. He has a savior complex."

"Alright. I'll see what I can do," Bastian says. He kisses her on the cheek and says his goodbyes, waving her off. She's not wrong. Andres does tend to take too much on as if he thinks that if he has a hand in everything, he can maintain some semblance of control. It's a habit he developed from his childhood, where he so often fended for himself or helped his parents hold it together as his brother slowly faded away. His comfort zone is caring for others and giving them all he has with little in return. Of course, he'd see Justin and Laura having a baby as another responsibility for himself. Bastian supposes that keeping him distracted and giving him a new focus outside of Justin's life changes is the least he can do.

True to his word, Bastian goes directly into distracting Andres the moment he hears Andres's motorcycle turn down his street. As has become his habit, he hits the buzzer on his building's front entry without even waiting for Andres to ring him, then unlocks his apartment door, using the deadbolt to prop it open. From there, he removes his clothes and steps into the shower, leaving the bathroom door all the way open. What a burden it will be to keep Andres's mind focused on something other than work.

"Bastian," he hears Andres say through the running water, followed by the click of the door to his apartment shutting.

"In here!" Bastian calls out, peeking his head past the shower curtain and making eye contact with Andres through the steam.

Andres hastily unbuckles his belt. "It's one thing for you to buzz me in and leave your door unlocked while you're in the kitchen; it's another for you to be naked and waiting in the shower." His pants fall around his ankles.

"You don't look like you're complaining that I'm waiting for you in the shower." Bastian looks him up and down and pauses at Andres's pants on the floor. "Besides, I can recognize the sound of your motorcycle from blocks away."

"Could've been anybody's motorcycle," Andres reasons, his shirt slightly muffling his voice as he pulls it over his head, exposing his broad pecs and perfectly defined abs in the process. Bastian feels himself begin to rise to attention.

"Nope," Bastian counters. "I always know when it's you. You have a very distinct sound."

"Been paying close attention to my sounds, huh?" Andres slides his briefs off. He pushes the shower curtain to the side and steps in, quick to get under the water and even quicker to get Bastian's face cradled between his palms.

"I know all your noises," Bastian says and licks the droplets of water from his lower lip, his eyes staring directly into Andres's before Andres brings their lips together in a sweet, wet kiss.

"Do you now?" Andres challenges, running one thumb across Bastian's lower lip and reaching his other hand down between the two of them.

"Yes," Bastian says, his breath slightly hitching when he feels Andres wrap his fingers around both of their lengths.

"All of my noises, huh?" he asks, his fist moving languidly up and down. "I think I might have a few that you haven't heard yet."

"Is that a challenge?"

"It's a promise," he says and spins Bastian around, holding him firmly around the waist with one hand while the other takes Bastian's hands to splay them across the tiled wall. "Is this alright?" he whispers into Bastian's ear.

"It's more than alright," Bastian says and presses his ass against Andres's front. He can feel Andres's erection slide between his cheeks, and it practically makes him preen for Andres to take what he's made clear that he wants. They haven't done this yet, but this feels right, and it's definitely something that Bastian is craving. When Andres finally slides inside, Bastian listens as they both sigh. Andres is right, Bastian's not heard that sound before.

•♥•♥•♥•♥•♥•

The next morning is much the same. It seems after a full night's sleep, Andres is just as eager for a repeat—albeit dryer—performance of last night's activities as Bastian is. When Andres rolls Bastian onto his back and spreads his thighs, Bastian is more than happy to comply. From his position, he can watch as Andres prepares them both. Again, they let out the exact same satisfied sigh, as if they were always meant to be this way—Andres taking control and diligently making sure all of Bastian's needs are being met.

That diligence isn't reserved for only in the bedroom. After sex, Andres is out of the bed, grabbing a soft towel from Bastian's cabinet, and wetting it with warm water like he lives here. He gently wipes the mess they've made off Bastian's stomach, then kisses him on the forehead and is at the coffee pot setting it to brew before Bastian has even had a chance to rise and offer to do it himself.

With the coffee brewing and the towel tossed into the laundry hamper, Andres slides back into bed and scoops Bastian into his arms, kissing the back of his shoulder and making Bastian shiver in a terrifying but extremely pleasant delight. He's ruined now, and he knows it. When the relationship goes sour, and Andres has decided that Bastian is not the person that he has made him out to be in his head, Andres will move on and eventually find someone perfect who can live up to the wonder that Andres is. Whereas Bastian will be lost in his memories of mornings spent with strong arms around his body and the smell of coffee brewing in the air while basking in the sated afterglow of a good fucking.

CHAPTER 10

> Any chance you can get off work early tomorrow?

Bastian frowns at the text. He knows without looking that he's already booked until close.

> Can't. I'm booked.

Hanging his head, he hits send. He and Andres have been going back and forth since Andres left his place for work Sunday afternoon, trying to find a time when their schedules are in sync.

> Damn.

Bastian huffs out a laugh at Andres' response as he feels the same. He watches the tiny dots on the screen flash as Andres types more.

> I'd like to take you on an actual date one of these days.

> Me too.

An actual date, one that doesn't end with Bastian getting his heart broken in front of his bowl of noods or dealing with some blowhard questioning his fitness routine, would be a nice change. He's not about to complain to Andres about this. He knows from years of listening to Andres regale him with stories about women and the occasional man who was more upfront with his feelings throwing an absolute fit at Andres simply for him having a work schedule that kept him busy every society-sanctioned evening designated for date nights.

Bastian doesn't care about that. Dates on Friday nights are meaningless to him when he has to work a long day on Saturdays. And dates on Saturday nights are exhausting after a long week of being on his feet and entertaining people from behind his chair while fluffing up their hair and egos. A proposed impromptu Thursday night date sounds far more appealing. He flips to his schedule to see what he's working with—Vivienne Paul, lesbian florist extraordinaire. She's booked for a root touch-up and a cut, a two-hour-long appointment. She's usually pretty flexible with her schedule, and Bastian hatches a plan. He pulls out his phone and texts Andres again.

Never mind. I'm freeing myself up right now!

Really?!?

> *Yes, really. So you better knock my socks off with something grand.*

> *Oh, I'll be knocking your socks off. That's a promise.*

> *Good.*

Bastian slides his phone into his pocket and heads down to the reception desk.

"Hey, Oliver," Bastian says, and Oliver looks at him suspiciously. "Can you do me a favor?"

"Maybe," Oliver says, like any good receptionist who has dealt with stylists' requests or been on the other end of a lousy phone call with a client who can't listen to reason. "Depends on what you need."

"Could you call Vivienne, she's my six o'clock tomorrow, and ask her to come in Saturday morning instead. I'll come in early for her. It shouldn't be a problem."

Oliver narrows his eyes at Bastian. "How early?" he asks. "I'm opening on Saturday, and I really don't want to have to come in extra early that day. Saturdays are long enough as it is."

"You can come in at your regular time. You won't even notice Vivienne and I are here. You know her; she's so pleasant, and she'll likely bring us a couple of bouquets to place around the salon.

She'd be doing you a favor, really. One less stop for you to make to spruce up the place for Saturday's wedding party."

"That's true." He narrows his eyes at Bastian again. "Then who am I putting in her place for Thursday?"

"Well, Martha Stewart, of course," Bastian says like the answer should be obvious.

"Martha Stewart doesn't exist," Oliver says.

"Sure she does!" Bastian counters. "She runs a very successful home goods empire and gets high with Snoop Dogg on the weekends."

"I meant, she doesn't exist as one of our actual clients."

"Oliver, just because she's never actually made it to one of her appointments, that doesn't mean she's not a client."

"You know one of these days Mitchel's going to catch onto your little game," Oliver warns. "And I'd really like to not be caught up in it with you."

"Where's your sense of team spirit?"

"Anywhere that doesn't involve me getting fired."

"You won't get fired. Mitchel won't even notice," Bastian assures. "He'll be well on his way to ripping his weekend rails by the time Martha doesn't show up to her appointment."

"Bastian," Oliver whines out his name. "Come on."

"Then don't use Martha if you're so concerned. Make up any old client to go into that two-hour spot."

"Fine." Oliver finally gives in. "But you owe me."

"That's a good lad." Bastian pats him on the head and then walks back up the stairs. "I'll bring you coffee and breakfast on Saturday."

"Damn," Bastian says, making a show of checking the time on his phone and looking believably disappointed in his client's inability to show up. He starts packing up his station.

"Getting blown off?" Laura asks from beside him as she puts the finishing touches on her client's fringe.

"Looks like it." Bastian sighs and rechecks his watch. Out of the corner of his eye, he can see Mitchel still looming, taking in the hustle and bustle. "Fifteen minutes late," he says a little louder than he normally would in order to make himself heard throughout the room. "Even if they do show up, I won't have enough time for their appointment anyway."

"That's a real shame," Laura says, and Bastian is pretty sure he can hear her trying not to laugh. He gives her a warning look and a discrete angling of his chin in the direction of their eavesdropper. "Didn't this same client blow you off a few weeks ago as well? It's really too bad they're making a habit of it."

"You know, it really is," he says. "I'm gonna have to have Oliver make a note in their profile. This is unacceptable." He closes his station drawer and hits the lock on it right as a familiar set of tailpipes begins to rumble the windows. Wincing, he hopes that his boss is out of touch with his staff enough not to know who those tailpipes belong to. Mitchel gives Bastian a once-over and then walks towards the breakroom and attached office. Bastian lets out the breath he was holding.

"You may as well go enjoy your night off," Laura says. "Perhaps jump on the back of that motorcycle I hear rumbling outside. I'm sure the owner of it is very charming."

"And smoking hot!" Marny adds from across the room.

Bastian glares at the both of them.

"Go have fun, Bastian," Laura says in a hushed tone. "We'll see you tomorrow."

"Goodnight, ladies!" Bastian trills, giving himself one last look over in the mirror. Satisfied with what he sees—hair in place, black skinny jeans perfectly tight to show off his spindly legs, and a cream-colored second-hand Balmain turtleneck—he turns on his heel and swiftly strides away. He's practically running down the stairs when he hits them and passes Oliver at the desk with a solute and a wink. Then he's out the door.

Andres is, of course, waiting for him, looking cool as can be with his thighs straddling the motorcycle, its engine still rumbling. "Hop on!" he says, patting the seat behind him, and Bastian doesn't hesitate. Andres cranes his neck to look over his shoulder and gives Bastian a quick kiss, then says, "Hold on tight!" and puts the bike back into gear.

Bastian gives him a good squeeze around the middle. "Where are we going?"

"Art Institute is open until eight tonight, so I thought we'd start there, and then, if you're not too cold, make the ride into Pilsen for tacos and Mexican Chocolate milkshakes. After that, your choice of my place or yours."

Bastian's grin is hard to hide as Andres rounds the street corner to shoot over the river and into the Loop and then to the Museum on Michigan Avenue.

"We could go someplace fancier for dinner if you'd like," Andres says.

"No way. When one of the city's leading restaurateurs makes a dinner suggestion, you don't question it. Besides, I love grabbing tacos in Pilsen, and we haven't been there since last summer."

"Good," Andres says and pats Bastian's hands before he hits the throttle. The deep rumble of the engine reverberates off the city's skyscrapers.

Bastian hooks his chin over Andres's shoulder as he takes it all in—the evening commuters heading home, the fountain and plaza outside of the Daley Center, the giant Picasso statue, the old Marshall Field's building that has been shamefully turned into a Macy's, and then Millenium Park situated next to the vast, brick building that houses one of the world's most extraordinary collections of art and the largest selection of post-impressionist paintings in the world. The bronze lions with their green patina stand sentry and seem to watch as Andres parks the motorcycle across the street.

Once parked, they hurry across the road, dodging traffic hand in hand, running up the museum's steps, and then Andres is holding one of the large, heavy glass doors open for Bastian to walk through. Like he always does, Bastian looks and admires the magnitude of this building as the echoes of people's heels resound on the marble floor. He could happily live in this museum, take in all the paintings and sculptures every day, and trace his fingers over the glass display cases containing centuries-old pottery, jewelry, armor, and textiles. He could fall asleep reading in the library's antique leather chairs and wake up to explore this place end to end every day and still never tire of seeing it all.

"We only have about an hour and a half before this place closes," Andres says, giving Bastian's hand a gentle squeeze. "So a visit to the Chagall glass, then off to the O'Keeffe, some Warhol, the Rene Magritte, a few minutes in front of the Seurat, and then a finale surrounded by Monet?"

"Sounds like you have this place mapped out," Bastian teases and lets Andres guide him by the hand towards the steps leading them down to the display of stained glass windows perpetually illuminated by lights that mimic the afternoon sun.

"I wanted to make the best of our time," Andres says. "So I double-checked the map."

"You listed all my favorites," Bastian says. "What about you? What do you want to see?"

Andres stops midway down the stairs and looks over at Bastian. "Only you," he says as if the answer should be obvious, as if the answer is in no way terrifying and too pure and too good to be true. He touches Bastian's cheek. "Most alluring work of art in this building."

Bastian wants to melt into the floor as Andres turns and continues down the steps. How did he get so lucky to have this man as his best friend? How did he get so lucky to have this man holding his hand in one of the world's most extravagant places? And when did he get so stupid as to fall for him?

"These are works of art," Bastian corrects Andres as they enter the hall of glass, the room bathed in the blue light reflected through the windows. They stand in the middle and let the colors separated by intricate rod-iron patterns tell the story of music, painting, literature, architecture, theater, and dance. These aren't the stained glass windows of churches depicting religious figures. These are works of Americana set to pay homage to the gods of new. And Bastian, being the creative that he is, takes each panel in as intended.

From there, it's back up the stairs and then up another set to reach the benches situated to view the giant Georgia O'Keeffe painting that hangs high in the museum like the sky that resides above the clouds painted on the canvas. The day may have faded into night outside, but the setting sun lives forever in the brush strokes between the clouds, blending the sky seamlessly from light blue all the way down to deep pink nearing orange.

"There's something so comforting about this one," Andres says as he loops his arm around Bastian's shoulders.

"It's like floating through a dream."

"It is," Andres says and pulls him closer then rests his head against Bastian's as they continue to take the exorbitantly large painting in.

"Andres?" A distinctly feminine voice breaks their peace, and Andres jolts slightly away from Bastian. They're still touching, but their semi-private and intimate moment has been broken.

"Oh, Nicole," Andres says. "I didn't see you there. How are you?"

"Good," she replies. She eyes Bastian and then looks back at Andres. Bastian looks her up and down. She's dressed in head-to-toe Chanel, and her ombre hair cascades down her back in perfect waves. "Where've you been? I haven't heard from you in a while."

"The usual," he says and places his hand on Bastian's thigh. "Work and spending time with this one."

"And you are?" she asks, looking back at Bastian.

Bastian sticks out his hand. "I'm Bastian—"

"Oh." She places her hand into Bastian's and shakes it. "I've heard about you. You're Andres's best friend."

"Yeah," Bastian says, feeling stung as he lets go of her hand.

Andres squeezes Bastian's thigh. "Listen, Nicole," he says. "It's good to see you." He pauses and turns to look back at Bastian for a second. "But Bastian and I have places to be. I'll see you around."

"Oh ... alright," she says, then takes one last glance at the two of them. She seems to notice Andres's hand on Bastian's thigh. With a meek shrug, she says, "It was nice to meet you, Bastian."

"It was nice to meet you, too." Bastian, looking away from her, subtly rolls his eyes. He briefly wonders if she has a list in her closet similar to Bastian's that Andres is about to have his name added to.

"Come on," Andres says, rising once Nicole is well on her way. He grabs onto Bastian's hands and attempts to pull Bastian to his feet. "What's wrong?"

"Who was that?" Bastian asks.

"No one."

"She didn't act like no one."

Andres takes a deep breath. "She's just someone I saw a few times when you and Ryan were still together."

Bastian eyes go wide. "But you're not seeing her anymore?"

"Did it look like I was seeing her anymore?" Andres cocks an eyebrow.

"Well, no," Bastian says.

"Good. Cause I'm not. I only have eyes for you." He tries to tug Bastian to his feet again, but Bastian remains firmly planted in his seat. "Come on. Let's go. Time's running out."

Bastian looks up at Andres, trying to read any hint of a lie in his voice or his words. He sees none, but he's still not wholly convinced. Nicole looked to be much more in line with what Andres should be spending an evening at the Art Institute with.

"Okay." He sighs and lets himself get pulled to his feet.

Andres's lips spread into a relieved smile as he pulls. "Up you go. We're off to Magritte's Banquet and then a quick stop by Warhol." Now that Bastian is standing, Andres pauses and leans forward to give him a soft, settling, and reassuring kiss. When he pulls away, his look is playful and mischievous. "Or perhaps you'd like to save the Magritte for last, and we can plot an art heist on our way to the modern wing?"

"We better go see it first," Bastian says. "I'm not above art theft, but I doubt the Cook County lockup has milkshakes."

"They do." Andres laughs. "But they're not ones you'd like."

"Let's avoid those and go see the Magritte now."

"As you wish," Andres says and grabs onto his hand. They then turn together and head off to the modern wing to see the treasures held inside.

"I can see why you like this one so much," Andres says once they stop in front of one of the many Rene Magritte paintings hanging on the gallery walls.

The Banquet—technically part of a series, but this one stands alone—is Bastian's favorite painting. Like the O'Keeffe, this one also features a sunset, but far bolder in color and contrast. The sun shines directly through the trees, boring a hole through the center of them, making visible what should be invisible. That perfect orange circle directly in the middle of the painting helps calm Bastian's unease as he focuses his attention on it.

"This painting is like you," Andres says, breaking the moment of shared silence.

"How so?" Bastian asks, not taking his eyes off the center point. He wishes he could be that circle—the sole center of focus for once in his life.

"Like the sun, you refuse to remain hidden by the trees," Andres says. "You carved your own path."

"I'm not sure that's necessarily true about me," Bastian says, letting his eyes rove around the entire painting. "I'm nothing special. I'm simply a hairstylist making money off of peoples' vanities."

"You do way more than that," Andres says. "You make a difference in your clients' lives. I've seen how you can transform someone and make them walk down the street with confidence in their step. Most people in this world can't say that they do that kind of good."

Bastian continues to observe the painting thoughtfully while he digests Andres's words. It's been a long time since he's thought of what he does in that sort of way. After a few moments of comfortable silence, he looks at Andres. "I don't see how that makes me like the painting, though."

Andres looks at him. "You, like the sun, shine through the trees and warm and light up those around you."

"I think you're getting me confused with you," Bastian says. "You're the one people can't resist. You're the one that has this city at your fingertips."

"That could be you too," Andres says and places an arm around Bastian's shoulders, pulling him towards his side. "You only have to ask for it."

"I'm not like you, Andres," Bastian says. "I don't have your resources, your charm, or your connections. I have a certificate that says I completed fifteen hundred hours of tedious and sometimes disgusting beauty school."

"A far more admirable feat than four years spent on an uppity college campus drinking beer and chasing tail." Andres laughs. "And my connections are yours as well. My offer still stands. If you want your own salon, even without Laura involved now, you can have it."

"We'll see," Bastian says to placate him and hopefully get Andres to drop the subject. He lets his head slump against Andres's shoulder, his eyes going back to lingering on the painting, that orange circle being the only thing keeping him grounded.

Andres's offer is tempting. It would be nice to be his own boss, and not only so he wouldn't have to make up a fake client to clear a few hours of his life for an impromptu date to keep him as present as possible in Andres's world. The salon life is grueling at times, and salon owners, particularly ones like Mitchel, who have never worked behind a chair, can be harsh and unsympathetic to what they do all day. They see stylists as machines, able to crank out thousands of dollars in a week's worth of hair services without even breaking a sweat. Which, of course, they can do, but the burnout one feels from years of having to work like this is fast approaching and hiding barely out of sight below the surface of Bastian's cutting cape. If he were his own boss, everything he made would be his. He could cut back his hours, he could take time for himself, he could have a vacation that didn't take place during an off-season. But if he takes Andres's money, utilizes his connections, isn't he putting himself into someone else's pocket? As he's learned over the years from watching the elite treat simple folks like him as cogs, that is the last thing he needs. He'd rather be able to do it independently with the meager savings he has managed to accumulate. Even when the dream was to do it with Laura, and they were going to need Justin to pay a fair share, Justin is at least her soon-to-be husband. There are legalities and built-in safety measures in place with that contract, and no Nicole's to throw it off kilter.

"Come on," Andres says. "Let's start to make our way to the exit and through the final two exhibits. We have tacos calling our name."

And what delicious tacos they are. Good enough that Bastian can finally let the incident with Nicole leave the forefront of his mind. He supposes it's not really the tacos that do it but the way that Andres has been sure to remain solely focused on Bastian and Bastian alone since they've arrived to wander down 18th street.

"Do you remember when we first came here?" Andres asks.

"I do, actually," Bastian says, a smile pulling at his lips. "Your mom brought us after a trip to the Museum of Science and Industry."

"Yeah," Andres says, a sort of somber smile tugging at his own lips. "To make up for that field trip Julian didn't get to go on." He laughs lightly and shakes his head. "The two of you were so mesmerized by the baby chick exhibit."

Bastian brings a hand to his heart. "How could we not be? They're so cute."

"Yeah," Andres says. "Cute enough that you haven't eaten meat since."

Now it's Bastian's turn to laugh. "I can't help it. All I see is their cute little faces."

Andres regards Bastian thoughtfully. "I think I know how you feel," he says. "I'd give up anything if it meant keeping you happy."

"Anything?" Bastian questions, his mind briefly slipping to Nicole from earlier. He shakes it off, keeping his eyes focused on Andres.

"Anything and everything," he says, reaching between them to grab Bastian's hand. "You about ready to get out of here? I have a feeling I have some proof of my dedication I need to do to you back at my place in my bed."

"Is that so?" Bastian questions, a smile lighting up his face. He tosses the paper his food was wrapped in into a nearby garbage can. With one eyebrow raised and his smile turning into a smirk, he jokes, "I guess it's a good thing we ate light then, huh?"

"Very good thing," Andres says, then picks up the pace to get back to his motorcycle parked a few blocks away.

CHAPTER 11

"Any news from my six o'clock?" Bastian absently asks Oliver while standing at the reception desk and tapping a message to Andres on his phone.

Are you coming to get me?

Oliver rolls his eyes at Bastian. "Do your imaginary clients ever call with an explanation for their whereabouts?"

Bastian shrugs, his eyes still on his phone. "No. I'm doing my part in making this look believable."

"Your little charade stopped being believable after the third Thursday in a row you pulled it," Oliver says as the phone rings. He picks up the call. "Thank you for calling Salon Azure Blue. This is Oliver speaking. How can I help you?"

Bastian shrugs again right as a text comes through from Andres.

I'm stuck at work. Can you meet me at Graze?

Yeah, sure. Bastian's feet are tired and sore, and walking the eight blocks to Graze from Salon Azure Blue sounds exhausting. Andres isn't even supposed to be at work. Thursdays are his night off, which is why Bastian has been playing this dangerous game of the magical disappearing client for the last month.

Oliver hangs up the phone and looks back at Bastian. "Will you be bringing me breakfast again on Saturday for this?" Oliver asks. The phone rings again before Bastian can answer him. It chimes twice, denoting it's an intra-salon call and not a customer. He holds up a finger at Bastian and answers it. "Front desk ... Yes ... He's still here."

Bastian's heart starts to beat faster. *This can't be good.*

"... Okay. I'll tell him." Oliver hangs up the phone and sucks a breath through his teeth. Wrinkling his nose, he says, "Mitchel would like to see you before you go."

"Fuck," Bastian mutters.

"I told you he'd catch on." Oliver's expression is smug.

Hanging his head, Bastian walks back up the stairs to the salon's top floor and makes his way into the office, briefly locking eyes with Laura in the breakroom before he closes the office door behind him.

"Sit," Mitchel says, pointing at the chair farthest away from the door.

"I'd rather stand," Bastian says, preferring to remain above Mitchel in physical stature at the moment and to have easy access to the exit in case immediate vacating of the premises is necessary. He places his hands into his pockets and leans against the door.

"Very well," Mitchel says. He turns to look at the office computer. "I can't help but notice there has been a bit of an anomaly in your books lately."

"Really?" Bastian plays dumb. "How so?"

"To start, it seems that your Thursday, six o'clock time slot is cursed," Mitchel says, pointing at the computer screen directly at the aforementioned cursed time slot.

"Hmm ..." Bastian hums, purses his lips and nods. "I'm sure it's nothing more than the typical start of summer cancelations. You know how it goes? Restaurant patios open up, and suddenly, everyone has more important plans."

"Once, maybe twice, yes," Mitchel agrees. "But three times? That's officially suspicious."

"Is it?" Bastian questions.

"Yes."

Bastian swallows.

"Anyway," Mitchel continues. "Since it's too late to fill this empty time slot tonight, I won't. So you better go enjoy yourself. Because this is the last Thursday night you'll be having off, ever."

"Alright," Bastian says, nodding his head, before he turns on his heel and leaves, making the walk to Graze even more arduous.

With each step, he internally curses himself for playing with fire. Though it could have gone way worse, he hates that he's walking through the streets of Chicago with his tail tucked between his legs like a dog that's been scolded by its owners. It's simply not fair. He's a fully grown adult, and yet his time and life is still being dictated by others. It's not only his boss. It's everyone. It's his clients making ridiculous demands for their hair. It's his mother guilting him into Sunday dinners. It's his girlfriends' insisting they know what's best for him and a long list of loves on his closet wall of boys who never made an ounce of effort to make Bastian a real part of their lives or take him seriously.

Truthfully, it's Andres too. Why is Bastian the one who has to risk his job to make time for them to go on proper dates? Sure, he's only a hairstylist and not some big-time restaurateur, but that shouldn't mean his career should take a back seat. He has his ambitions as well.

Perhaps the most annoying thing about this whole situation is that his ambitions for his career and his life require more than what his job is providing for him. He works damn hard on his feet all day for ten hours a day, five days a week, and still he has nothing to show for it except a discount designer wardrobe and a studio apartment in a neighborhood he's in danger of being priced out of.

Maybe it is time for Bastian to swallow his pride and take Andres up on his financial offer? It's an option Bastian is almost fired up enough to take by the time his tired feet enter the threshold of Graze. Only, Andres is laughing at the bar, his hand on the shoulder of a man in a fancy suit. *Never mind.* He wants to punch whoever this is that is more important to Andres than picking up Bastian at the salon. Accepting money from Andres will do nothing but muddy the waters of friendship more than they've already been muddied.

"I'm here to see Andres," Bastian says as he walks up to the hostess station. They wave him by, and he weaves through the crowd towards Andres, watching him chat with the man, the two sipping on identical whiskeys. He lightly taps Andres on the shoulder once he gets near enough to him. "I thought you were working?"

"Bastian," Andres replies, startled, then looks at his watch. "Excuse me," he says to the man, "I have to get going. But it was nice talking to you."

The man looks Bastian up and down, then extends his hand to Andres. "Yes," he says. "I'll be in touch."

"Sounds good," Andres says, then turns away from him, places an arm around Bastian's shoulders, and begins to lead them back through the crowd. Self-consciousness rises in Bastian, and he tries to ignore the feeling in the pit of his stomach that he is being watched and judged by everyone around him.

"What took you so long?" Andres asks earnestly once they step outside.

"I got held up at work."

"Did a client come in?"

"No," Bastian says and removes himself out from underneath Andres's arm. "I got scolded by the boss for rearranging my life for *you* while you get chatted up by some dude in an expensive, and might I add, ill-fitting suit, at your bar."

Andres steps back, looking stunned. "I wasn't getting chatted up," he says. "That was one of the Wrigleys. You know, the family that giant-ass baseball field a few blocks north of your place is named after that makes parking in Boystown a nightmare. He's looking to invest in our next restaurant."

"Since when do you need investors?"

"Since always," Andres says. "Look, the more money that gets poured into this business, the better it'll do. It's a pretty basic concept."

"Some of us aren't as business savvy as you," Bastian bites back.

Andres takes a deep breath and looks directly at Bastian. "Why are you being like this?"

"Like what?" Bastian asks, stung as to why this is being turned around on him.

"Accusatory."

"I'm not being accusatory!" Bastian says. Then again, he had jumped to conclusions, and Andres has never given him a reason to be suspicious. That being said, neither had any of his other boyfriends and look how that turned out.

"Honestly, there was nothing going on. It was nothing but business talk." Andres pauses and makes a step towards Bastian. "And boring business talk at that. I'd much rather have been with you."

Bastian, whether from already having had a rough night or not wanting to risk losing Andres over his own insecurity, feels his shoulders slump as all fight leaves him. "I'm sorry," he says. "It's been a long day."

Andres closes the gap between them and pulls Bastian into his arms, holding him possessively. "Do you want to go back to my place and tell me about it?"

"I want to go back to your place and forget about it," Bastian says, his voice muffled by Andres's shoulder.

"Alright." Andres gives him a tighter squeeze. "And I'll make it up to you this weekend. I owe you a proper date."

"No, you don't," Bastian says, letting himself fully relax into Andres's arms. The exhaustion of his day fully catching up to him. "Just come to my place Saturday night after work at a decent hour."

"Okay." Andres laughs into his ear. "I'll see what I can do."

Bastian checks the time on his phone. It's officially well past midnight, and he is struggling to keep his eyes open after a very long day made longer by him going into the salon at eight instead of nine to make up for his missed client on Thursday. He texts Andres.

Will you be here soon?

After a few short seconds of waiting, Andres is texting him back.

Sorry. Still at work. Would you rather I sleep at my place instead of yours?

Bastian considers this. He's tired, but he's off work tomorrow, and he'd much rather wake up late in bed with Andres than by himself. Besides, Andres will have to leave for work in the early afternoon and waking in separate beds inconveniently cuts into their time together.

No. I'll wait up.

Bastian texts back in defeat.

Leaving in five. I'll make it up to you.

It's fine.

Bastian puts his phone down on the bed next to him and rubs his eyes. The harsh light—even on dark mode—has made them water and burn that little bit extra, so phone scrolling to pass the time and keep him awake is out. Perhaps a movie will work better, but he worries that it will end up lulling him to sleep. Rolling over onto his side, he flings the blanket off himself and sits up, turning to place his feet on the floor, then rubs harshly at his curls, not caring if he musses them up even more than they likely already are.

Tea, he decides, and an episode of *The Good Place* watched from his chair instead of his bed will have to do. Perhaps Chidi has some ethical lesson for him as to why it's important to be selfless and stay awake, even if he is getting grumpy.

Bastian knew what he was getting into as far as their schedules were concerned when all this started. This is most certainly not the first time during Bastian and Andres's relationship that Bastian has found himself in a position where he's forcing himself to stay awake when all he really wants to do is go to sleep. At least now, there are cuddles, lazy kisses, and at least one orgasm promised for his efforts in wakefulness.

As he waits for the electric kettle to boil, he reaches into his junk drawer, filled with pens and hair ties he'll never use but Andres might, paper clips, matchbooks, and his spare set of keys, which has sat in that drawer since he moved into this apartment almost five years ago. He pulls the latter out and places them on the center of the kitchen table. It's a simple solution to these late-night dilemmas and not suggestive of anything more.

Sure, this is the first set of keys that Bastian has ever intended to present to anyone, and he's never received a set from anyone else, but honestly, this is not a big deal. Not a big deal at all. This is about Bastian being able to fall asleep on Saturday nights when he's exhausted after a long work week and Andres being able to let himself in. Andres should have always had a set of keys to Bastian's apartment long before they even began sleeping with each other.

He's sipping the last dregs of his ginger tea, the hot porcelain long cooled in his hands, when he hears the familiar rumbling of Andres rounding the corner. *Finally.* He swallows what's left of his tea, places the mug in the sink, and goes to stand by the door and his buzzer to let Andres in.

"You look dead on your feet," Andres says as he walks through the door, placing a kiss on Bastian's forehead as he passes. Bastian finds himself loosely wrapped in Andres's arms the second the door closes. "I'm sorry I kept you waiting. Long night at Graze, and then there was a fiasco at Partager that I had to take care of as I didn't want to wake Justin. And I'll have to deal with it tomorrow again before they open for dinner service as the sous chef walked out at the end of the night for some issue he was having with Alex, and it's never a dull moment." He stops and takes a breath, then brings a hand to Bastian's jaw to angle him to look at him. He's smiling at Bastian, and he takes another breath. "Hi," he says, then leans in and kisses him. "Much better," he says against Bastian's lips when they pull apart.

"Much better, indeed," Bastian says, then turns himself onto Andres's shoulder to stifle his incoming yawn. "Sorry you had such a bad day. That sounds awful. But really, you should have Justin take some of this on tomorrow. You can't be at two places at once."

"But I can try," Andres says with an exhausted smile that match-es the way Bastian is feeling.

"You shouldn't have to. He's your business partner," Bastian says. "And besides, if you're thinking that Justin needs the day off because he has a pregnant Laura to attend to, you're wrong. I work next to her every day, and she's growing tired already of having Justin following her around like a mother hen. You'll likely be doing her a favor if you have him tend to the issues at Partager."

"True, he can be a handful," Andres says and walks them both towards the bed, depositing Bastian onto it when the backs of Bastian's knees hit the mattress. "But Justin has never worked the kitchen, so he's useless for the Partager problem, and Graze is my baby. I don't really want to subject the staff there to Justin running amuck. Simone can handle it until I come in to close the place down at the end of the night."

"You need to hire more managers," Bastian says around another yawn.

"And you need to go to bed," Andres says, placing another kiss on Bastian's lips. "Go to sleep. I'm gonna take a shower, and I'll quietly crawl in when I'm finished."

"Don't you want company in the shower?" Bastian asks, yawning again.

"I always want company in the shower. But I want you to go to sleep more." He kisses Bastian again and starts to back away from the bed.

Bastian falls over onto his side and pulls the blanket and top sheet up to his chin. With his eyes closed, he calls out to Andres as he walks away, "Andres, before I forget, there's a set of keys for you on the table. Next time, you can let yourself in."

"Okay." He hears Andres say as he falls immediately to sleep.

When he wakes the following morning, he finds that the set of keys to his place has been replaced by a set to Andres's.

With the keys exchanged, everything is more straightforward. A simple text of, *My place or yours?* sent by either of them is all that it takes to kick the night off. Bastian no longer has to try to stay awake when Andres is coming by his place or sit at Graze to wait for Andres to get off so they can go back to Andres's. Bastian can go to the restaurant, eat dinner, have a drink, then walk the few blocks from Graze to Andres's condo and luxuriate in Andres's jacuzzi tub while he waits for him to come home, which is what Bastian is doing right now.

Bastian loves Andres's condo. Everything in it is brand new. The floors don't creak, the appliances are modern, the countertops granite, and the cabinets are bamboo. It's been meticulously decorated with walls painted in rich grays and blues, perfect for displaying Andres's choices in art. When the walls aren't satisfying Bastian's eyes' needs, there's the view of Chicago that is unobstructed from Andres's floor-to-ceiling, living room windows. And then, of course, the view of Andres himself once he gets home from work later.

That is arguably the best view. There is something so sexy about a man who is content in his home—a man who has picked out every piece of furniture for both style and comfort. It's not that Bastian prefers Andres's place over his. It's that it is a different place entirely. While charming in its own way, Bastian's apartment feels juvenile. Andres's condo drips with class and luxury, but not in an obnoxious way. It doesn't feel like living in a museum, as Andres's childhood home did. In that place, Bastian was afraid to touch anything. He hardly ever felt like he was allowed to breathe in there, let alone run around and play with any sense of vigor as any normal kid would. Bastian is sure that's why Andres has gone to such great lengths to make his home not only livable but inviting and warm.

Each room has features one would never have thought they needed. The floors are all heated, so even barefoot, his toes never get cold. There's a fireplace in both the living room and the bedroom—not that it's needed now that summer is here, but when winter settles back in again this year, Bastian is sure to take advantage. The kitchen is always stocked with food and anything he would need to make a meal. Just like the appliances, everything is of the best quality and brand new, except for the well-seasoned Le Creuset cast iron skillet that lives on permanent display on the extensive Viking range.

The furniture is plush and soft in dark tones, with bold blankets and pillows always within arm's reach. The television is a massive seventy-eight inches and equipped with 5.1 surround sound. The shades draw down with a remote, casting you into your own private world or lift to reward you with a personal viewing of the city surrounding you from twelve stories up.

Bastian's favorite place—outside of Andres's bed, of course—is the bathtub. It's big enough for two but not so big that they don't have to configure themselves into each other's arms. The jets submerged in the water can be adjusted to a variety of strengths, and most important of all, the tub is heated, keeping the water at the exact temperature he sets it. Bastian has set the water to a very warm one-hundred and four degrees. It's sure to leave him pink all over if he ever decides to leave it. He supposes, as he takes a sip of the glass of red wine he brought into the tub with him, that Andres will persuade him to come out when he gets home—after he's had his wicked way with him inside of this tub, of course.

Bastian grabs his phone, holds it up high and away, angling it perfectly to highlight where he is but not necessarily show anything he shouldn't, and snaps a picture, then sends it to Andres.

Get home soon. I'm starting to prune.

Well, we can't have that. Leaving now. See you in five.

True to his word, Andres is walking through the bathroom door a few short seconds past the five-minute scheduled arrival. He eyes Bastian up and down in the tub.

"Like what you see?" Bastian asks, taking another sip of his wine.

"Can't see much with the bubbles covering most of you." Andres smirks. "I guess I'll have to climb in and explore what's hiding in there."

"Something you're sure to like." Bastian takes another sip of his wine, emptying the glass. He holds it up for Andres. "Mind getting me a refill before you join me? The bottle and a spare glass are on the counter between the sinks."

Andres grabs his glass and refills it slowly before he hands it back to him and pours one for himself. Then, he begins to remove his clothes. All the while, he keeps his eyes on Bastian, and Bastian thanks the gods for the hot water he's been relaxing in so he can use that as an excuse for the blush that is creeping up his cheeks thanks to Andres's hungry gaze.

When Andres gingerly slips into the water, sliding himself behind Bastian, he does it with a sigh that sends delighted shivers down Bastian's spine.

"How long have you been in here?" Andres asks, his lips hovering around Bastian's ear.

"Oh, long enough to have a glass of wine," he says, though the truth is it's been about an hour.

"Must have been a large glass," Andres teases as he holds up and examines the fingers of Bastian's right hand.

"You do know I like a heavy pour."

"Don't we all."

Bastian rests his head against Andres's chest. "How was the rest of your night?"

"Uneventful," Andres says. "I spent most of it willing time to move faster so I could get back to you and do this."

"Only this?"

"Maybe something a little more than this," Andres says. His voice is husky as it rumbles through his chest, causing the air to vibrate around them.

Bastian takes a sip of his wine and then places it beside Andres's on the wide tiled edge of the tub.

"Hmmm ..." Andres hums as Bastian runs his hands down Andres's thighs that are caging him right now. His fingers drag through the layer of coarse dark hair and eventually settle at the junction where Andres's thighs meet his hips. From there, he lifts himself, using his grip on Andres's body for leverage, and carefully turns inside Andres's arms, meeting his lips in a slow, languid kiss as he settles himself to lounge against Andres's front, situating them chest to chest.

"What would Justin do if he knew his business partner was having lurid thoughts about a naked man in his tub while he's supposed to be working?"

"Nothing," Andres says with one hand resting on Bastian's back, the other giving Bastian's ass a firm squeeze and supporting him in the water. "Because unlike you and your co-workers, there are some details about our lives that we do not divulge at work."

"Pfft." Bastian scoffs. "As if restaurants aren't a hotbed of HR nightmares."

"At least we're not reading centaur porn in the kitchens during lulls in orders," Andres teases and brings his other hand to Bastian's other ass cheek and pulls him closer, effectively sliding their shafts together.

"Oh, we're onto minotaur porn now. Very sexy," Bastian says with one eyebrow raised high and self-mocking.

"I doubt that," Andres says and brushes some of Bastian's drying curls away from his eyes. He looks at Bastian. "I'd much rather have my explicit fantasies of what I have planned for you."

"That's hardly appropriate work talk, even for a salon," Bastian says.

"Oh, I didn't mean that I'd express them out loud. What you and I get up to is for me and you alone." He slides his hand to cradle the side of Bastian's face, and Bastian can't help himself from leaning into his touch.

Bastian opens his eyes wide and nibbles at Andres's thumb which is pulling gently at his lower lip. "So I should stop writing that erotic novel I'm crafting about us?"

"Why write it when we can live it?" Andres asks and cuts Bastian off with a kiss before Bastian can answer.

It's not only the evenings that work out better with keys. The mornings run smoother as well. From Andres's place, Bastian can walk to work in fifteen minutes instead of needing to take the "L." That's only when Andres isn't ready, willing, and insisting on giving him a ride. Which most days, Bastian is happy to take him up on. But today, the sun is shining and summer has made its arrival, so Bastian decides to walk and enjoy the scent of brownies wafting from the nearby chocolate factory.

The beginning of June brings with it two things: the official kick-off of oppressive summer and International Mister Leather, otherwise known as IML weekend. Muscle and leather daddies, along with humidity, descend upon the city like a storm front, mingling together in one giant three-day-long party, ending in time to kick off Pride Month. While it may not be Bastian's fetish, he does enjoy the joviality the event brings to all corners of his metropolitan playground. There's a party and an event for everyone, and as Bastian makes his way to work from Andres's, walking through the West Loop to River North, he sees glimpses of the unbridled celebration that is intermingling with the mundane around him. These are the regular neighborhoods. If history serves as a bellwether, Boystown is likely already overflowing with even more gay men than usual celebrating their lives proudly in the streets.

Even as he stops at Brew, he sees evidence of the weekend's activities. He covertly snaps a picture of the leather-clad couple standing in front of him in line and sends it to Andres, then deletes the picture from his phone.

> *The leather daddies have arrived. Should I let them buy me a cup of coffee?*

> *Considering your coffee is always on the house at Brew, I think that would be an unnecessary effort.*

Bastian laughs to himself. For as kind as he is, Andres has never been one to share. He's likely lying in bed, lips pulled tight and heat rising into his cheeks, cursing himself for not insisting a little bit harder that he'd give Bastian a ride to work.

> *I don't know. They look like they could be a good time.*

Bastian, forever the brat, sends back.

> *Doubt.*

This is all he gets in return from Andres as he steps up to the register to place his order.

"Hi there," he says to the young blond behind the counter. Her name tag denotes her as Haley. She bats her eyelashes at him, attempting to bark up the way wrong tree. She must be new. "Large iced coffee, topped with almond milk and a vegan, black forest donut, please."

"Hey, Bastian," Padma, Brew's manager, says from behind the espresso bar. She looks to the girl at the register and informs her, "Bastian is on the house. Always."

The girl nods, then turns back to Bastian and flashes him another grin as he drops a few dollars into the tip jar.

Bastian steps to the side to wait for his order and resumes texting Andres. Taking pity on him, Bastian decides to drop his teasing, opting to attempt to make weekend plans instead.

> Are you planning on going to any of the parties?

> I can probably get off work early enough on Monday to make it to the Black and Blue Ball if you want to go?

Bastian bites at his lip. The Black and Blue Ball is the most extravagant and expensive party of the weekend.

> I'm not sure I can afford it.

> It's not like you'll have to pay to get in.

> Can you get us in for free?

It's kind of a ridiculous question. Of course, Andres can get them in for free, and even if he couldn't, it's not as if he'd let Bastian pay for anything anyway, even if Bastian were to protest. But Bastian never wants to assume or overuse Andres's connections. When he does, it always leaves him feeling uncomfortable and inadequate.

> Yeah, I'll make the calls.

> Thanks!

Bastian sends back and, thinking about how raucous Boystown can get during IML weekend, decides to ask,

> Can I spend the weekend at your place? My neighborhood is bound to be a disaster.

> Isn't that why you live up there?

> No. I live up there for the history.

Which is true. Or at least part of the truth. Admittedly, when he moved into his first apartment in Boystown at nineteen, it was because he wanted to live in the thick of all the action. He wanted to be near all the gay bars and clubs and vibrant gay-owned businesses, and he was naive enough to believe at the time that those things only existed within the confines of the blocks that made up Boystown. Now he realizes that gay life thrives throughout the entire city, and he can, in fact, live anywhere he pleases and have it not make him any less gay. He decides to add a joke.

> And my first-ever walk-in closet.

> I have a walk-in closet.

Andres texts back.

> *That you have filled with shoes.*

Bastian chuckles, thinking about the shelves upon shelves of pristine shoeboxes organized meticulously in Andres's closet.

"Here you go, Bastian," Padma says, passing him his coffee and donut. He juggles them in his hands to still be able to hold his phone and bids Padma a goodbye as his phone buzzes again.

> *True. But I can clear out a shelf or two for you if you wanna bring some clothes back with you later.*

Bastian's body buzzes as he reads the message, a warmth bubbling through him that he quenches with a sip of his iced coffee. Fumbling one-handed with his phone and backing out of Brew's front door, he types back.

> *Alright. I'll try not to mess up your curated shoe collection when I unpack.*

With the message sent, he tries not to fret too much about the implications of what moving some of his clothes into Andres's place could possibly mean.

As he promised, Andres has cleared out a few shelves from his closet and left an entire rod empty for Bastian to hang some clothes.

He's flipping through the items that he had brought with him after work on Saturday, trying to pick out what he wants to wear tonight to the Black and Blue Ball, and is feeling a few things. This closet is obviously much too large for only one person, but Bastian isn't entirely sure how comfortable he is helping Andres fill up the space. Andres has worked hard for it, and it feels somewhat rude to claim a section of his home as Bastian's own. Never mind that it's been given to him.

He shakes off the feeling and intrusive thoughts, reasoning that it's his subconscious not used to this sort of thing. After all, no one else has ever given Bastian a section of their closet. Hell, Ryan got bent out of shape when Bastian had left a toothbrush. It's perfectly reasonable to be apprehensive when it comes to marking your metaphorical territory with a few hangers' worth of clothes.

"What are you wearing?" Andres asks as he enters the closet wearing nothing but a towel. He wraps his arms around Bastian's waist and looks over Bastian's shoulder at the section of the closet partially filled with Bastian's things. Andres's breath tickles his ear, and a few drops of water that Andres must not have dried off are sticking Bastian's back to Andres's chest. He's tempted to call this whole evening off and suggest they stay in and lounge around on the sofa with a familiar movie or TV show playing on the giant screen. That is a strange feeling in and of itself, almost as strange as seeing a few of his things hanging in Andres's closet. Bastian has never felt at ease enough in someone else's space to have the urge to stay in their home on a regular basis. Not even during the long Chicago winters when stepping outside is an affront to your entire existence.

"Not sure." He sighs and leans heavily against Andres, trusting his friend's arms to hold him up as he's done for most of Bastian's existence. Even in the past, when Andres needed support, like when his brother was passing, the positioning was still the same. Andres finds comfort in caring for other people, and Bastian has found himself on the receiving end of Andres trying to distract himself from his own life for damn near twenty-five years. A quiet part in the back of Bastian's mind worries that's all this is. Andres diving into Bastian, trying to avoid his own issues. From what Bastian can see—outside of overworking himself and a long-strained relationship with his parents—Andres has nothing that resembles an issue at all, and his time spent with Bastian has felt nothing short of genuine and authentic. But there is always that doubt, that fear, that lingers in the background of someone who has repeatedly been spurned.

Andres reaches around him, pulls Bastian's green and gray five-year-old Burberry trousers off the shelf and a tight black T-shirt off its hanger, then hands them to Bastian. "This will look nice tonight," he says and places a kiss on Bastian's cheek before he pulls away and removes his towel.

Bastian lets his eyes linger on Andres's nakedness and again strongly considers suggesting that they stay in. He shakes it off.

International Mister Leather only happens once a year, and it only happens in Chicago, and the Black and Blue Ball is a big event. Besides, Andres has already called in a favor with his connections at the Metro, ensuring their admittance into the VIP section.

He begins to change into the clothes, his eyes lingering on Andres, who is still standing completely nude, like it doesn't affect Bastian at all. He winks at Bastian as he pulls a pair of Gucci pants off the shelf and a simple white button-down from its hanger. "I was thinking," Andres begins, "since you have to work tomorrow, we can call it an early evening, and I'll give you a ride to work in the morning."

"That would be nice," Bastian says, though internally, he's guessing that even if they do call it an early night, he's not going to be getting any extra sleep. He and Andres can't seem to keep their hands and mouths off each other once they're in bed for the evening. Or once they wake up in the morning. Or when one of them gets in from work, which was the case only fifteen minutes ago.

"Good," Andres says. "Not that I'm not looking forward to going out tonight. It's just been so nice to stay in lately."

"It has." Bastian laughs, amazed at how Andres always seems to echo his thoughts. Not that he should be surprised. The two of them have seemingly been sharing a brain cell since they were five.

"It's funny," Andres continues. "I never really thought my life could be like this."

"Like what?" Bastian asks. Andres is not one for leaving life to chance. How could anything take him by surprise?

"Like this." He gestures between them. "Easy, companionable."

"I could make things difficult if you'd like," Bastian says. "Add a little spice if this is feeling easy."

"Don't you dare," Andres says, zipping up the fly of his pants. He steps to Bastian and scoops him back into his arms, placing a loud and firm kiss on his cheek.

"But you like it when I'm a brat." Bastian pouts.

"Do I?" Andres questions him with an eyebrow raised.

"Don't you?" Bastian asks, spinning himself in Andres's arms to rub his ass against Andres's crotch. That earns him a soft spank.

"Behave, or we are never getting out of here tonight," Andres says with a throaty growl and spins Bastian around again to kiss him on the lips.

Finally, after another slight delay in leaving, Bastian, with a drink in his hand, looks down onto the partygoers below from the second-floor balcony. Hordes of men from all walks of life are mingling and dancing together, various degrees of undress among them. It's like stepping into a Tom of Finland art piece. There are the leather men, young and old, like the ones who started this whole event in the seventies, men in complete designer suits, and those who look barely old enough to be here wearing nothing but a jockstrap. It's a variable cornucopia of men dancing and writhing together in unfettered debauchery. A full-on celebration of men and unbridled masculinity. Their revelry is revealed with each flash of the bright strobe lights that moves in time with the signature Chicago House music coursing through the Metro's state-of-the-art sound system. None of them have a care in the world right now as they celebrate the lives they've carved out for themselves. It's not the best party that Bastian has ever been to. It's no trip to the Dolphin for gay night from the days of his youth, but it's still a good time, and Bastian bops along to the beat of the music with Andres at his side. Given the way everyone in the room seems to know who Andres is, he could've organized this whole event.

That's the thing about Andres. He's a celebrity in his own right—one of the biggest who's who of Chicago. Tucked inside either of their apartments, Bastian can forget this. But out in the open, with someone stopping them every five feet or calling Andres's name across the bar, Bastian is continuously reminded that he's a nobody.

He has to laugh to himself when an old private school acquaintance of Andres's, Antony Dayon, that Bastian has met countless times, turns to him after addressing Andres and asks, "Who are you?"

"This is Bastian. You've met before," Andres says before Bastian has a chance to respond. Andres looks at Bastian and makes a jerking-off motion toward the guy, making it clear what he thinks of him.

Bastian bursts out laughing again, and Antony looks back and forth between the two of them, clearly bewildered that he has missed the joke. This is easily the fourth time that Bastian has met Antony. The second since he and Andres started doing whatever it is that they are doing that hasn't been defined yet. Like they do every time this happens, he and Andres laugh it off, and Bastian pretends like it doesn't annoy him to no end.

"He's always been such an ass," Andres says into Bastian's ear. "He's trying to get me to promote that new vodka that's out. It's vodka. They're all basically rubbing alcohol anyway."

Bastian lifts his drink. "Speaking of, do you think you can get me another rubbing alcohol and soda, please?"

"Of course I can." Andres kisses Bastian on the cheek. He steps away, and Bastian resumes looking over the balcony.

He can see a handful of familiar faces below. Some ex-boyfriends whose names have been cemented in ink on his wall, a few guys he's gone out on a date with here and there, a selection of Grindr hookups, and even a client or two. There's some surprising faces—local celebrities, athletes, and heirs to old million-dollar fortunes who will shimmy back into their closets once this party, and, subsequently this weekend, are over. It's a bit like playing gay *Where's Waldo* from above.

A tap on his shoulder catches him off guard. Turning, he smiles, expecting to see Andres with his refilled drink.

"Hey, Bastian," Ryan Andrews says, taking Bastian entirely off guard. "Fancy seeing you here."

"Hey, Ryan." Bastian's mood suddenly sours.

"I wasn't expecting to see you tonight."

"Why not?" If anyone is out of place here, it's Ryan. For all his talk during their breakup about not wanting to be tied down for the summer, he's not exactly someone known as Mr. Social. Bastian had to practically beg him to go out at all when they were dating, and it was nearly impossible to get Ryan to come to Bastian's instead of Bastian always having to go to him.

"I meant up here," Ryan teases, but Bastian doesn't miss the smugness. "My company was in charge of advertising this year. It's been VIP access all weekend for me."

"How nice," Bastian says, desperately wishing that he had a full drink to take a sip from.

"It's been a *wild* couple of days," Ryan says, his shoulders bobbing awkwardly to the music. Looking at him now, Bastian can no longer remember what he ever saw in him. Underneath the soft reddish glow of the lights, music thumping in the background, Ryan has never looked more unappealing. He leans in towards Bastian and murmurs into his ear, "You look good."

"Thanks," Bastian says, and it's his turn to sound smug this time.

"Are you here with anyone?"

"I am," Bastian says as he sees Andres making his way back over to him from the bar with two drinks in his hands. His lips pull up into a smile that he didn't direct them to do.

"A pity invite from your best friend Andres doesn't count as someone," Ryan says, his tone mocking. Bastian's smile falls.

Refusing to look at Ryan, Bastian keeps his gaze focused on Andres as he makes his way through the crowd. He watches as people stop in their tracks to get a look at him or lean in and whisper something to their counterpart, or most annoyingly, reach to grab onto Andres and pull him into conversation and playful flirting. Andres, like he always does, commands a room simply by being in it. And this, mixed with what Ryan said moments ago, along with the awkward encounter with Antony before that, has Bastian feeling rather small and quite ready to go home.

"It isn't pity. We're dating," Bastian says, still not even bothering to look at Ryan.

"That's a laugh," Ryan says, following it with a literal laugh.

Bastian turns his head and raises an eyebrow at him. "Jealous?"

"Not even a little bit."

Bastian, all remaining traces of joy leaving his face, focuses his gaze back on Andres. Andres seems able to read his thoughts or, at the very least, his expression. He cocks his head to the side and furrows his brow in concern. Bastian takes a breath, forcing a smile back onto his face on the exhale, then nods his head to the left to indicate Ryan standing beside him. Andres repeats the gesture in understanding and quickens his pace to cross the final ten feet to get back to Bastian.

Bastian takes his drink from Andres and sucks up a third of it through the too-thin straw.

Andres, not bothering to pay attention to Ryan, kisses Bastian's cheek as he swallows. "You about ready to get out of here?"

"So ready," Bastian says.

"Good." Andres smirks. "We can have more fun just the two of us anyway," he says and whisks Bastian away to enjoy the rest of the night in.

CHAPTER 12

"The wedding has been moved to August twenty-third, and instead of the two-week honeymoon in Maui we were planning, Justin and I will only be going up to his parents' Lake House in Door County for five days. I'm not even missing a full week of work," Laura says to her client, who is clearly faking excitement at Laura's news.

Bastian isn't surprised. He's been listening to poor Laura relay this information to her clients all week. This has to be the fifteenth time he's heard this, minus the first time she told him the new plan during a meetup for coffee before hitting up the Pride Parade at the end of June. He spins his client's chair while he's blow drying so he can better give Laura support by making eye contact over the tops of their clients' heads when she needs it. She looks at him appreciatively, knowing what he's doing, and smiles kindly as she continues to explain.

"And then the baby's due the week before Thanksgiving."

Laura's client lets out a sigh that is audible even through the sound of Bastian's running blow dryer. "Right before the holidays? That's not very convenient."

"Yes ... well ... I do intend to work all the way up until the week the baby is due."

"That's assuming nothing goes wrong. You never know with this sort of thing," her client says with no trace of worry for Laura or her baby's wellbeing. Years behind the chair has Bastian's, and likely Laura's, instincts honed to when someone's concern is purely selfish. Besides, a large portion of the clients at Salon Azure Blue make sure their stylists know whenever possible that they are, in fact, beneath them, even though everyone needs a haircut from time to time.

"I know," Laura says and subtly drops her head back for a brief moment.

"And I'm sure you'll need to cut back on hours."

"Possibly. But I'll make that decision if and when the time comes."

"And will you be honoring standing appointments over new ones when the time comes to cut back? I don't want to show up here and not know who will be doing my hair."

"I assure you, any changes to your appointments you will be made aware of." Laura looks at Bastian.

He lowers his blow dryer away from his client's hair and tucks it under his arm, making sure the hot air blows directly at Laura's client's face while he takes his time sectioning off his client's hair to begin styling it with his round brush.

Laura's client shifts uncomfortably in her chair. "And when will you be returning?"

"I will return to work the first Tuesday in February," Laura says as plainly as possible.

"February?" Laura's client questions. "That's a bit long, don't you think?" "It's less than three months," Laura says, and Bastian has never wanted to spray hairspray directly into a client's eyeballs more. And this is saying something considering the nightmare people and the microaggressions he's had to deal with in his years behind the chair. Maybe it's more that he's had to listen to Laura explain in the gentlest terms possible over and over again that she has a life and hopes and dreams outside of the salon to her clients, who are all more concerned about their complimentary bang trims than they are about Laura's wellbeing.

"And Bethany, here," Laura continues, gesturing over her shoulder to Bethany, who has been acting as Laura's shadow since Laura informed Mitchel that her life had taken an unexpected turn, "will be available for all your needs while I'm gone." As if Laura didn't already have enough on her plate, it's now her job, which she won't be compensated for, to make sure that Bethany is ready to step behind the chair and take on Laura's clientele while she's on maternity leave without the slightest hiccup. "I assure you, you will be in excellent hands."

"But she's new." Laura's client scoffs. "And my hair is complicated."

This, Bastian has to roll his eyes at. Everyone thinks their hair is
unique, that it requires a certain finesse. Which, sure, a perfectly
executed precision haircut and color makes a difference, but it
means nothing if the client goes home and uses Pantene to wash
it and Aquanet to finish it.

Bethany catches his look this time and has to stop herself from
snickering. In any average salon, Bethany would already be working behind the chair. She and Lizzie have a natural gift for seeing
what is possible with someone's hair and how to execute it. At this
point in both of their training, it's only a matter of fine-tuning
them and them patiently waiting for a chair to open up that they
can take.

Poor Lizzie. She'll have to continue to wait for her opportunity.
She was a good sport about Bethany being offered the chance first,
even if that chance is still four months away.

"I promise you," Laura says, the brightest, most confident smile
she can muster on her face, "that Bethany will be up for the task.
Right, Bastian?"

Bastian spins his client in his chair to face the mirror again
and steps to stand behind it, blow dryer still running as he lets
down another section to style. He makes eye contact with Laura's
client through the mirror and puts on his most sarcastic smile, face
scrunched up, cheeks making his eyes squint. "That's right!" he

exclaims way too brightly. "Laura and I have been working with her every day."

"Regardless," Laura's client says. "I think I'll have Oliver downstairs set up all my future appointments with another, more experienced stylist when I check out today. You understand, don't you, dear?"

"Of course," Laura says, but Bastian doesn't miss the slight hint of annoyance in her voice. Telepathically, Bastian sends Laura the vibe to make sure she messes up this woman's bangs.

"This is excruciating," Laura says as she sits beside Bastian in the breakroom and hangs her head between her hands. Feeling sorry for her, he cuts the black bean burger that Andres dropped off for him in half, then slides the wax paper over and between them so she can eat with him. She looks up at him gratefully and says quietly, "Thanks."

"I hope you got a little scissor happy with the length on that last one," Bastian says and takes a bite of his food. "She was awful."

"Yeah." Laura takes a small bite and thoughtfully chews. "I really wasn't expecting that out of her."

"Especially when one considers how gung-ho she was about you getting married," Bastian points out.

"Right?!" Laura exclaims and forcefully shoves four French fries into her mouth.

"They're all the same," Bastian continues to commiserate, his voice taking on a thick, sarcastic tone. "I can't believe you haven't met someone yet! Oh, is he the *one*? When's the wedding? You know what happens next? A baby! And then they shit all over us when those life occurrences play out."

"At least when you and Andres get married, you'll be able to avoid a lot of this."

"Excuse you, but who says Andres and I are getting married?"

Laura rolls her eyes. "Don't be so self-sabotaging, Bastian. The man is head over heels for you, and you for him. It's a matter of time."

Bastian wrinkles his nose at her declaration. Sure, things have been going well with Andres, great actually, but a wedding seems a bit excessive to be thinking about. He's only even voiced the idea that they were dating once, and that was in an attempt to shut Ryan up. Joking about a wedding feels an awful lot like jumping the gun and likely jinxing this whole thing, which has probably been cursed from the start. "Andres and I are not getting married."

"Famous last words."

"We're not!" he says and throws a fry at her.

She catches it and eats it. "If you change your mind, since they wouldn't give us our deposit back, we have the rooftop of Tribune Tower still booked for the last Saturday of October," Laura says as if this settles it and takes another bite of her portion of Bastian's lunch. "Fuck, these burgers are good."

·❤·❤·❤·❤·❤·

Just like she had managed to do before with her 'See what I mean' and then her 'You're dating Andres Wood,' Laura's words of a wedding, no matter how ludicrous, have decided to take up residence in Bastian's head rent-free as he journeys back home to Boystown for the night. Bastian has never even thought of marriage outside of preparing his clients' hair for it. All those years of special occasion styling and color matching to make sure the wedding photos were perfect have left Bastian a bit jaded about the whole concept. At least half of his clients have made Bastian dread every single one of their appointments leading up to their wedding day by giving him an ever-expanding list of impossible hair demands and freakouts over the smallest of details and boring him beyond belief with talks over bland catering food have ended in divorce within the first five years—making the whole thing seem like an immeasurable waste of time and money. Each time, it leaves him questioning: if you love each other truly, is this entire show really necessary?

Worse yet, Laura suggesting it, for whatever reason, seems to hold more weight than when Andres offered it three months ago. Granted, it's not as if Andres proposed back then as they sat beside each other at Graze. He simply reminded Bastian of a silly childhood promise that should've remained long forgotten by both of them. And Andres hasn't brought it up since. They're not getting married. They're barely even dating.

Yet, here, Laura's words sit and live in his brain, chewing at him and making him wonder what it would be like to stand at the top of the historic Tribune Tower and make vows to Andres.

He shakes it off as he flips on the lights in his apartment. It's been days since he's been home, having spent the last three nights at Andres's. With tomorrow being Saturday, booked beyond its gills and starting earlier than usual to squeeze someone in, Bastian decided it was best to sleep by himself in his bed and then smartly pack a bag with a re-up of clothes and supplies to be left at Andres's place.

His phone is vibrating in his back pocket before he's even had a chance to shut and lock the door. He sighs when he sees it's his mother. He's been ducking her calls for days, finding himself in various stages of undress each time her name appears on the screen. Explaining to his mom that he's breathless because Andres is attached to his neck by his lips is a conversation he'd prefer to avoid. He'd much rather keep his discussions with his mother polite and vague at best.

"Hey, Mom," he says as he answers the phone, tucking it between his ear and his shoulder so his hands are free to drop his stuff on the ground and fiddle with the door.

"Sebastian, darling, is that you?" she says with false astonishment.

"Haha, very funny, Mom," Bastian says. "I'm sorry, I've been busy this week."

"Too busy to pick up the phone when your mother calls? What if I had something important to say? Or there was an emergency?"

"Then you would've left me a message or sent me a text," Bastian says.

"That is true. It does seem like the best way to get a hold of you these days is to text. But it wouldn't kill you to call your mother from time to time."

"It's just easier, Mom," Bastian says as he throws the clothes that he brought back with him from Andres's into the little stackable washer and dryer in his tiny laundry closet. In theory, he probably could've washed these at Andres's, but he does feel bad getting the hair clippings that embed themselves into his clothes stuck in Andres's washing machine, no matter how many times Andres laughs and tells him it's fine.

"What are you doing, darling? All I hear is wrestling and banging on your end."

Be glad that's all you're hearing, Bastian thinks, remembering all the times this week his mother has called him at the worst possible moment. "I'm doing laundry."

"Laundry? On a Friday night?"

"I told you, I've been busy."

"Busy doing what that it has you doing laundry on a Friday night? That's a Sunday activity."

"For you, maybe," Bastian says. "Why are we arguing about when I can do laundry?"

"We're not, dear. I'm only saying that it's odd that you're doing laundry on a Friday night."

"Is this what you've been calling me about all week?" Bastian asks. He's over this conversation and misses having Andres's lips all over him as an excuse not to pick up the phone.

Laughing, she says, "Of course not. I wanted to say hello, see how my darling boy is doing, and make sure you're still planning on coming for dinner on Sunday. You are still coming, aren't you?"

"That is the plan," Bastian confirms. "Unless you want me to stop doing my laundry now and save it to do on Sunday, a much better day for laundry, according to you."

"You're so silly. You know that?" she admonishes. "We will see you on Sunday? It has been over a month. July is nearly over."

"Yes, I'll be there," Bastian says, even though this conversation is making him not want to be there at all. Though, if he doesn't go, it will lead to her being more persistent until he does.

"And Andres too?"

Bastian rolls his eyes. "Yes, Andres is planning on coming."

"It's so nice to see the two of you boys together."

The color drains from Bastian's face. He hasn't told his mother anything that has developed between him and Andres. He doesn't want to have to listen to her shock when this inevitably blows up. What she doesn't know won't hurt her. "You say that like Andres and I haven't been best friends since we were five. Why wouldn't you see us together?"

"Oh, well, you know ..." she says and pauses like she's trying to find the right words, making Bastian worry even more that perhaps he and Andres haven't been as subtle as he had thought. "Sometimes those things fizzle out over time."

And *that* is exactly what he's worried about.

"What time do we have to leave?" Andres asks Bastian as he kisses down the column of Bastian's neck, his tongue dipping into the slight hollow between his collarbones.

"Soon, I guess." Bastian makes no effort to get them out of bed. He'd rather not stop Andres from the track that he's on. Besides, he'll be in a much better mood and far more patient with his parents if he's had an opportunity to get off before they make the ride down Lake Street to Oak Park.

"Should we put this on hold until we get back tonight?" Andres asks and, like Bastian, makes no effort to stop. If anything, he escalates the experience by shifting himself to slot flawlessly between Bastian's parted legs, bringing their erections to rest beside each other. He gives a little thrust to his hips that makes Bastian mewl. "Like that, huh?" He thrusts again, and Bastian arches off the bed to meet him. "Yeah, you like that."

Bastian is gone in full-blown ecstasy. So what if they're a little late for dinner?

·♥·♥·♥·♥·♥·

"Sorry we're late." Bastian kisses his mother on the cheek. "Andres got caught up." He has to stop himself from laughing as Andres narrows his eyes at him from where he's standing behind and out of sight of Bastian's mother and shaking Bastian's father's hand in hello.

"No problem, boys," she says, kissing him back.

"Yes, no problem," Bastian's dad agrees while looking Bastian directly in the eyes.

Bastian gulps, feeling like he's been caught in trying to pull a fast one. The look he's giving Bastian has him feeling like he's sixteen again and getting caught climbing out of his second-floor window to sneak off to see the nineteen-year-old barista from the Starbucks around the corner.

"Yes, I apologize," Andres says and swoops in to steal a hug from Bastian's mother that has her gleefully giggling like she's the one that holds Andres's affections. Young or old, it doesn't matter. Andres has that effect on everyone, including happily married, middle-aged mothers. "Can I help you in the kitchen?"

"Oh no, sweetheart." She pats Andres on the chest. "It's almost finished. You go make yourself comfortable." She turns to look at

Bastian. "But you, Sebastian, come with me, please. My bangs are hanging in my eyes."

"Why didn't you tell me? I'd have brought my shears," Bastian says, exasperated.

"Oh, no need for that," she says, leading him into the kitchen. Bastian gives Andres a quick look as Andres is being led into the living room by Bastian's father, presumably to watch whatever game is on.

"Um, yes, need for that," Bastian corrects her. "I can't trim your bangs with kitchen shears."

"I'm not asking you to do anything fancy, Sebastian," she says. "I only need you to make it so I can see again."

"Fine," Bastian says. "I think I have my shears from beauty school upstairs in my old room somewhere unless you've moved them around."

"They're in your desk drawer," she says and resumes tending to the food cooking on the stove. "I use them to trim Randy when I can't get him into a groomer."

Bastian lets out a sigh and walks back out of the kitchen to head up the stairs to grab the shears he hopes haven't gone dull or rusty from trimming dingleberries off the dog.

Once upstairs and alone in his childhood bedroom, Bastian is hit with another wave of nostalgia that, thankfully, isn't laced with memories of his father's scolding. It's a wonder what his mother must think whenever she enters this room and why it is that she hasn't cleared it out to turn it into something more useful than a makeshift museum of all the dumb phases Bastian went through in his adolescence. He was happy growing up here. Well, as happy as a child prone to bouts of anxiety and depression could be. Rummaging through his desk drawers thrusts him right back into the feelings of the Bastian of old. The Bastian who lived in this room and dared to dream of a glamorous life he still hasn't found. The Bastian of old who is still very much ever-present in the Bastian of now. He may have grown, he may have moved out on his own, but he remains in a lot of ways the same insecure boy who is always second-guessing himself and wishing so desperately for another boy to come along and deem him enough.

Except maybe he's had that all along. There has been a boy in his life who has always seen him as enough as he is. For years, Andres has been there for him as a friend, but as a partner, a lover, he is invariably so much more. Bastian has learned from experience that he's not able to keep someone's affection when it comes to love. Friendship seems to be the only way he's ever been able to hold onto anyone.

Digging and looking for his old D-grade shears, he stumbles across a stack of photos taken of him and Andres across their entire childhoods spent together. He pulls the top one from the stack, recognizing it immediately as the one his mother had texted him a shot of a few weeks back.

"What are you doing?" Andres's voice surprises him. He hooks his head over Bastian's shoulder and wraps his arms around him from behind, sighing against his ear.

"My mom wants a bang trim," Bastian says as Andres takes the photo from his hand.

"Julian," he says with a low, soft voice, drawing out his brother's name. He squeezes Bastian a little tighter around the middle.

"Yeah," Bastian says, not sure of what else to say.

"Your mom must have taken this," Andres says. Juanita and Walter Wood had put their cameras away once Julian got sick, always preferring to remember him as he was before he began to fade away. "Do you think she'll mind if I keep this?"

"I think she'd want you to have it," Bastian says, remembering his mother had asked him weeks ago if he thought Andres would like to see it. He can't believe he had gotten that so wrong. All these years, he's been trying to protect Andres from unexpected reminders of Julian, but maybe what he's wanted all along was to see him everywhere. "We can ask her if she has any more."

Andres looks intently at the photo in his hand. "Nah, just this one for now," he says, then slides it into his back pocket before pulling and turning away from Bastian to quickly wipe his eyes. He stops and stares at an old CD rack filled with hard copies of all the music Bastian now enjoys digitally. He laughs softly and says, "Not much use for these anymore."

"I don't know why my mother won't get rid of everything. It's kind of freaky, isn't it?" Bastian asks, not sure how to tread in the waters around this seldom-seen, vulnerable state of Andres.

"I think it's sweet." Andres shrugs.

"You wouldn't say that if we were in your childhood bedroom," Bastian says, wincing when his eyes land on an old photo of Justin Timberlake hanging on his wall. How he took his side over Britney's all those years ago, he'll never know.

"My childhood bedroom has collectible antique furniture in it and about a decade's worth of dust. We wouldn't even be able to breathe in there." Andres lightly laughs as he does another quick wipe of his eyes, then turns to face Bastian again. Stepping forward, he brings one hand to Bastian's cheek and gently brushes his thumb across Bastian's cheekbone. "I always felt more at home in this room with you, anyway," he says, then dips down and kisses Bastian lightly.

Bastian feels himself go weak in the knees. Whether it's from the kiss, the words, the emotionally charged state they're both currently in, or the heady combination of all three, he's not sure. Regardless, when he leans heavily against Andres as their lips pull away, he's as grateful as he's always been for Andres's steady presence in his life. Maybe he was dumb to have not seen the possibility of what they could have become all those years ago. How could he have been so blind during all those nights that Andres would spend here curled beside him in his double bed as opposed to sleeping on the floor where most other boys' best friends would've chosen to spend the night? And why has he been so stubborn and stupid as not to accept what Andres has been offering this whole time? Instead of choosing Andres and the feeling of home that comes with him, Bastian has consistently chosen to give his heart away to boys who treat him like garbage instead of like a treasured presence in their lives.

Standing here with Andres, memories of their shared past swirling around them, Bastian knows at this moment, as Andres's soft lips press lightly to his again, that he loves him. He genuinely loves him, and he's been a fool not to have seen it sooner. But if his past experiences with what he thought was love have taught him anything, he knows the best course of action is to keep his mouth shut and not say anything. The L-word tends to scare people off.

CHAPTER 13

I t turns out that pretending not to be in love with Andres Wood is a lot harder than Bastian expected. It's hard to live in denial when the man continues to send Bastian lunch at work, pick him up and drop him off, or lounge around in companionable silence while watching movies and reruns of favorite TV shows on their days off. It's hard not to scream out, "I love you!" when Andres is puttering around the kitchen in his gray sweatpants and simple T-shirt, preparing coffee and making breakfast. It's harder still to control his words when Andres's hands and lips are all over Bastian's body, making him cry out in complete bliss as he comes.

It's hardest when Andres has his hand in his as they shop at the small local boutiques and designer pop-up stores on Milwaukee Avenue. The August sun is shining on them, warming Bastian's cheeks with a nice summer glow, and there's a light breeze blowing through his hair. He enjoys the feel of it as they dip in and out of air-conditioned storefronts, looking for sales or new releases.

While the clothes and shoes are all eye-catching, his favorite thing to see is the people they walk past, taking a look at Andres and then curiously checking out the man who belongs to the hand that he is holding. Bastian enjoys the looks he gets from people who are silently judging—more accurately hating—him for being in this position. Andres is *the* catch of Chicago, and here Bastian is, walking hand in hand with him through one of the city's hippest neighborhoods. All those years of dating the Ryans of Chicago have earned him this privilege. He's not about to give it up by jumping the gun and saying too much.

He's heard the stories and seen it firsthand, laughing with Andres when Andres regaled him with all the times he's had to leave a date mid-dinner because the person on the other side of the table said I love you too soon. Or when he's had to cut and run after a night of passion because some fool had the gall to say I love you at all. While Bastian has dreamed of hearing someone else say those three simple words to him, Andres has run away from them faster than his motorcycle speeding down Lake Shore Drive.

Reading people is one of Bastian's specialties. It's one of the qualities that makes him a remarkable hairstylist. He can anticipate people's needs, and he can read their subtle cues. He knows when to speak, and he knows when to keep his mouth shut. And this is a time to continue to play it cool.

The task grows a little harder when he sees an ex-bartender of Graze walking towards them, smiling broadly as she calls out Andres's name.

"Hey, Samantha," Andres says, letting go of Bastian's hand to wave.

"How are you?" she asks, petting Andres's shoulder and completely ignoring Bastian.

"I'm good. Just out with this one," he gestures at Bastian, "enjoying the day."

Samantha finally acknowledges Bastian's existence. "You're Bastian, right?"

"I am," he says, then looks her up and down. "I remember you from Graze."

She drops her head back and lets out a laugh, then petting at Andres again, she says, "Best job I ever had. It's almost a shame I gave it up for this one to eventually ghost me."

"I didn't ghost you," Andres says.

"You most certainly stopped calling me." She trails her hand down his arm and lets her fingers linger above his wrist. The same wrist that was attached to the hand that was holding onto Bastian's a few minutes ago. She locks eyes with Andres and regards him thoughtfully, then pulls her hand away and brings it to flip her low ponytail over her shoulder. "Let me know if a position opens up at Graze again. I'd love a second chance."

"I'll keep you in mind," Andres says as Bastian clumsily takes his hand, trying to reclaim his territory.

Samantha's eyes briefly flick to their awkwardly linked fingers before she takes her gaze to Bastian. "Hold on tight to this one," she says. "He'll slip right out of your fingers if you're not careful."

"I'll do my best," Bastian says, all traces of confidence gone.

Samantha leans into Andres's space and gives him a cursory kiss on his cheek. "It was good to see you," she says, then struts away from them like she didn't just drop a bomb onto Bastian's day.

Andres, for his part, seems unbothered. "Let's stop in Supreme real quick," he says, lacing their fingers properly, then tugging at Bastian's hand and pulling him to the front of the line where the door guy lets them in with a nod and a "What's up," to Andres.

The walls inside are covered in street art from local artists and portraits of celebrities wearing signature Supreme logo tees. There are racks of these T-shirts, hooded sweatshirts, and rare, hard-to-find pieces of outerwear, and shelves of what they came to see. More accurately, what Andres wants to see: a display full of the latest limited-edition sneakers that are only sold here and at a handful of other locations in the country. Andres is already holding onto a white, low-top Nike Air Force One with red laces. His eyes are narrowed in on the stitching and tiny details.

"Do you have these in size thirteen?" Andres asks the guy behind the counter, and Bastian hears the metaphorical record scratch silencing the entire store's chatter at Andres's request. Half the patrons turn and look at Andres questioningly, no doubt stunned that Andres is looking for a specific size instead of taking what he can get his hands on for his collection. That's the thing about sneakerheads; they hardly ever wear the shoes that they buy. They hoard them in their closets or sell them on the gray market for a profit. But Andres is not such a man. Andres will wear these proudly and somehow keep them pristine in the process. Bastian has no idea how he does it. But then again, Andres doesn't spend his workdays around hair clippings and hair color flying about in every direction.

"Maybe," the sales guy says, looking at Andres. He walks into the backroom, and Andres continues his appraisal of the shoes on display.

"Here. For you," Andres says, holding out what, at first glance, appears to be a simple plain black leather sneaker. It's not until Andres turns it in his hand for Bastian to see the back that he notices the bright red Supreme logo emblazoned across the heel. "These would be nice for you at work."

"Mitchel would hang me from my ankles off the fire escape for wearing those," Bastian says. Although, the thought of potential workplace doom doesn't stop him from touching the shoe in Andres's hand or relishing in Andres's thoughtfulness. Especially after their run-in with one of Andres's ex-flings outside.

"You wear those Nike Blazers I got you all the time," Andres points out.

"True. But that's a much slimmer shoe, and they don't have a fire engine red billboard across the back. Far easier to hide what it is." Bastian shrugs.

"Do you like these, though?" Andres hands the shoe to Bastian this time. "Because if you do, it's worth trying to wear them to work. Your feet will be happy. And if your boss gives you shit, then oh well, you have a new pair of shoes for going out dancing."

"As if I go out dancing that often anymore," Bastian says.

"I thought you and the girls were going to Smart Bar for Laura's bachelorette?"

"That is the plan." Bastian lifts his left foot and holds the shoe beside it, checking to get a feel of what it would look like on him.

"They'll look good," Andres says. "I'll get them for you."

"You don't need to do that." Letting go of Andres's hand, Bastian checks the price tag and gulps but reaches into his back pocket for his wallet containing his credit card anyway. Andres stills him, placing a gentle hand on his wrist, preventing him from pulling it from his pocket. "Andres, come on. I can buy my own shoes."

Andres grabs a hold of Bastian's hand again and squeezes it. "I know you can," he says, then asks the guy behind the counter to grab the shoes in size ten when he returns with the ones that Andres wanted for himself.

Annoyed as he was at Andres's insistence to buy them, Bastian can't help but note while he stands behind his chair, working on the sixth client of the day with barely a moment to pee between any of them, how happy his feet are in his new shoes. He's even more pleased to note that their existence has slipped right past his boss's nose, disguised by Bastian's choice to wear a wider-legged pair of black pants today. Once again, Andres was right. Bastian will have to keep this in mind the next time he even thinks about questioning the man's logic.

"What are your plans for the weekend?" Bastian asks his client as she sits back in his chair after having been shampooed by Lizzie. It's the new blond girl from Brew, Haley, that he met a few weeks ago. Apparently, Padma had informed her that Bastian was *the* best in the business and that she needed to see him ASAP for any and all hair needs. Which would be fine if she hadn't treated every single one of Bastian's visits to get coffee like they were her own personal consultation time.

"Oh, nothing much," Haley says, looking and smiling at him in the mirror. "Just work and errands and stuff. Though I have a date on Saturday."

"Well, that sounds fun," Bastian says, thinking about how unfun it actually sounds. "Who's the date?"

"Someone I work with. He's really nice. I'm excited about it."

Bastian runs through the list of employees he knows at Brew in his head. It's a small staff—only a handful of baristas and Padma.

Although, Bastian supposes that Andres, Justin, and Alex all make their occasional appearance there as well. Not that that matters. Justin is obviously spoken for, Andres is as well, and although Alex is single, she doesn't seem like her type. All that being said, the only male barista Bastian can think of that works at Brew is gay. He knows from personal experience as they drunkenly hooked up a handful of times last summer before Bastian started dating Ryan.

Suddenly, a series of encounters flash through Bastian's mind. *Samantha from the weekend. Nicole from the art institute. The Wrigley heir laughing with Andres at Graze. All the hands and arms pulling Andres this way and that at IML. Even the server from that first night when Andres proposed dating.* With the blood draining from his cheeks in paranoia, Bastian tries to play along.

"I know that feeling," he says, trying to remain cool. After all, it is entirely possible that she could be talking about anyone who works with her. And if this girl is naive enough to think dinner or drinks with her gay co-worker is a date, that's her problem and not Bastian's. Besides, she does have that fresh-from-Iowa girl-next-door air about her. These small-town interlopers only stay naive for so long. "First dates are always exciting."

"I hope it goes well. I really like him," she says. Looking thoughtfully at Bastian in the mirror, she asks, "What about you? Are you seeing anyone?"

Bastian swallows his laugh. "I am. He's great. We're boring, though. Tell me more about your guy."

"I don't really have much to tell yet except that he's older," she says. "But I'll report back the next time you come into Brew."

Bastian, afraid of what he'll find out, decides not to continue pushing. Sure, he's had a few instances in the past few months reminding him of how desired Andres is by all, but Andres has always been forthright with him in the event that Bastian becomes ill at ease. That thought alone calms him a bit. Changing the subject, Bastian looks at Haley through the mirror and says, "Tell me, where are you from?"

"I'm from Iowa," she says, her eyes lighting up. *Called it.* "I moved here this spring. It's amazing!"

"Uh-huh. It sure is," Bastian agrees and lets himself get lost in the meditation of her haircut while she dives into her entire life story from start to finish for Bastian as if he cares. It's fine, he's happy to have her talk, and he knows all the right moments to interject with a hum of agreement or a nod or a well-placed OMG. Clearly, she's in need of some attention. A few months away from living in mommy and daddy's nest will do that to these young ones barely old enough to order a drink when they go out.

At some point, she finally runs out of things to say about herself and circles back to Bastian. "Are you from here?"

"I am," Bastian says. "Born and raised."

"How come all Chicagoans say that?"

Bastian tilts his head to the side. "What? That we're born and raised here?"

"Yeah."

"I guess because there's a difference between those of us who were raised in these streets and those who weren't."

"How so?" she asks as if she feels slighted by Bastian's statement.

"We have thicker skin." He shrugs. "And grit and fortitude. We have to in order to survive winter here."

"We have winter in Iowa," she says.

"Not like we have here." Bastian laughs. "You and I will circle back to this conversation in January."

"It's that bad, huh?" she asks.

"Yes." Bastian laughs again. "But you get used to it. And it makes summer that much more special when it comes around."

"Is that why there's so many street festivals and parties here?"

"That's part of it for sure."

"Are you going to any parties this weekend?"

"I'm going to Laura's," he gestures to Laura working beside him with his cutting comb, "bachelorette party, and by that, I mean I'm taking her out to dinner at Cafe Ba-Ba-Reeba and then dropping her pregnant ass off at home so Marny and I can go dance our unpregnant asses off until five a.m. at Smart Bar."

"Hey!" Laura exclaims. "I want to go to Smart Bar."

"Sorry, Laura. No preggers allowed," Marny says from across the room as she works on her client's fade. "You'll scare the gays and lesbians off with your het-ness."

"That sounds like something I need a shot for," Laura says with a pout.

"Isn't that one of the arguments against vaccines?" Bastian jokes.

"Yes." Marny laughs. "It's part of our gay agenda."

"I'm hardly showing." Laura tries to reason. "Maybe I can come with you for a little bit. I'll wear a flowy top."

Bastian stops his cutting and looks at Laura gently. "You're welcome to join us for as long as you like. It is your party, after all."

"It doesn't feel like it."

"Oh, quit whining," Bastian says. "You know we wouldn't ever leave you behind."

"Wait," Haley says, interrupting. "You're my boss Justin's fiancé, right?"

"Sure am," Laura says.

"You're lucky. He's so nice," Haley says. "He and Andres have been very welcoming to me. We should all go out sometime."

Bastian almost chokes on his spit. *Who does this girl think she is?* He's about to ask when Laura butts in. "Oh, no, honey. Justin and Andres don't fraternize with their employees."

"Huh." Haley shrugs.

Bastian, knowing quite otherwise about Andres, is once again feeling very ill at ease.

"Hop on," Andres says to Bastian, patting the seat behind him on his motorcycle. "I escaped work for a bit. Thought I'd give you a ride."

"You came to pick up little old me?" Bastian questions. He makes a show of looking around him as he steps away from the salon's entrance.

"Yes, you! Get over here." Andres pats the seat again. "I have dinner for us in the saddlebag."

"Hmmm ..." Bastian plays at thinking about it as he walks towards the bike, eying the seat behind Andres, the spot he has come to refer to as 'his' seat. He twists up his lips and raises an eyebrow in question. "What's for dinner?"

"Two of Alex's latest concoctions for the ramen joint we're opening next month."

Bastian's eyes go wide, soft, and pleading. "You brought me noods?"

"Yeah." Andres smirks. "And there's soup too."

"And you say I'm the incorrigible one," Bastian says, laughing, as he climbs onto the back of the motorcycle. Once there, with his arms around Andres's waist, he finally shakes off the feeling Haley left him with earlier. She's just some dumb girl from Nowhere, Iowa. She's no one Andres would ever be interested in. "Thanks for coming to get me."

Andres squeezes Bastian's thigh and turns his head to meet Bastian's lips with a quick kiss. "You're welcome. It's good to see you."

"You saw me this morning." Bastian gives Andres a second kiss.

"This morning was a long time ago."

"You're ridiculous."

"And you're irresistible," Andres says, then turns his attention to the road and puts his bike into gear, pulling away from the curb. "My place or yours?"

"Yours, I guess," Bastian says as they cruise through traffic. "It'll give us more time together, right?"

"Buys us an extra hour together, at least."

"We can do a lot in that hour," Bastian says.

"Not as much as I would like," Andres replies, his voice gravelly. He pulls one hand away from the handlebars to give Bastian's thigh another squeeze. His large hand lingers there, gently digging into Bastian's flesh through the fabric of his trousers. He gives Bastian's thigh one last little pat before bringing his hand back up.

Once inside, with the food divided between them, they settle onto Andres's couch to eat in comfort, and Andres goes old school and local, putting Common's *Like Water for Chocolate* to play on the turntable. "How was your day?" he asks as he hands Bastian a glass of red wine before sitting beside him.

"It was fine." Bastian shrugs. "I did one of your employees' hair today."

"Oh, yeah! Which one?"

"That newer barista at Brew."

"Haley?" Andres questions, his head tilted to the side thoughtfully.

"Yeah," Bastian says, feigning indifference. He twists his chopsticks into his broth and pulls out a scoop of noodles. "She seems like she needs a lot of attention."

"She's a sweet kid," Andres says. "A bit clueless. But she makes a hell of a cup of coffee."

Bastian scoffs. "She always gives me oat milk instead of almond milk." He's lying. She's made that mistake only once.

"That's a fireable offense for sure," Andres says. "That type of error cannot stand."

"Seriously though, who hired her?" Bastian asks and pulls some bok choy out of his broth to eat.

"She was an Alex hire. She's his cousin or a friend or something. I'm not entirely sure."

"That explains it." Bastian rolls his eyes.

"What did she do? Ask you to make her look like a Phoenix or some shit in your chair today?" Andres laughs. "I can feel your disdain for her from across the couch."

"I don't think she's up to your usual caliber of employee."

Andres places his food on the coffee table and leans across the couch. "I'll let you sit in on interviews from now on," he says, then places a placating kiss on Bastian's forehead.

Bastian dips his chopsticks back into his food. He's not sure why he's so bothered by her. He barely knows her, and Andres has most certainly never given him a reason to dislike her. Yet, there's still this nagging feeling in his gut that has his hackles raised. He's heard far too many stories from behind his chair of his clients' tales of love woebegone. He's had too many instances in his own love life where he's let his guard down, only to lead to him getting burned. He's watched movies and TV shows and listened to songs, and all these instances and examples have all pointed to one conclusion—trust no one and be prepared for the rug to be pulled out from under you. Especially when you think you're in love. There are Haleys lurking everywhere, waiting for their chance to steal your happiness. It's cruel that falling in love with someone leads to this kind of conclusion and constant looking over one's shoulder in preparation for that love to be ripped apart. Alas, it's where Bastian finds himself after one hour spent with some silly, young, conventionally attractive girl in his chair.

"So, Laura's party tomorrow." Andres interrupts Bastian's train of thought. "Is she excited?"

Bastian takes a breath and swallows a sip of his wine, hoping to bring some color back to his cheeks and praying he doesn't look as haunted by his intrusive thoughts as he feels. "She is."

"Is there anything I can do to make it smoother for you all?"

"I don't think so," Bastian says and runs a quick checklist through his mind. He has reservations for them at Cafe

Ba-Ba-Reeba, and Andres has already called in a favor to put them on the list at Smart Bar so they can skip the line. Their sound system and the DJ lineup they have spinning all night is sure to draw a quick above-capacity crowd of House heads and every gay with the night off imaginable in the city to Smart Bar's doors. "I wish you could join us."

"Me too," Andres says with a relaxed smile on his face. He squeezes Bastian's foot that's up on the couch beside him. "Can I interest you in joining us for Justin's on Sunday?"

"A day at Wrigley Field?" Bastian winces. "I think I'll pass."

"Is it too late for me to pass as well?"

"You planned it!" Bastian teases, even though he knows that a day spent at Wrigley Field is Andres's worst nightmare. He may like sports, but Cubs games draw a particular crowd of drunk tourists and suburbanites looking to hold onto a piece of Americana long gone.

"It wasn't my idea," Andres says. "It's what Justin wanted!"

"After all these years that you two have been friends, you couldn't get him to give up his silly North Shore loyalty to the Cubs." Bastian shakes his head at Andres.

"How on earth did I end up business partners with a die-hard Cubs fan?"

"You went to private school with him and lost all your street cred."

Andres brings a hand to his chest. "Are you challenging my street cred?"

"You are going to a Cubs game this weekend." Bastian laughs. "You're not leaving me much to challenge."

"You little shit," Andres says, placing his food back down on the coffee table. He leans towards Bastian again and takes Bastian's bowl from his hands as well, then scoops him up and places him into his lap.

Bastian yelps in surprise and laughs out loud. "I wasn't done—"

Andres cuts him off with a kiss, effectively earning back his street cred and Bastian's ever-expanding affection with the curve of his lips and a few swipes of his tongue. All thoughts and suspicions of Haley are stuffed back down for Bastian to worry about later if, for some reason, they're given cause to return.

Checking his watch, Bastian frowns at the time. His next client is now fifteen minutes late. If they don't show up soon, he'll be cutting it close with finishing them and making the reservation he and the rest of Laura's bachelorette party crew have at Cafe Ba-Ba-Reeba. *Just my luck,* he thinks. He sighs and stands up off the windowsill by his station that he's been perched on, waiting for his client's arrival. He quickly makes his way down the stairs to where Oliver is sitting behind the reception desk.

"Any word from Caroline?" he asks.

"I tried calling her a few minutes ago. She didn't pick up. Should I call again?"

Bastian chews at his bottom lip. Typically, a last-minute blow-off like this on a Saturday would be annoying but welcomed if it meant he could take his tired ass home. Today, he can't even do that as they're walking to the restaurant from here, and even if he went home, he'd have to turn around and come right back anyway. He thinks of Andres. Maybe he's available for a cup of coffee.

"Nah, we can call it," Bastian says. "If she shows up or you hear back from her, reschedule her for another day. Alright?"

"Yeah. I can do that," Oliver agrees, clearly relieved. He was probably hoping that would be Bastian's answer.

Bastian taps the desk twice, then heads back up the stairs, pulling his phone out of his back pocket as he goes.

> Got blown off. Want to meet me for a coffee?

The response is almost immediate, and Bastian sighs in relief before he reads it. That sigh, however, quickly turns into a frown.

> Wish I could. Work emergency. See you later tonight at your place?

> Yeah. I might be late. But make yourself at home.

> Okay. Have fun tonight.

Bastian frowns again, shuts off his phone, slips it into his back pocket, and goes to clean up his station. A cup of coffee with Andres would've been nice. Still, once he's finished cleaning, he settles for a bit of pregame boozing at the salon, grabbing a beer meant for clients out of the refrigerator, and settling into the backroom to entertain himself on his phone while he waits for Laura, Marny, Bethany, and Lizzie to finish up for the day.

First, he scrolls through Gay Twitter, laughing at memes and ogling all his favorite gay pornstars and amateurs with their thumbnails of OnlyFans clips. He raises his eyebrows when he recognizes his upstairs neighbors in a few of the trending tweets containing images and GIFs. He sends a link to Andres.

> *Good thing we spent the night at your place last night.*

The last two nights they'd spent at Bastian's, they'd laughed at the reoccurring argument from the couple upstairs over where to put their ring light to best illuminate the action for their shaky cell phone footage. It's nice to know that they're finding some success.

He doesn't hear back from Andres, which isn't a surprise. After all, Andres told him that there was a restaurant emergency. The poor man is likely knee-deep in a clogged grease trap or a busted beer line or anything in between. Bastian hopes that Andres has a laugh when he sees the clip.

From there, Bastian takes a sip of his beer and opens up Instagram. He takes a selfie of himself with the beer at his lips, then quickly posts it, the caption reading, *'When your client no-shows.'*

Like always, his notifications begin to blow up, and he goes through those quickly, responding to the comments from clients and other hairstylists expressing their disapproval of his predicament. Clients are vowing never to do that to him, and hairstylists are noting their disapproval at how inconsiderate clients are with stylists' time. There are a few people on there informing him of how cute he is, and he smiles to himself, absorbing the ego boost.

It's then that he sees it. A notification from yesterday that he must have overlooked. He's been tagged in a new photo. He checks it and rolls his eyes. Haley. It's a picture of her sitting at the bar at Graze last night, hipsters and other Friday night revelers around her. The caption reads, *'Looked cute, might delete later. Thanks for the cut @hairbastian!'* He desperately wishes that she would have deleted it later, even though her hair does look stunning.

Bastian, being a bit of a glutton for punishment, and though he is loath to see her in his notifications, clicks on her handle to see the rest of her feed. It's morbid curiosity, really—an opportunity for him to find more reasons to dislike her. Unfortunately for Bastian, the reasons come quickly, as he's met with selfie after selfie of her. She clearly knows how to post for attention. There are pictures of her out and about taking in Chicago's sights, eating and drinking at restaurants, and working behind the espresso bar at Brew. All of them look like she has her own personal camera crew following her around.

Her general existence exasperates Bastian. Eventually, he notices that she has a particular penchant for hanging out at Graze and, while there, manages to capture pictures of Andres nearby. He's in the background of nearly all of them, and in one, she has the gall to catch him smiling and expressive in his happiness, captioning the photo, *'Handsome, isn't he?'*

Yeah, he is fucking handsome! And he's mine. His stomach sinks. With his brow furrowed in anger, indignation, and hints of humiliation, Bastian clicks on the comments, instantly regretting it but unable to stop himself.

'He's so cute!'

'You're so lucky!'

'Where can I order one of those?'

Bastian's heart rate picks up and sends his thoughts racing with it, bringing suspicion and worry to the forefront of his mind. *It could be nothing,* he tells himself. *Or ... it could very much be something.*

Closing out of Instagram, he switches over to Google and looks up the phone number for Graze. If there's an emergency, they'll tell him, and he has nothing to worry about. He's only being paranoid and dumb and looking for a problem where there is none. It'll be funny, and he can have a laugh about it with the girls at the party.

"Graze. How can I help you?"

"Hi, this is Bastian. Is Andres available?"

"Sorry. He's not in tonight."

"He's not?"

"No. Sorry. Can I help you with something else?"

"No." He hangs up the phone.

Bastian has never felt so dumb. He puts his phone down and holds his head in his hands. How did he let this happen to himself again? How did he let himself get sweet-talked to look past the truth? He's no one special. He's a hairstylist with nothing to his name but an over-priced pair of shears, an imposter wardrobe bought on credit, and a list of names documenting his repeatedly broken heart on his wall. Even with that long list of names, he's learned nothing from his past. His need for love and approval to keep him afloat has doomed him to fall for another man's lies once more.

He thought it was different with Andres. He thought Andres was different. He made Bastian feel like he was the only person that mattered. Bastian had believed him despite everything in his being telling him not to. Who's to say that Andres hasn't made everyone he dates feel this way? They all seemed so eager to have him back as their own. Who's to say he doesn't make Haley feel this way? Who's to say Bastian is better than anyone else Andres has ever dated? He's not. He's just dumb enough to believe that he is.

He slams the rest of his beer and begins to pace the backroom, getting angrier and angrier the longer he thinks about the pictures and comments that he's seen. He can't breathe back here, and he feels like he wants to scream. He needs air, and he needs it now. Grabbing his phone, he runs out of the salon's breakroom, down the stairs, and out the front door. The sunshine stings his eyes which are already burning with frustration and the threat of falling tears, and he can't decide if he wants to scream, cry, or throw up.

"Why, the fuck, me?" he asks no one.

The universe answers his call, for at this moment, the sound of a familiar engine breaks through his spinning thoughts, and Bastian looks to the right, catching Andres rounding the corner that Brew is located on with Haley sitting on the back of the bike in Bastian's seat.

Some restaurant emergency, he thinks and promptly throws up.

CHAPTER 14

M ore out of a sense of self-preservation than any form of social decorum, Bastian swallows his humiliation and sits with a placid smile on his face, joking and laughing along at Laura's bachelorette dinner like everything is fine. He tries to forget the image he saw of Haley sitting on his seat behind Andres on the motorcycle. He tries to forget her idiotic Iowan friends' comments on her Instagram photo of Andres. He tries to reason with himself that this is all nothing, that there is a perfectly good explanation, that *his* Andres would never do such a thing. But self-doubt, anxiety, and years of a heart repeatedly broken at the hands of others has Bastian's mind spinning, and he can't catch a moment's rest.

The only thing that seems to be helping is copious amounts of sangria. He pours himself another glass out of the shared pitcher and continues to pick at the small plates of tapas-style Spanish food they're splitting.

"You good?" Marny whispers into his ear.

"Absolutely!" Bastian lies, holds up his glass of fruit-filled sparkling wine, and takes a giant sip.

Marny looks at him skeptically but doesn't say another word. It's not as if Bastian isn't prone to the occasional foul mood. If he seems off, he reasons that's none of her business, but he does attempt to make his smile appear more genuine and authentic as he reaches and grabs another scoop of paella, then some bread with goat cheese. After all, he will need something else in his stomach to soak up all the sangria if he wants to make it through tonight.

He'd initially thought that Laura, being pregnant and all, was going to be the one who would want to call this an early evening. However, as they step out of Cafe Ba-Ba-Reeba, she's the one ordering two Ubers large enough to transport the entire bachelorette party of nine up north to Smart Bar in Boystown, a place where last call isn't until five a.m.

Bastian doesn't want to go to Smart Bar right now. He wants to track Andres and Haley down and make them tell him what is going on. Make Andres say the words out loud that Bastian's internal monologue has been making up for him and playing on a repeated loop so much that they may as well be the truth at this point. After, with confirmation from Andres that Bastian has been right this whole time, that dating each other was the worst idea in history, he wants to go home and do the one thing he vowed he never wanted to do: add Andres to the Boystown list of heartbreakers.

"Get in," Laura says, nudging Bastian's lower back with her clutch purse.

Taking her direction, he shakes away his intrusive thoughts, puts on his best smile, and laughs tightly as he climbs into the back seat of the black SUV that has come to pick them up.

"Seriously, dude. What the fuck is with you?" Marny asks him under her breath when she slides into the seat beside him.

"I already told you. Nothing, I'm fine," Bastian whispers back.

"You look like you've seen a ghost, and you're practically ignoring all the living beings around you. Snap out of it before Laura catches on. You're lucky she hasn't already."

Laura looks over her seat at the two of them behind her. "What are you two whispering about?" She narrows her eyes. "You don't have a surprise up your sleeves, do you? I swear if you two assholes got me a stripper or something, I'm going to make you both Godparents of this baby."

Bastian and Marny both put their hands up in defense and cringe together.

"Oh, you two are the worst!" Laura wags her finger at them. "Just you wait. My baby is going to steal your hearts!"

"Sure, Laura," Bastian says, and Laura reaches over the back seat to swat at him. He ducks out of the way and comes up laughing, the first genuine laugh he's had all night. "I'm kidding. I'm kidding. You know I already love the mini you, but don't ask me to change its diapers."

"I would never," she promises, then adds with a wink, "besides, I think that's a job Andres is more suited for."

Bastian's heart falls through the chassis of the SUV and onto Clark Street, where it gets run over by tonight's traffic at the mention of Andres's name. It takes his laughter with it. In an attempt to cover, he rolls his eyes and tilts his head to the side. "You're gonna trust Andres with your baby?"

"Absolutely!" Laura says. "I'd trust Andres with my life."

Bastian offers her a feeble smile and wishes he could jump out of the SUV's back hatch. He feels Marny's knee nudge against his.

"You know I'll babysit for you," Lizzie says, interjecting herself into the conversation and thankfully catching Laura's attention.

"Me too," Bethany chimes in. "When I'm not too busy taking care of all of your picky-ass clients, that is." Laura, Lizzie, and Bethany all start laughing and engage in a conversation about babies that Bastian will never understand.

"Alright. Let's hear it, Bastian. How'd you fuck it up with Andres?" Marny asks him once the other three women are distracted.

"Excuse you." Bastian scoffs. "I don't know what you're talking about."

"The hell you don't. What dumbass thing did you do?"

"What makes you think that it was me that did something dumb? Andres isn't this perfect being that you all make him out to be."

Marny grabs hold of his hand. "I know that," she says, her tone dipping into gentle. "But he's so clearly smitten with you." She pauses and takes a deep breath, then brings two fingers to his chin to direct him to look at her. "And let's face it, you have a tendency to self-destruct at the slightest provocation."

"I do not!"

"You do, though," she says at the same time that Laura looks back over her seat at them and says, "You do not what?"

"Self-destruct," he says, and Laura laughs at him. "Ugh. I don't know why I'm friends with you two."

"Because you love us," Laura says and lifts herself in her seat, high enough to reach back and grab his other hand. "And because no matter how much you fuck up, we always have your back. Now quit pouting." She squeezes his hand. "And don't think I haven't noticed your sour mood."

"Alright," he says and smiles genuinely at her. After all, after Andres, Laura is his best friend, and Marny falls in line right behind her. Hell, even Bethany and Lizzie have weaseled their way into his heart. With Laura getting married next weekend and then having a baby in a few months, he'd do best not to alienate himself from all of his friends by pouting all night, even if all he really wants to do is curl up under a blanket and pretend he doesn't exist.

However, once at Smart Bar with a drink in his hand and the bumpity-bump of the bass of the DJ's carefully selected and spun-together records reverberating out of the speakers, Bastian is reminded quickly that he does, indeed, exist. The handful of men ogling him by the bar or stopping in their steps while they dance as he walks by is enough of an ego boost to bolster his self-confidence and put some things into perspective.

It now dawns on him that he may be taking this whole thing with Andres too harshly and the wrong way. At no point in their perceived coupling over these last few months has either of them clarified what they were to each other or confirmed if they were indeed a couple. No one had mentioned exclusivity. Neither one had used the word boyfriend. Bastian had smartly kept the L-word in his back pocket. So what is he so upset about? In theory, he should be thrilled. This turn of events has freed him up to do as he pleases. He doesn't answer to Andres. He owes him nothing. So what if Andres is out with Haley right now? It's not as if they'd ever declared themselves as boyfriends or exclusive. Sure, Bastian was under that impression, but he'd also been under the impression that Ryan was going to be his forever before this whole debacle even got started. Clearly, he can make mistakes and jump to conclusions when it comes to the status of his relationships.

So with renewed vigor and a determination to have a good time, Bastian swallows his drink down in one very long sip through his straw, orders another one, and then hits the dance floor with everything that he's got, letting himself get spun around and ground against, and pulled into corners, nooks and crannies, and bathroom stalls to get kissed and groped and forget about the fact that he was dumb enough to believe that he had fallen in love with Andres Wood.

Waking the following day, Bastian is sure of exactly two things. One, this is not his or Andres's apartment, and two, he has royally fucked up. He takes a deep breath and mentally notes that everything but the shoes he was wearing last night are still on. "Thank fuck," he mumbles to himself and adjusts to sit on the couch he's woken up on alone.

"There's coffee if you want it," the voice of Ryan says rudely as he steps into view and sits beside Bastian on the couch.

Bastian shakes his head no and swallows thickly, last night's whiskey and sangria still coating his tongue. "Did we?" he asks, gesturing between them. Given the state of his clothing, he's pretty sure the answer is no, but he needs to double-check.

"We did not," Ryan says. "And you look like you don't want to now, either."

"Definitely not," Bastian says. He grabs his phone off the coffee table to check the time. It's dead.

"It's nine-thirty," Ryan answers for him.

"Fuck," Bastian mumbles.

"Have somewhere you need to be?" Ryan asks with a snort.

"Yeah. Home. Why am I here?" Bastian snaps as he grabs his shoes from underneath the coffee table and begins to slide them on his feet.

"After your little girlfriends left last night, you were hanging all over me—and everyone else who crossed your path—so I figured you wanted to have some fun." He pauses and takes a sip of his coffee, the smell of which is making Bastian want to vomit whatever is left in his stomach from the night before. "And then you passed out on the couch, crying something about Andres before we so much as even made out."

Andres. Bastian brings his hands to his face and rubs harshly. He wants to be with Andres. Even if it's simply because the haze of his hangover is softening the edges of why he was so upset with Andres yesterday.

"I gotta go," he says, rising from the couch and sliding his dead phone into his back pocket.

"I'll see you around, Bastian," Ryan says, not even looking away from the television he's turned on.

"I hope not," Bastian says under his breath and walks out Ryan's apartment door, letting it slam in the process. The jolt the slam gives to his system is both painful and deserved, and he feels the lingering effects of it the entire walk home.

At least the gods have some mercy on him for his walk, or maybe it's the early-ish hour of the day. The sidewalks are relatively empty, and there's minimal traffic on the streets, making it easy for him to cross and not have to stop on the seven-block walk from Ryan's to his place.

Bastian's relieved when he rounds the corner onto Aldine Street and sees Andres's motorcycle parked outside his Boystown building. He wants to slip into his arms and pretend like yesterday and last night didn't happen. For a brief moment, he even reasons with himself that he can deal with Andres not taking their relationship seriously as long as he can go back to waking with him on occasion. He can ignore the other flings that Andres has if he can still have some of Andres for himself as well.

"Did you have fun last night?" Andres asks from where he's seated wide awake in Bastian's reading chair. He looks like Bastian feels: worn out, like he hasn't slept a wink. Mostly, he looks sad as he keeps his eyes on Bastian and runs his hand through his hair.

"Not really." Bastian gently closes the door behind him and wants to run to Andres. He wants to plop himself onto his lap and snuggle in where he should be, but there's something defensive about the way Andres is seated. He's slightly hunched forward, crowding the space where Bastian would typically sit when presented the chance.

"There's tea on the counter for you," Andres says, and Bastian looks, catching the mug of steaming liquid in his eyeline. He grabs it and takes a sip—peppermint, perfect for soothing his queasy stomach, but it does nothing to ease his nervous heart.

"Listen..." he says but doesn't really know where to begin. In theory, he doesn't need to begin anywhere. If their relationship is casual, he doesn't owe Andres an explanation, yet he feels like he does. And he definitely thinks Andres owes him one. Or at least he thought he did. But seeing Andres right now, tired and visibly distraught in the reading chair by the bay window, Bastian suddenly finds himself feeling very guilty.

"I'd have come and got you last night if you had asked," Andres says. "Though, you'd have had to pick up your phone to ask me."

"My phone died," Bastian says, but he's not sure when his phone had run out of battery. He has a vague recollection of seeing Andres's name pop up on his caller ID at some point and thinking he had no interest in being Andres's backup plan for the night.

"I know you didn't go home with any of the girls. Did you at least stay someplace safe?" Andres asks, concern in his voice and his eyes pleading even underneath their sadness.

"I spent the night at Ryan's," he says. "But nothing happened, I swear. I passed out on his couch."

"Ryan's," Andres repeats and closes his eyes. He takes a deep breath that seems to suck all the oxygen out of the room, then opens his eyes back up and looks directly at Bastian. The hurt in his eyes reaches Bastian in his soul.

"Nothing happened. I swear," Bastian says. "And I didn't think you were coming here last night anyway."

Andres looks at Bastian, confusion plain on his face. "I told you yesterday I'd come here after work. And even if I hadn't, did you think you could get away with going home with another guy? How often have you done things like this since we've been together?"

"How often have I?" Bastian questions, his temper flaring along with his guilt. Sure, he made a mistake by going home with Ryan, but that's nothing different than Andres being out with Haley when he said he was at work.

"Yes, Bastian," Andres says. "Is this something you have done before? I thought I could trust you."

"Trust me?" Now Bastian is heated. How dare he question Bastian's trust. Bastian, who had given himself over to Andres when Andres was getting cozy with his young, pretty employee. "You're the one who was cozying up to that hussy Haley that you have working for you!"

Andres looks like he's been shot, stunned at having been caught, and Bastian oozes smugness.

"Oh, you thought I didn't know about that!" Bastian says. "It may have taken me a while to catch on, but I figured it out."

"Figured what out?!" Andres has the gall to ask.

"That you and Haley are seeing each other." Bastian pauses and points directly at Andres. "You're all over her Instagram, and I saw *you* yesterday with *her* sitting on *my* seat on the back of *your* motorcycle, riding through River North with her arms wrapped around you. You're not even smart enough not to take your little side piece for a joy ride past my work."

"Side piece?" Andres asks. "What the fuck is going on?"

"You've been caught. That's what's going on. I know you're seeing her as well as me."

"What!?" Andres rises to his feet. "What the fuck are you talking about? I'm not seeing Haley. You're the only person I've ever wanted to be with."

"Stop lying, Andres! I saw you!"

"What you saw was the work emergency I told you about yesterday," Andres says, his voice firm. "Haley's father had a heart attack. She needed an emergency lift to O'Hare to catch a last-minute flight back to Des Moines. She wasn't going to make it by train, and the motorcycle cuts through traffic faster than a car. You know that as well as I do. It's why I own the damn thing!"

Bastian feels the blood drain from his cheeks.

"And if you did think something was up, why didn't you ask me?!" Andres yells. "I'd have told you the truth like I always do."

"But her Instagram ..." Bastian is grasping at straws. He was so convinced yesterday that he was right about this. The evidence was there.

"Who gives a shit about her Instagram?" Andres asks.

"You were on it," Bastian says. "Her friends, they were all talking about how hot you are and how lucky she is."

"And you believed some twenty-year-old's Instagram over my actions towards you every day?"

"I ... I don't know." Bastian, feeling very stupid, hangs his head. Andres is right. His actions should have spoken louder than any doubts Bastian's insecurities have managed to plant in his own head.

"Fuck." Andres sounds exhausted. "I love you, but I don't know if I can do this anymore."

Registering what Andres said, Bastian snaps his head back up, and panic begins to set in. "What do you mean?"

"I have loved you for so long. For years, I have loved you and watched you choose to get treated like dirt over me—"

"I didn't know—"

"And that's on me for not saying it sooner," Andres interrupts him, "but I can't watch you do it any longer."

"But these past few months—"

"These past few months, you've fought being with me at every turn. You only ever wanted to admit that we were dating when it was convenient for you." Andres rubs harshly at his cheeks. "And I let that happen. That's also on me. I never pushed you to say it because I figured you felt it. I showed you every day what you mean to me."

"That's not fair," Bastian says, though he knows that it's true. He has made this difficult. He did try to hide it. He didn't want to admit it. But it was all because he was scared. Scared of this moment right here.

"No. What's not fair is me giving you my heart again and again for you to choose to blow it all up instead of attempting to love me back." Andres grabs his keys off the counter. "I gotta go. First pitch gets thrown at eleven."

"Will you come back after the game?"

He pauses at the door and looks over his shoulder at Bastian. "I need a break from you." He walks out the door without looking back.

"Andres! Please!" Bastian tries to beg, but Andres doesn't come back. Bastian remains frozen in place until he hears the roar of Andres's motorcycle outside driving away.

Sad, humiliated, and angry at himself for being so stupid and stubborn, Bastian begins to pace around his apartment. He's mad. He's hurt. He wants to blame anyone for this but himself. He blames Haley, Ryan, and even Laura's unborn baby. He blames Andres for leaving him when all those years ago, he promised him that he never would. He promised Bastian he'd always be by his side, and now he's gone.

Heartbroken, Bastian storms into his closet and grabs the pen dangling from the woodwork to add Andres Wood to the list on the wall. And that's when he sees it: written in Andres's elegant scrawl on the bottom of the list is his own name, Bastian Russo.

CHAPTER 15

astian doesn't know how long he sits and stares at his name written on his closet wall. He doesn't know what time he finally stands up and goes to brush the remnants of whiskey from his teeth, wishing that the bristles would take the words of vitriol he wants to say about himself with it. He's not sure which carton of take-out he opens from his fridge in a piss-poor attempt to get a meal into his system. All he does know is that the screen on his phone remains blank of notifications throughout all of it.

Technically, he doesn't even remember when he managed to plug his phone in to charge. He only knows that he will remain tethered to it all day and that each time he checks it to find the screen blank it will lower his heart another level.

Rechecking it again and seeing nothing from Andres, he wonders how it is that he could've gotten this entire situation so wrong. Having it laid out to him in such a cut-and-dry manner from Andres has made the gravity of his mistakes and hasty conclusions that much more heavy. Andres was right on all accounts. He was the only one who had a measure of the situation. He was the only one who had a measure on Bastian, and Bastian hates himself for having misread everything.

Looking at it now, with fresh—albeit hungover—eyes, Bastian can see his mistakes. He did try and push Andres away from the start. He had fought him at every turn. He had denied that they were together. He let all the run-ins with Andres's admirers cloud his reality. He let his bad luck in love and inability to see himself as someone worthy of the kind of love Andres was unquestioningly providing get in his way. His whole life, people had told him that he was his own worst enemy, and not once had he ever listened to or believed them. Now, he sits in his lone chair by the window, his knees curled into his chest and a mug of tea long gone cold in his hands, replaying all the mistakes he made with Andres from the start.

He picks up his phone and texts Andres again.

> I'm sorry. Nothing happened, I swear.

He holds his breath and bites at his lip when he sees the three tiny dots appear. Finally, Andres is ready to accept his apology. He just needed a few hours to cool off.

> I believe you, Bastian. But this is bigger than whatever did or didn't happen with Ryan.

Bastian chastises himself for being naive enough to believe that Andres was going to cave so quickly, even if Andres has always given in to whatever Bastian has asked of him in the past. It's not only these last few months but years of friendship leading to this text thread.

> I'm not lying to you. You can trust me.

He tries to explain again feebly.

> I said I believe you, and I do trust you. But that's not the point. The point is you don't trust me. And I can't continue with this if that's the case.

Panic begins to rise again. He needs to fix this, but he has no idea how. Instead, he practically fumbles his phone as he quickly types another message.

> I do trust you. I always have.

It's not a lie. Bastian has always trusted Andres. Or, at least he did before they started dating. In fact, he did up until—he checks the time—precisely twenty-four hours ago. It was this time yesterday that this entire disaster was put into motion.

> You obviously don't.

Bastian's thumbs are quick on his screen.

> I do! I swear!

> *If you did, we wouldn't be in this mess. You wouldn't have gone looking for any little reason for there to be something wrong between us.*

Bastian's skin goes cold. Andres is right again, of course, but Bastian hadn't realized it until right this second. He'd been so convinced that something would go wrong that when things were looking too good to be true, he started looking for anything he might have been missing. And the stupid anxiety that he's been conditioned to feel by every shitty past relationship has manufactured an entire scenario that Bastian used to blow up his own happiness. He threw the metaphorical hand grenade onto his own life. Not Andres, not Ryan, not Haley, not Laura. Him. He pulled the pin, and now he's left living amongst the shrapnel.

> *I fucked up. I'm sorry. I love you.*

> *I love you too, Bastian. But right now, I'm not sure that's enough.*

From there, Bastian's phone goes dark. Well, dark outside of phone calls and text messages from anyone and everyone who is none the wiser to Bastian's plight. He ignores them all and opts for internet scrolling instead. He goes into full sleuth mode and hops back onto Haley's Instagram to see where and how he went so wrong again. In the first picture, she's with her father, who's hooked up to myriad machines with a weak smile on his face. The caption reads, *Get well soon, Dad.* The picture posted before that is a cliché shot taken from an airplane window of the sun lighting the sparse clouds. He doesn't bother reading the caption of that one, sure that it will be some long melancholic dribble about the fleetingness of life. As if a twenty-one-year-old knows anything about that. From there, he goes straight to the photo that sent him on a collision course with heartbreak. He almost chucks his phone across the room when he sees it. *Too bad this ones taken,* she had added to one of the comments. All he would have had to do was press his finger onto the tiny line that reads *read more replies* yesterday, and maybe his anxiety and learned mistrust of everyone wouldn't have kicked into high gear.

He stares for a few moments at the picture and studies Andres's smiling face. He looks so happy and carefree, fully confident, and with a glow to his cheeks that his stubble can't even shadow. Bastian checks the date and tries to remember. Bastian was at Graze the night this was taken. He'd probably just left to head back to Andres's for a bath and an evening of lounging—likely crossing paths with Haley and not knowing it—as he waited for Andres to come home.

Unlike the mistaken conclusions he'd come up with the day before, Bastian realizes now that *he* was likely responsible for that broad smile on Andres's face. It doesn't seem so farfetched. He remembers leaving and flirting insatiably with Andres on his way out the door, covertly kissing him under cover of the alcove that leads to the delivery entrance and leaving Andres with promises of salacious activities once he got home. Had he known that night the position he'd be in now, he'd have dropped to his knees right then and there and given Andres a proper reason not to have to question Bastian's dedication to him.

However, this doesn't seem like the type of thing that Bastian can fix with a blowjob. That's basically been the scotch tape that has held Bastian's love life together in the past, and look where that's gotten him: a thirty-year-old man with massive trust issues and a need to always try and run damage control with his skilled mouth instead of his words. Sure, Andres had clearly been enjoying their sex life, as had Bastian, immensely so. But in these past few months, Andres had always seemed happiest and most content when they had their clothes on. Yes, there'd been some urgency to his kisses and moments when he was attaching his lips to Bastian's neck before they'd even closed the door, but that was usually in response to Bastian being a terrible flirt and tease and getting Andres all riled up. Bastian has mistakenly taught himself to believe that that is where his worth lies due to having been conditioned so by every relationship or casual hook-up of his past.

Which is ridiculous. Suddenly, he hears Andres speak to him from the past, not during their relationship, but from their friendship before. Moments of Andres telling him that he's worth more than what he thinks. That he doesn't need to drop what he's doing because some man on an app is showing him an ounce of interest, be the guy who caters to the needs of every man he's seeing, or that he has to make concessions and give up his free time or his sleep to make sure said man is sexually satisfied. Only now that he's had a taste of how good things can be can he see how toxic the way he was living before had been.

Everything with Andres had simultaneously felt so foreign and yet so inexplicably right. Bastian had fucked up from the beginning, and he realizes it now. He'd assumed the worst of Andres, and in so doing, he exposed the worst of himself. There has to be a way to fix this, he reasons, but he doesn't know what that way can be. This is something he is out of his depth with. He's in unfamiliar territory.

All he does know as he flips through Instagram, going back to his general feed, is that Andres looks absolutely miserable in the first photo he sees. Justin must have posted it at the end of the baseball game. It's a shot of Justin with all his boys, all red-faced and in varying degrees of drunkenness, except for Andres, who looks ashen with what Bastian knows is the falsest of smiles on his face. Bastian frowns. That's his fault. He put that there. And it looks so wrong on Andres's ordinarily warm and handsome face.

A text from Laura appears at the top of his screen as he's studying Andres and committing that hurt look to his memory so he has a reminder of what an asshole he is capable of being.

> *Tomorrow. 10 am final dress fitting. You better be there.*

Angry with himself for being the catalyst that made his worst fears come true, Bastian tosses his phone onto his bed without answering Laura's text. He hangs his head and tugs harshly at his curls. He will fix this. Unfortunately, he has to get through Laura's fucking wedding first.

"Did Andres stumble in last night as drunk as Justin did?"

It's the first thing out of Laura's mouth the moment Bastian enters the store. Not "Hello." Not "How are you?" Not "Thanks for coming." Just a punch to the gut that makes him want to double over and forget he exists. Instead, he puts a smile on his face and says, "Nah, he went back to his place last night after the party."

"Sometimes I wish Justin had his own place to go back to," Laura says with a laugh. "I'd get way more sleep that way."

"It can be quite nice," Bastian says, even though right now he knows that he would give up ever having a full night's sleep again to ensure that all of his nights are spent from here on out in the arms of Andres.

"You okay?" Laura asks him like she's only now gotten a good look at him.

"Yeah. I'm fine," he lies and grabs one of the complimentary mimosas from the coffee table as he sits on one of the plush sofas and watches Laura get bustled into her dress.

She furrows her brow at him.

"Really, Laura. I'm fine," he reiterates. "It's just a bit early for me to be on the Gold Coast on my day off."

"That's fair. Do you want to get lunch after this?"

"Sure," Bastian says, even though it's the last thing he wants to do. He's existing underneath such a thin façade of happiness that he's worried even a light interrogation by Laura will have him crack under questioning and spill the beans of his calamitous mistake. Gracefully admitting that he has done something wrong is not one of Bastian's strengths on the best of days, and most certainly not on the tail end of having his heart broken.

"Great!" she says. "Call Andres! Let him know we'll be at Graze in about an hour."

"Let's go someplace around here," Bastian says, his heart rate kicking up in total apprehension of calling Andres for anything other than forgiveness at this moment, much less a favor. She looks at him quizzically. Sighing again, he offers a feeble explanation, "I have to go back up to Boystown today. You know what a pain in the ass that is from the West Loop."

"Have Andres take you."

"He's not my personal chauffeur," Bastian says.

"I know that." Laura rolls her eyes, then goes back to looking at herself in all the mirrors, checking how she looks from every direction as the seamstress pulls, prods, and pins the fabric. She runs her hand over the roundness of her belly, which has been very carefully concealed within the layers of gauze fabric and silk. She drops her hands and looks at Bastian. Her eyes are soft. "Does this look okay? I don't look too pregnant?"

"You look beautiful," Bastian says, taking a moment to really take her in. Having opted for a less traditional look, she is a vision in pale rose gold. The entire ensemble is delicate and flowing. It fits her like a glove in the places that it should. It doesn't necessarily hide that she's pregnant, but really, is that even the point? If anything, the dress presents Laura and the baby inside of her as the gift that they are. Justin is going to melt right there on the spot.

"Do you think so? I feel so unlike myself lately that I can't be an objective judge."

Bastian rises to his feet and walks over to the low plinth that she is standing on. The seamstress, seemingly proud of her work, steps away, and Bastian grabs onto Laura's hand. He holds it high above her, and she takes a little twirl, the fabric flowing and billowing around her. "Prettiest bride I ever did see," he says. "And lord knows I've seen more than my fair share of brides for a man who has no interest in them."

She stops her twirl, looking all weepy-eyed, and wraps her arms around him, the extra height of the plinth making it possible for her to drape her arms over his shoulders. "Thank you, Bastian," she says, her voice thick and heavy.

"You're welcome. But don't go getting all emotional on me, or I'll take it back," he teases and squeezes her a little tighter around the middle, careful not to hold her too close, and either wrinkle the dress or smoosh the baby.

"Sorry," she says and wipes her eyes over his shoulder. "I'm a non-stop crybaby these days."

"Mood," he says before he can stop himself.

The rest of the week goes by in a fog of last-minute wedding problem-solving, an overbooked schedule at the salon, and hours upon hours of checking and rechecking his phone, waiting to hear anything from Andres.

It's not as if Bastian isn't trying. On Monday, after returning home from the dress fitting, he texted Andres to invite him to his place after work. In retrospect, he shouldn't have been surprised or stung when Andres said he'd be going home to his own bed. That had been the norm for their Monday routine as of late, except Bastian had taken up the habit of being in Andres's bed when he'd walk through the door. The real sting happened when Andres didn't tell him to go ahead and make himself at home at his place.

Then came Tuesday—a long day after a lonely night of no sleep. Bastian had tried again. This time reaching out with a phone call that was never answered.

Wednesday, he tried calling again. Again, Andres didn't pick up, but at least sent him a text message back.

> Really busy at work. I'll call you in a day or two.

Thursday, day one. No Andres

Friday, day two. Bastian shuts his lights off to go to bed, and still no Andres.

By Saturday, Bastian has pretty much given up. He's tired. He's barely slept all week. His eyes are red, and he has a headache that is slowly and steadily trying to kill him. He wishes it would move faster. The only solace he has is that he has managed to keep his breakup—if that even is what this is—a secret from everyone. Since Laura hasn't metaphorically entered stage left to beat him with a baseball bat for screwing up his life the week of her wedding, he can only assume that Andres has remained mum about all of this as well. Of course, it would be nice if Andres would pick up his fucking phone to tell Bastian that. Or better yet, pick up his phone to tell him that all has been forgiven.

He's packing up his station when his phone finally buzzes in his back pocket. He sucks in a breath before he grabs it, hoping beyond hope that it's Andres. He doesn't get so lucky.

YOU FUCKING IDIOT!

Bastian doesn't need any further explanation. Laura has obviously found out the bad news.

Laura's wedding day, like most, starts early, and Bastian is up and out of his apartment by nine to get to Laura and Justin's River North condo on time to get them ready. Slung heavily over his shoulder is his pride and joy: a Yves Saint Laurent leather bag he found at the Brown Elephant resale shop with which he keeps full of all of his supplies—two curling irons, one box of bobby pins, a tail comb, one pick, one smoothing brush, his Mason Pearson Denman brush, and every product in his arsenal that will keep Laura's hair in place as well as make it shine. For Justin, he has his edge clippers to make sure his hairline is crisp and his trusty box of pomade to hold the groom's hair perfectly in place. With the weight of the bag on his shoulders and the sight of the tiny Prius coming to pick him up, he's relieved he had the foresight to drop his suit off at their place earlier in the week instead of having to carry it now. This ride in the Uber from his place to theirs is likely the last moment of peace he will have all day.

Too bad he can't enjoy it. Like every other opportunity he's had to sit and be still this week, his mind travels to Andres. Initially, he'd been looking forward to this day. It was a chance to get dressed in his best and to stand proudly alongside Andres as their friends got married. To smile and laugh, and to be led out onto the dance floor and spun around the room in Andres's arms.

Now, he's not sure what to expect. Will Andres be at his side? Will Andres clink his glass in a toast? Will Andres proudly waltz Bastian through the crowd and make it clear that they are meant for each other? Right now, he can't even get Andres to answer his phone calls. He doubts Andres will even slide him his slice of chocolate wedding cake so he can see Bastian smile at the chance to eat more of his favorite treat.

Pulling his phone out of his pocket, he decides to extend an olive branch. Well, another olive branch.

> Come to Laura and Justin's place if you want your hair done for the wedding.

t's a small offering, and he feels kind of stupid even suggesting it. It's not like he's going to take his one-inch curling iron to Andres's hair and perfect a few well-placed tendrils to hang against his cheeks. But he could smooth it for him. Tie it back nicely in a low ponytail or leave it loose so it grazes Andres's shoulders just so. He could tousle it a bit and use his fingers in Andres's hair to speak to him. It's the magic of the hairstylist, the ability to read people through your fingertips. To touch someone and settle all that ails them with the simplest connections. He could do that with Andres today if Andres would grant him ten minutes.

> *Can't. Too much to set up at Partager with us closing the place for the reception tonight.*

"Damnit," Bastian says under his breath upon reading Andres's feeble excuse. There goes that idea. But he's not to be deterred.

> *If you change your mind, come on by, or I can bring my stuff to the church if you want.*

From there, he's back to square one with Andres, receiving nothing in reply. He sits listening to "Smalltown Boy" by Bronski Beat on his headphones and idly scrolls through Twitter for the rest of his ride to Laura's.

"Bastian, I love you, but you're a fucking idiot," Laura says as she swings open her condo door.

Bastian wrinkles his nose and glares at her. "Do you think I don't know that?" he huffs out and walks briskly past her, heading straight for the guest bedroom where he'll be working with Laura hot on his heels. "Why do you think I was so against this to begin with?"

"Don't try and act like the victim here. You and I both know that this one is on you."

"I'm not acting like a victim," Bastian says, even though he does feel like a victim of life in general.

"You are, though," she says. "And that's half the problem." Catching up to him, she grabs him by the shoulder and turns him around with a force he never knew she had in her. She grabs him by his cheeks and holds his head steady to keep his eyes focused on her, and his heart wants to sink through the floor with how much he misses having Andres's large hands cradle his face this way. "You're always so wrapped up in the what-ifs and any potential impending doom that you create situations for you to be the victim. And every time you do it, it's Andres who comes running to pick you back up. To dust you off and make you feel whole again. But he can't do that this time!" Letting go of his face, she jabs a finger into his chest. "You have to address whatever it is that's wrong inside of you on your own this time. Otherwise, even if he does take you back, you're going to repeat the same mistake again and again." She pauses, takes a breath, and finally looks at him gently. "I want this for you. Everyone does. Even Andres. But you need to dig deep and pick yourself up for once."

Unable to look at her and face the truth of himself anymore, Bastian drops his bag to the floor and hangs his head. "I know," he says. "But I don't know if I can do that."

"You can," she says and ruffles his curls. "Now go get set up. I'll pour us both a cup of coffee."

As suspected, Andres doesn't come to Laura and Justin's. He doesn't text Bastian to bring his supplies to Holy Name Cathedral to fix his hair before the ceremony. He exists as a ghost in the wedding party, preparing everything he can in places that Bastian can't see him in, but to his frustration. Even with all of this, or maybe because of it, the sight of Andres standing at the marble and wood altar of the historic cathedral takes Bastian's breath away as he leads the bridal procession to their places. He's a vision in a black suit, and Bastian's heart hurts when Andres gives him the saddest of smiles as Bastian takes his place at the front of the church. The only thing keeping Bastian from leaping toward where Andres is standing is the knowledge that Laura will skin him alive for making a big gay love proclamation that will likely get them kicked out of the most prominent Catholic Church in all of Chicago before she has a chance to say, "I do." Besides, he doubts that's what she meant when she told him to pick himself up for once.

Still, that doesn't stop him from being highly distracted throughout the ceremony. His eyes keep flitting towards Andres, each time hoping that maybe Andres will be looking back at him. He thinks he catches him at least once. It's unlikely the blush that sweeps across Andres's cheeks has anything to do with the priest's sermon. He's dutifully looking forward and away from Bastian regardless.

When the ceremony is over, and the guests are milling about, socializing, and taking in the historic site before they make their way to Partager for the reception, Bastian is being ushered around by the photographer for staged pictures and frustratingly being placed away from Andres in all of them. It's like some mad conspiracy. Had Andres phoned ahead and specifically requested not to be in the same frame as Bastian unless it was necessary? He doubts it, but it feels like he's being danced around and avoided purposefully.

By the time they make it to Partager in separate cars, Andres is off to the back of the restaurant and entirely out of Bastian's sight.

"Is he working this wedding so he can avoid me?" Bastian asks into Laura's ear.

She fixes him with a stern look that says what she doesn't want to have to say out loud, "Not my problem today."

"Right." He nods and lets her go back to greeting guests and accepting kisses, hugs, and congratulations at the door. He turns on his heel and walks away, off to get a drink at the bar to hopefully take the edge off.

"You wanna talk about why you and Andres are dancing around each other?" Marny asks him as she stands at the bar with a drink.

"I don't know what you're talking about." He grabs a glass of champagne and takes a sip.

"Fuck you, you don't." She laughs. "It's obvious something is up with the two of you."

"Nothing is up." Bastian takes another big sip. "We had a fight, is all." She shakes her head at him. "What did you do?"

"Why do you assume it's something I did?" Bastian asks.

She just looks at him, her face completely neutral, and he wonders why all the women in his life have the ability to scold him without even speaking.

"Fine. I may have accused him of cheating on me."

She raises an eyebrow at him.

"And I also went home with Ryan after Laura's bachelorette party."

"You what!?" she yells and smacks him behind the head.

He reaches up and smooths his hair down on reflex. "Nothing happened with Ryan. I fell asleep on his couch."

"God, you're dumb," she says and pulls him into a hug anyway. "Are you alright?" she asks, and Bastian realizes that she's the first person to ask him that yet.

"Not really," he says and sucks in a breath. "He's barely talked to me all week. And even that has only been over text. And he's been avoiding me all day, and I don't know how to fix this."

She lets go of him and hands him a second glass of champagne. "Why don't you start by bringing him this and talking to him?"

"As if he'll let me anywhere near him."

"Don't turn around," she directs and lowers her voice. "But he's behind us by the wedding cake. And he's staring at—"

"My ass?"

She smacks him gently again. "No, you horny little shit." She pauses and tilts her head thoughtfully, looking over Bastian's shoulder. "Maybe he is a little bit. But his look is too sad for him to be thinking about anything sordid."

"What do you mean, sad?"

"What do you think I mean?" she asks, completely exasperated. "He looks like he misses you."

"Really?"

"Yes. Really." She gently shoves him by the shoulders. "Now start fixing this!"

"Okay," he says with a deep breath that sets his shoulders back and straightens up his spine to make him look, but not feel, more confident. He turns on his heel and immediately spots Andres where Marny said he would be. His sudden turn around seems to have startled Andres, and he gives him a weak half-smile in apology as he takes the six strides it takes to reach him.

"Here," he says and hands Andres the glass of champagne.

"Thank you," Andres says as he takes it.

Bastian holds up his glass in cheers. "To the bride and groom, or ..." he lets the sentence trail off, not quite sure how to say what he wants, which is that he's sorry for the nine hundredth time. That he's an idiot. That Andres deserves better than Bastian, but he wants him to choose Bastian anyway because the two of them together is the only thing that has ever made sense.

Andres looks at him sadly and clinks his glass. "To love," he says, holding Bastian's gaze for a beat before he looks away and takes a long sip of his drink.

"Listen," Bastian begins. "I know that this is—"

"Can we put a pin in this?" Andres asks, cutting him off. "I have to go check on something in the kitchen."

"Yeah. Sure. Whatever you need." Bastian shifts his gaze to stare at his shoes. "I'll be around if you need me."

As Andres walks off, Bastian stares at his retreating back and thinks how strange of a thing that was for him to say. Not that it's not a nice offer. It's, indeed, the correct offer. It's only, Andres hasn't needed Bastian, or anyone really, for help with anything since Julian died. It's like Andres buried that part of himself with his brother. Looking at him now as he walks, his posture slumped heavily forward, it's like fifteen years of bottled-up vulnerability has been let loose around him.

It occurs to Bastian that everything Andres has done in the years since Julian died has been designed to keep him from feeling outwardly vulnerable ever again. He's avoided serious relationships. He's avoided his parents. He's poured himself into work. Pursuing a relationship with Bastian those few months back is the first genuine risk of the heart the man has taken. He knew what he was risking. He knew what the possibilities could be, yet he trusted Bastian fully with his heart, only to have him smash it with his own insecurities.

He chugs the rest of his champagne, then places the empty glass down on a nearby table. He charges into the kitchen and finds Andres hovering over a steaming taurine of soup. Without any warning, he grabs Andres's face, cradling his cheeks between his palms in the manner he has grown to enjoy Andres doing to him, and kisses him soundly. For a split second, he thinks he's made a mistake until Andres wraps an arm around his waist, pulling him in, and kisses him back with the same intensity.

"I'm not giving up on us," Bastian says when they pull apart. "We made a promise to each other when we were kids, and I intend to keep it."

"I thought you said this was a bad idea," Andres teases him, and the fact that he makes a joke right now, even if it's a feeble one, fills Bastian's lungs with more air. He hasn't fixed anything yet, but it's a start.

The corner of Bastian's lips lift into a cautious smile, the first genuine one he's felt all day. "Turns out," he says, "that it happened to be the best idea."

"Is that so?"

"Yeah, it's so," Bastian says and spins out of Andres's hold to the faint sound of the band beginning to play on the other side of the wall separating Partager's kitchen from the front of the house. He tentatively grabs Andres's hand. "Come dance with me."

Andres hesitates, looking around the kitchen. Seemingly finding nothing to distract himself with, he lets Bastian pull him along.

Once on the dance floor, where the band playing their rendition of "Leather and Lace," Bastian lets Andres take the lead. It's not their most graceful moment of dancing together, but to Bastian it is their most significant. There's weight to it, and he worries that once the band switches songs, this small moment of connection will be gone, and they'll be back to where they were before Bastian took the reins for the first time in his life and truly grabbed onto what it is that he wants.

That kiss, that moment of honesty from Bastian, feels like it flipped things, if not right side up, at least part way on its side. They're not back to where they were before Bastian's pole vault to conclusions, but they're also not back to where they were before this whole experimentation in childhood friends to lovers got started. They are in a softer, more precarious place of hesitant touches and gentle words whispered into Andres's ears as they dance.

"I really am sorry, you know," Bastian says as the band begins to segway into something more lively and appropriate to melt into the background as the guests enjoy their meals.

"I know you are." Andres begins to pull away, his arms firm, keeping Bastian from tugging him back into his embrace again, clinging to him and never letting him go. "But it's my turn to insist we take this slow."

"We can go at whatever speed you need," Bastian says, the irony that he's repeating Andres's words from months ago not lost on him at all.

Andres nods his head and gives him a small smile. He then turns to walk off the dance floor, leaving Bastian to trail behind him toward their table. It's disorienting, and Bastian feels wildly off balance as he tries to subtly chase after Andres for the first time in their adult existence. But he doesn't let it deter him. At dinner, he lets his hand brush against Andres's. During dessert, instead of Andres offering Bastian his piece of cake, Bastian shares his. Through all of it, he finds reasons for his fingertips to trail down Andres's arm or his lips to whisper words and observations delivered to only Andres's ears to hear, bringing forth that special, amused smile that has always been reserved for Bastian. In those rare moments, whenever Andres dares to reach across the fractured but slowly mending space between them, Bastian leans into his touch, no longer concerned about what anyone would have to say about the two of them being together. Instead, he wants to proclaim that Andres is his and he is Andres, even if they're taking it slow.

He finally understands how nervous Andres must have been feeling this entire time. He finally understands his gestures and offers of money and leaps of faith to jump through Bastian's hoops to make Bastian happy and to put him at ease. It occurs to Bastian for the first time since this all started that Andres had as much to lose as Bastian did, perhaps even more. For Andres to have put this all on the line, to risk losing Bastian as his one constant since they were five, he must have felt something deeply. He must have had the same realization that Bastian is having now, one that is making his heart burst from the inside: they were never meant to just be friends. Just being friends was never going to be enough. And the love that is possible between them is worth risking everything for.

CHAPTER 16

Waking the next morning, Bastian knows two things. One, that he still has a lot of work to do in proving himself to Andres. And two, he's still incredibly relieved that Andres invited him back to his place at the end of the night. He's still relieved that he was granted a gentle goodnight kiss by Andres before he spun Bastian in his arms to spoon him much like he had since they were innocent kids who assumed that all friends did this sort of thing at sleepovers. As he lies awake, loosely held in Andres's arms, he tries not to chastise himself for not having seen where they were inevitably headed sooner. Like two ridiculous star-crossed lovers residing in the same constellation, Bastian now knows that he and Andres have always been destined to end up right here. If only Bastian had listened to the lessons of destiny and fortune from the fables of old instead of believing the drivel that society has levied against him in colorful infographics and catchy slogans for not fitting perfectly into the white picket fence mold. Andres is his proverbial Prince Charming, not the monster under the bed looking to ruin his life.

With that in mind and his stomach beginning to rumble, Bastian very carefully extricates himself from Andres's hold. Then, quiet as a mouse, he shuffles from Andres's bed to the kitchen to start breakfast for them.

Breakfast and coffee has been Andres's thing. But today, waking slightly hungover from one glass too many of champagne and with sore feet from the loafers he danced all night in without socks, Bastian hobbles and silently winces his way around the kitchen to make the grand gesture of a post-wedding breakfast.

Not sure where to begin, he opens Andres's refrigerator and is met with mostly empty shelves. No meats—which Bastian doesn't eat, but Andres does. No leftovers. No breads or baked goods. There isn't even the usual stockpile of fruits and vegetables that Andres tends to have on hand to whip up something fresh and delicious for Bastian to fuel him for his long days on his feet. All he sees are some eggs, almond milk, the typical selection of condiments, and a chunk of cheese that Bastian is afraid to touch because its packaging denotes it's imported and likely exorbitant in price.

No matter. He pulls out the eggs and milk. There are two completely brown bananas on the counter beside the fridge. He can make a simple batch of muffins, assuming Andres hasn't somehow managed to let his dry goods cupboard go bare like he did the fridge in the wake of Bastian's stupidity.

Though finding the dry goods proves to be more complicated than Bastian had thought, he swears they were in the high cabinet next to the fridge, but that cabinet is full of glassware. Maybe they're in the Lazy Susan that spins out, attached to the door of his corner cabinet next to the stove. No such luck. That's reserved for mixing bowls and bakeware, which, luckily for Bastian, he does need. Unluckily for Bastian, he accidentally topples the entire stack of stainless steel mixing bowls, causing a very loud clattering sound in his attempt to only pull out the medium-sized one that he needs. Wincing, he restacks the fallen bowls and slowly closes the cabinet, praying to the kitchen gods that he didn't wake up Andres.

He pauses and sucks in a breath but doesn't hear any stirring from the bedroom. Slowly letting out his exhale, he continues with his task, laughing a bit at himself for being so ridiculous. This is Andres. He's not going to kick Bastian out of his kitchen for dropping mixing bowls. Or is he?

"No," Bastian says to himself in affirmation. "Andres isn't like the rest."

Bastian frowns. That's a thought he should have had months ago when Andres first expressed an interest in dating. He should have given Andres the grace to be Andres without letting Bastian's experiences with those whose names decorate his closet wall taint his motives. He should have trusted Andres to be the same Andres he has known and loved his whole life. He should have trusted Andres's actions towards him instead of the actions of those around Andres. Sure, Andres may have cast others aside, but he has never once, not in the twenty-five years of knowing him, cast Bastian aside. And he most certainly wouldn't start now because Bastian is making too much noise in his kitchen (which seems to have a microphone in every corner amplifying every sound that Bastian makes as he works).

Finally, after an absurd amount of tiptoeing, Bastian does manage to get the muffins in the oven, then switches gears to make coffee in Andres's overly complicated machine. He's watched Andres do this enough; this shouldn't be that hard. But alas, it is, and after many false starts, Bastian finally hears the whirring sounds of the machine percolating water into the coarse grounds. "Success," he says quietly to himself. He leans his forearms on the counter so he can watch the clear coffee pot fill and make sure it doesn't end up overflowing.

"It smells good in here," Andres says, surprising Bastian and pulling him from his intense observation of the coffee that is finally finished brewing.

"Thanks," Bastian says, turning to see Andres as he makes his way fully into the kitchen. Like Bastian, he's still in his sleeping clothes from the night before, looking perfectly rumpled. Bastian turns back around and pours them each a cup of coffee, then adds a splash of almond milk to his. Pausing, he looks over his shoulder at Andres, silently asking how he takes his. He should know this. And he assumes it's black, but he isn't entirely sure. Andres nods at him and reaches for the mug, and Bastian exhales. "I hope you don't mind. I used two of those old bananas for muffins."

"I don't mind," Andres says over the rim of his mug, keeping his eyes locked on Bastian's. "Thank you for this," he says, then bites at his lip after he swallows, looking slightly nervous.

Bastian knows that look. Not because it's ever graced Andres's perfectly angular face before, but because Bastian has worn it many times himself. It's the look of apprehension. Of 'can I accept these nice, simple gestures of love and affection and caring from another without fear of it being ripped from me again later.' Bastian's heart clenches at the sight of it. Andres was never supposed to wear this look.

"That was fun last night," Bastian says, breaking the momentary silence and hoping to put Andres fully at ease around him again. He takes a sip of his coffee and leans heavily against the counter, sure that if he has to keep seeing this look on Andres's face, he'll collapse from the weight of it.

"I think your muffins are done," Andres says and steps toward the oven.

Bastian takes a sniff. Sure enough, the air is fragrant with the smell of cooked banana, cinnamon, and sugar. He cuts in front of Andres to reach the oven first and makes a show of bending over as he opens it to pull the muffins out. With the muffins in hand, he quickly straightens and winces. With things so tenuous between them, Bastian isn't sure if being an insatiable flirt is still allowed.

"Tease," Andres says with a soft, unsteady laugh and backs away from Bastian.

"Sorry," Bastian says, placing the muffin tin on the stovetop. He chances to take a look at Andres. "Old habits, you know?"

Andres takes another sip of his coffee and locks eyes with Bastian once again. His expression has changed to something more warm and fond. "Some habits don't need to be broken."

Bastian tilts his head to the side, and his lips turn up at the corners. "Like what you saw then, huh?"

"I've always liked what I see when I look at you."

"Even still?"

"Yes, Bastian. Even still," Andres assures, laying some of Bastian's current worries about them getting back on track to rest.

Marny approaches Bastian as he steps into their workroom at the salon the next day.

"You two are back together?" she asks.

He walks swiftly past her and goes straight to his station. "I mean, I think so," he says. "We haven't really discussed it. But we hadn't ever made it official before, either."

"And you don't see that as a potential problem?"

"What do you want me to do? Present him with a corsage and ask him for his varsity jacket so we can proclaim ourselves as," he brings two fingers to either side of his head, "'going steady'? We're adults. That hardly seems necessary."

"This coming from the man who not even two weeks ago made it very clear with his actions that it was indeed very necessary," Marny says.

"It's not necessary now." Bastian huffs in annoyance to mask the lingering fear he didn't want to bring to work with him. "I know where my heart lies. It lies with him, and I have no interest in seeing anybody else."

"Okay. That's great and all," Marny says, moving her hands in circles between them. "Glad you told me. Glad that you finally know what it is that you want. Did you bother to tell Andres this?"

"I don't have to."

"Umm, I kind of think you do."

Bastian rolls his eyes at her. "Who got married and designated you the new Laura?" "Laura, actually." Marny laughs and pulls her phone out of her dress's pocket. She flips her finger over her screen a few times as she walks over to Bastian, then shows him her phone.

> Make sure Bastian doesn't do anything stupid while I'm gone this week.

Bastian frowns. "You two have no faith in me."

"Oh, we have faith in you." She repockets her phone. "Faith that you'll be a complete dumbass again."

"And to think I was gonna stay late to cut your hair today," he says as if Marny's words and her and Laura's conspiring haven't stung him. "I guess I'll go home early then."

"You wouldn't dare," Marny says.

"Oh, yes, I would." Bastian laughs and returns to setting up his station for the day.

"Fine. If you're going to hold my much-needed haircut hostage, I won't tease you anymore. But promise me, Bastian, you'll tell him all this."

"Alright! I'll tell him. Have a little faith in me for once, please."

She kisses him on the cheek as Lizzie arrives to tell them that their clients have arrived. "I believe in you," she says, and Bastian believes her.

It's not easy to get Andres alone while he and Bastian seem to be working double time to make up for Laura and Justin's honeymoon absences. Still, Bastian manages to find a few moments within the chaos to at least say hello and check-in. While those interactions are nice and serve to settle Bastian's soul, confirming to him that they are, thankfully, still on speaking terms and on the right track, none of those moments are good for doing what he promised Marny. He can't make love and commitment proclamations over text while his clients are being shampooed, or while the restaurant is making the change over from lunch to dinner service, or while he's on a fully loaded Red Line train.

It's on one of those trains, frustrated and pressed far too close to someone who's far too sweaty for public transportation, that Bastian decides he's had enough of this dance of trying to find time in his and Andres's days for them to see each other face to face and have a meaningful conversation. He pulls out his phone, pauses Depeche Mode's, "Never Let You Down Again," and texts Andres.

> Any interest in an impromptu date at Lincoln Park Zoo today?

> What time?

> Whatever time you can make it.

> In an hour?

> Perfect. I'll see you soon.

Bastian texts back, a relieved smile planted firmly on his face as he gets off the train at the Fullerton stop and starts walking toward the zoo.

Getting Andres to agree to an impromptu date with him is only half the battle. He still has to deal with work—a place he is supposed to be at in twenty minutes.

"Sorry, Oliver," he says with a slight laugh as he clicks on Salon Azure Blue in his contacts to call in sick.

"Thank you for calling Salon Azure Blue ..."

The color drains from Bastian's face, and he momentarily stops walking. The voice on the other end of the line is not Oliver's, but Mitchel's. Very quickly, he ducks into a nearby alley away from the crowded sidewalk.

"... How can I help you?"

Bastian fakes a cough as a horn honks nearby. Wincing, he says, "Hi. It's Bastian. I'm not gonna be able to make it into work today."

"Is that so?" Mitchel says, and Bastian can hear him aggressively clicking away on his mouse, likely pulling up Bastian's schedule for the day.

"Yes," Bastian says, collecting his resolve. This would have been easier with Oliver. Sure, he'd have been annoyed, but he still would have taken care of canceling Bastian's day and dealt with the brunt of the repercussions. But now, Bastian's chickens are coming home for their proverbial roost. *Fitting,* he thinks before continuing his feeble attempt at playing sick. "I've been fighting something off all week."

"You picked a terrible week to be sick," Mitchel says with zero sympathy.

"I know. And I do apologize." He fakes a cough again.

"You can stop with the act," Mitchel says. "I know you're not sick. So whatever it is you have planned for today better be worth it because you'll be doing all of these clients at half price to make up for your absence."

"Half price?" Bastian asks. "Since when is that the policy?"

"Since right now," Mitchel says. "And that half is coming out of your cut. So technically, you'll be making up all these appointments for free."

"What?" Bastian asks. "That's not fair!"

"Neither is calling in sick fifteen minutes before your book starts."

This Bastian rolls his eyes at. It doesn't matter if he called in sick fifteen minutes, fifteen hours, or fifteen days before his first client. The response is always the same. It's a sucked-in breath, followed by pursed lips and a judgmental tone implying that even if Bastian was having a medical emergency, calling in sick and fucking up Mitchel's influx of money for the day is beyond frowned upon.

"Are you still planning on not coming in today?" Mitchel asks.

Weighing his options, Bastian considers this for a moment. Losing eight clients' worth of pay is going to be quite the hit. If he hops back on the train, he can reach the salon roughly in time for his first client. But he's already committed to plans with Andres. And though he can't afford to lose out on the money, he also, as he recently found out, can't afford to lose Andres either.

Exiting the alley and picking up his pace towards the Lincoln Park Zoo again, he speaks his answer. Faking another cough, he says, "I really don't feel like I can make it in today," then hangs up the phone.

Like always, the sound of Andres's motorcycle approaching echoes off the buildings, and Bastian waits patiently, albeit a little nervously, at the west entrance. It's funny how now the mere thought of Andres's presence makes Bastian feel flustered, like he has to get everything right. More accurately, he *wants* to get everything right, he wants to be the person that Andres thinks he is—the person that Andres thought he was before he showed his true face as someone who is so distrustful of the world around him that anyone showing him the slightest bit of care is perceived as a threat.

Granted, the way that Andres looks as he dismounts his motorcycle—long, muscular legs stretching the fabric of his jeans, a loose white V-neck shirt showing a teasing glimpse of his bronze, sun-kissed chest, and dark designer sunglasses that he is now pushing up to rest amongst the wayward waves that have been windswept out of the knot securing the rest of his hair back—is a sight that should come with a warning. No wonder every person in Bastian's life thinks he's a complete idiot for having kept Andres as merely a supporting player for so long and then royally fucking it up the moment he decided to pull Andres off the bench. He's the complete package. Good-looking, successful, chivalrous, and honorable. Everything that Bastian is not.

He sucks in a breath and tries to play cool. "Hey there, good looking," he says and begins to walk towards Andres. "Let me holla at you."

Andres predictably laughs and shakes his head. "You are far too white to use that term."

Bastian gasps and acts insulted. "And here I thought I was too old and ten years too late."

"Well, that too." Andres laughs again, but he's looking at Bastian very fondly, and a shy smile pulls up his cheeks. It's adorable, and Bastian has never used the word adorable to describe Andres ever. But it's fitting in this instance.

Bastian extends his hand. "So, Mr. Andres Wood, may I interest you in a non-holla-ing stroll through the zoo on this fine late summer day?"

Andres looks down at Bastian's proffered hand, and Bastian holds his breath, scared for the briefest moment that Andres will refuse it. He doesn't. He grabs it and flips the grip, placing his hand on top, and Bastian lets out a breath around the smile pulling on his lips. This feels right and normal and exactly how things should be between them.

"Which way first?" Andres asks, tugging on Bastian's hand.

"North, I guess," Bastian says and gestures with a nod of his head.

Andres mirrors him and says with a laugh. "That way is south."

"Then south it is." It doesn't matter. He didn't ask Andres here to observe animals inside their makeshift habitats, no matter how nice they are. He asked him here so they could talk uninterrupted and enjoy something that resembles a date. Something that resembles their life from before Bastian mistakenly blew it all up.

"How pissed is your boss right now?" Andres asks as they approach the seals basking in the sun on the boulders surrounding their pool.

"Furious," Bastian says. "Serves him right, though. You know the only thing he gave Laura, besides an ulcer, for her wedding was one of his self-published, relationship self-help books?"

Andres lets out a full belly laugh. "Oh, God. Not the one with detailed advice and pictures on how to do naked couples yoga?"

"That would be the one." Bastian laughs as well. "The threat of getting a copy of that book is reason enough to make someone want to elope."

"That is what we told Laura and Justin to do from the start."

"I told her she should display it in the nursery on a shelf above the crib."

"You really are terrible," Andres says, still chuckling.

"Perhaps if I get fired for playing hooky today, I'll become a decorator instead of looking for a new salon."

"You could always open up your own place," Andres suggests again. "It doesn't have to be exactly like Salon Double Blue. It can be a place where you and a few other seasoned and established stylists who want to take control of their lives and schedules can work."

"Yeah, but I can't do that without Laura," Bastian says. "And she's in no position to add more stress and a new secret into her life."

"What about Marny?"

"Marny can't afford it either. Though I'd love to take her with," Bastian says. "We'll have to see how things shake out after the baby is born. Hopefully, Laura will have enough of her clientele left for us to return to our original plan."

Andres shakes his head. "The hair industry will always be a mystery to me."

"Well, it's a good thing you have restaurants figured out," Bastian says.

"Even that's getting old." Andres sighs. He pauses by the flamingos in the waterfowl lagoon. When Bastian looks at Andres, there's a serene smile on his face as he takes in the birds. "This schedule, the nights, the long hours, working on weekends and coming home smelling like alcohol and an industrial kitchen, it gets tiring, you know?"

Bastian shrugs. He does know. It's part of why he ultimately made the decision to come here instead of work today despite the repercussions. It's nice to be able to go somewhere with Andres to talk, walk, and simply be. They live in this vibrant city, but their chosen professions make it hard for them to go out and enjoy it together.

"I do know," Bastian says and realizes this is the perfect moment to say what he's brought Andres here for. He lets Andres continue to look at the birds, but he keeps his gaze focused on Andres's profile, which is relaxed and content in this moment. "But even with all that, the late nights, the scent of fries on pillowcases, the weekends spent at work, I still choose you."

Andres's chin falls towards his chest, and that shy smile from before creeps back into his cheeks. He gives Bastian's hand a firm squeeze and turns his head to look over his shoulder and face him. "I choose you too," he says, then continues their walk. "I always have."

"I know," Bastian says, leaning closer to Andres, their linked hands practically smooshed between them. "Well, *now* I know."

"I guess I should have realized that you would need me to be more upfront with how I felt from the start."

"You were pretty upfront." Bastian laughs, thinking about Andres stating that he wanted to be with Bastian and that Bastian couldn't be in safer hands.

Andres laughs with him. "Not upfront enough."

"But seriously though," Bastian starts, about to ask the questions he's been wanting to ask since the moment Andres suggested they start dating. "Why me? Why us? Why now?"

Andres pauses their walking. He lets go of Bastian's hand in favor of slinging his arm over Bastian's shoulders and leads them to stand against the wooden fence that keeps them separated from the camels and zebras grazing together on the other side. "It's like this," he says, taking a deep breath. "I've always wanted to be with you."

"You have?"

"Well, for at least as long as I knew that was a possibility," he continues to explain. "But after Julian, I couldn't bear the thought of losing you too. So I sort of ignored it. I figured it would go away and you and I could be just friends forever. But—"

"Eventually, that was no longer enough." Bastian finally understands. Unfortunately, though, for both of them, it took almost losing Andres for him to realize it.

"Exactly," Andres says with another light laugh. "And once Ryan broke up with you, I thought, 'This is it! This is my chance!' So I took it."

"And then I ruined it." Bastian hangs his head.

"Well, I wouldn't say you ruined it. You just didn't say yes right away like I had hoped."

"But I'm saying yes now," Bastian says.

"And I'm holding on tight and not letting you go."

CHAPTER 17

A ndres may have chosen Bastian, but Bastian is not about to get cocky and think that's enough. In their twenty-five-year-long relationship, never has there been a fissure, and though this first and hopefully only one is on the mend, it's still too fresh to assume that it's healed completely. Like any wound, no matter how severe, time is the best way to stitch it back together. The question is whether it's better to give it air to breathe and allow it to heal on its own or smother it with a Band-Aid for a quicker fix?

Bastian, it turns out, is constantly searching for a bigger and better Band-Aid. And it is time to pull out the biggest bandage of all. However, he is loath to do it, as it will lead to endless questions and proclamations from his friends that they always knew Andres and Bastian were meant for each other. Bastian is willing to endure the annoyance of his mother being proven right if it means he can hold onto Andres forever. At least that's what he tells himself as he gently knocks on Andres's door thirty minutes before they are due to arrive at Bastian's parents' house for Sunday dinner.

"I haven't had the locks changed," Andres says as he opens the door and lets Bastian inside. "You can use your key."

"I didn't want to assume." Bastian looks over his shoulder as he takes his coat off. "What if you'd been in here naked?"

Andres tilts his head at him. "That seems like more reason for you to use the key."

"Really?" Bastian says, eying Andres up and down. He looks good, like he always does, wearing a fitting pair of black jeans that hug him in all the right places and a tight, light gray high-necked sweater that's perfect for this late summer, false fall Chicago Sunday. Bastian would like to tear it all off of him and briefly weighs the pros and cons of arriving late to dinner. The pros are winning if Andres is willing. Sex is not something they have ventured back into in the few short weeks they've been knitting themselves back together. They've come close, but someone, mainly Andres, puts the brakes on it, stopping their make-out sessions and rolling Bastian onto his side to wrap his arms around him possessively for a cuddle instead.

It's funny, really, for all of Andres's talk at the beginning of all of this that they would go at Bastian's pace, coming out the other side, he finds that the roles have become reversed. Not wanting to push Andres at all, and after waiting for a beat too long anyway,

Bastian settles for simply giving Andres the softest of kisses in hello on his lips.

Andres hums against Bastian's lips before pulling away. "Are you going to be warm enough wearing that on the bike, or should we take the car?"

"Bike is fine," Bastian says. Sure, he'll be chilly, but he likes the intimacy that the motorcycle provides over the forced space created by the center console of a car.

"Are you ready then?"

"Yeah," Bastian says with a nod of his head and shrugs the coat that he needlessly took off back on.

Andres grabs his keys but pauses before he reopens the door to let them out. He looks at Bastian softly and pulls him wholly into his arms, kissing him thoroughly on the lips.

"What was that for?" Bastian asks, a bit dazed when Andres releases him.

Andres doesn't let go of him. "It's good to see you, is all," he says, even though it's only been three days since the last time they were in each other's presence.

"It's good to see you too." Bastian kisses him again, relieved that things, though admittedly far softer and sweeter and more chaste than they ever were before, are growing back to normal. With a bit of luck and a well-executed dinner with his parents, perhaps Bastian and Andres will take the next step of rekindling their relationship. A good fuck is sure to help seal this fissure closed forever, despite its reputation of doing the opposite. And maybe Andres is thinking the same thing when he places his hand on Bastian's lower back, gently guiding him out the door.

It's not only the way Andres had placed his hand on Bastian's back that has Bastian thinking that Andres's thoughts are on the same page. It's the way he finds multiple opportunities to run his hand up and down Bastian's thigh when his hand isn't needed to work the motorcycle's clutch. The way he looks at Bastian covetously when he gets off the back of the bike at Bastian's parents' house. The way he bumps shoulders with him, eliciting a giggle out of Bastian as they stumble up the walkway to Bastian's parents' front door. Now it's Andres who can't seem to keep his hands off Bastian, wanting to touch him whenever possible.

"Well, hello, boys," Bastian's mother says, swinging the door open for them before Bastian manages to pull his keys from his coat pocket. "It's been far too long since I've seen my sons."

"Mom," Bastian says, even though he is here on a mission to inform her that Andres is more of a part of the family than he'd previously let on.

"Oh, don't *'Mom'* me," she scolds and, despite her diminutive stature, somehow manages to pull them both into a hug.

"Hi, Mrs. Russo." Andres squeezes her.

"And don't you start with that 'Mrs. Russo' business," she says, kissing Andres on the cheek before she pulls out of the hug and ushers them inside. "I'm your mom, even if this stubborn son of mine won't date you."

Andres stifles a laugh into his shoulder, his cheeks blooming red in the process. Bastian wonders, not for the first time, how it was that he managed to be so blind and dumb about this in the first place. Laughing slightly himself, now, he figures this is as good a time as any.

"About that." Bastian wraps an arm around Andres's waist. He looks over at Andres, catching his eye and silently makes his intention clear, giving Andres a moment to back out of it if he wants to. Andres nods his approval, then loops his own arm around Bastian's shoulders. "I'm not stubborn anymore," Bastian says, his eyes locked on Andres's as he says it.

"Let's not go that far," Andres teases him.

"Shut it, you," Bastian says but tightens his grasp around Andres's middle. He looks back at his mother. "We're together. And I'm so freaking in love with him."

The squeal that his mother lets out quite possibly breaks the sound barrier and sends the dog running towards them, barking frantically. Bastian and Andres wince away from all the noise and manage to burrow further into each other, laughing as they do. "I knew it!" she yells out and jabs a finger at the two of them.

"Knew what? What's going on?" Dominic asks, descending the stairs with fingers in both of his ears. "I thought we were being robbed."

"Didn't I tell you?" she says, now pointing at Dominic.

"Tell me what?" He bends down and picks up Randy, tucking the dog at his side to get him to stop barking.

"These two," she gestures wildly at Bastian and Andres with her hand, "they're together."

"Oh. Is that all? It's about time they told us."

She turns and looks at him, stunned. "You knew!"

"Of course, I knew. They're as transparent as a glass door," he says, then lifts a hand and gestures at Andres. "I'm just glad he finally brought somebody home I actually like."

Bastian gasps as Andres starts laughing beside him. "I know the feeling, Mr. Russo."

With a clap to Andres's shoulder, his dad begins to pull Andres away from Bastian and his mother. "None of this 'Mr. Russo stuff', you know to call me dad. Now come on, let's watch the Packers beat the pants off the Bears."

"I'm happy for you, Sebastian," Annemarie says into his ear, then pulls him into the kitchen to help her with dinner as if the news that he and Andres are in love is the most natural occurrence in the world. Because honestly, it was.

Bastian climbs onto the back of the motorcycle and wraps his arms around Andres's torso.

"That went well," Andres says.

Still unable to stop himself from smiling, Bastian agrees. "It did."

Andres shifts the bike into gear, and they both give a final wave goodbye to Bastian's parents, who are watching them from the door. "I was thinking … do you mind if we swing by my folks' place before heading back downtown?"

"Of course not!" Bastian says quickly, hiding his shock that Andres is even suggesting this. He can't remember when the last time he saw Juanita and Walter Wood, and unless Andres has been sneaking in visits to his parents' place between shifts at the restaurant and chasing after Bastian, it's safe to say it's been quite some time for Andres as well.

"Good," Andres says. "We can make it a quick in and out."

"Alright," Bastian says, squeezing Andres a little tighter around the middle.

He keeps that tight grip for the entirety of their ride to Andres's parents' house. It's not far. In fact, they could have walked it like they did when they were children.

All too quickly, Bastian finds himself walking hand-in-hand with Andres towards the extravagant brick and stone Frank Lloyd Wright masterpiece that Andres grew up in.

Standing on the wide stone front porch, Andres uses the large, round brass knocker to knock on the solid front door. After two crisp raps, he drops his hand and looks to Bastian. "Looks the same, doesn't it?"

"Isn't that part of the deal with owning and living in one of these? You can't change anything?"

"Pretty much," Andres answers with a laugh. "Gotta maintain that historic curb appeal."

Hearing some commotion on the other side of the door, Bastian gives Andres's hand a squeeze. He wonders who it's going to be and, more importantly, wonders if they'll be happy to see Andres or put out by his unannounced intrusion.

"Andres?" Juanita Wood questions quietly as she opens the door. She's as elegant as ever in a pair of flowing black Dior linen slacks and white, button-down shirt. She looks exactly as Bastian remembers her. A tall, thin wisp of a woman even now still made for the runways. She is as intimidating as ever. And just like when they were kids, the only thing that gives her away is her eyes. Today, instead of compelling an expectation of perfection, they're tired and sad, and they are solely focused on her son. "What are you doing here?"

Shrugging, Andres stares hopefully back at her. "We were in the neighborhood. Thought we'd stop by ... We can go if this is a bad time."

"No!" Juanita says and shuffles away from the door, leaving it wide open. "Please, come in."

"Thanks," Andres says and lets go of Bastian's hand to nudge him in first.

Bastian has never really been all that comfortable around Andres's parents or in their home. He'd always been afraid they were silently judging him or worried he'd accidentally break some art deco window or vase that his parents wouldn't be able to afford to replace. They were never the warmest of people, even before Julian got sick, and he doubts that age has softened them at all.

"Is this Bastian?" she asks with a hint of a laugh in her voice as she takes him in, making Bastian feel like he wants to run out the door. That is, until she offers him the slightest smile that reminds him of how Julian used to grin when he knew a secret. "My goodness, child, you look exactly the same."

"Well, I wouldn't say *exactly*," Bastian jokes, relieved that this is going well so far.

"No, she's right," Andres says. "You never age."

"I hope I've aged some. Otherwise, this," he waves his hands between them, "is going to appear very inappropriate."

Andres fixes Bastian with a look, and Bastian feels his stomach drop. 'Sorry,' he mouths, and Juanita bursts out laughing, causing both boys to turn and look at her puzzled.

"Oh, please, you two standing hand-in-hand at the door is the least surprising part of this visit."

Bastian scoffs, but Andres laughs and squeezes onto Bastian's hand before letting it go to follow his mother as she leads them through the house towards the back, where Bastian remembers Walter Wood's office to be.

"Walter," Juanita says, pushing the already ajar door even more open. "Our son is here."

"Andres?" Walter questions as if it was possible for Julian to suddenly appear.

"Yes, Dad. It's me," Andres says. "We were in the neighborhood, and thought we'd stop by."

Walter rises from his seat, his form as tall and broad and looking so much like an older version of Andres with less luxurious hair and a pale instead of golden skin tone. "It's good to see you," he says and sounds like he means it. "It's been too long."

"Yeah," Andres agrees softly. "It really has been. I'm sorry about that."

Walter steps around his desk and claps Andres on the shoulder. "There's no need to apologize. I'm glad you're here now." He turns his gaze to look at Bastian. "Can I offer you boys a drink? I have a nice bottle of Pinot Noir we can open."

"Yeah, that would be nice," Andres says as his mom slips in between them and wraps her son in a hug.

An hour later, Bastian is holding on tight to Andres as they make their way back downtown. They haven't really spoken much since they left Andres's parents' house. It went surprisingly well, but he's not about to push. Though their visit was short, it was emotionally charged. Even without being a member of the family, Bastian finds himself pretty exhausted. He can only imagine how Andres is feeling, but the small smiles and few genuine laughs he'd let out while there are good signs. And the best sign of all is that before they left, Andres promised to come back again soon, and they insisted that he bring Bastian back again with him.

"Do you want to stay at my place tonight?" Andres asks Bastian as they zoom down Lake Street, the "L" tracks above them, and the pylons and metal rigging that hold the transportation system up all around them, making the journey back from Oak Park into city central feel that much more single-minded. As if even the city wants the two of them to stay on a singular track to their future together.

"That'd be nice," Bastian says into Andres's ear, and from this close, he can't miss how his words have lifted Andres's cheeks higher than they already have been since they left Andres's parents' house.

"Good," he says back and brings a hand to briefly rub at Bastian's thigh. Perhaps, Bastian thinks, he isn't exhausted at all. Especially if this means they take the final step in getting their relationship back to an intensely physical level.

It's a thought that Andres makes very clear is correct the moment he parks the motorcycle. He swats playfully at Bastian's ass when Bastian dismounts. He then puts his arm around Bastian's shoulders as they walk past the door attendant and make their way to the elevator, where he pounds on the up button repeatedly with two fingers. Once inside, he kisses Bastian hungrily and a bit sloppily as the elevator doors close.

They barely break apart from their kissing for Andres to fumble mindlessly with his keys to open the door. Once the door is shut and locked behind them, Andres practically carries Bastian to the bedroom. He lifts Bastian by the waist so that only his tiptoes drag across the floor.

Once in the bedroom, Andres slows things down, and Bastian, as he toes off his shoes, briefly worries that he has once again miscalculated about what this night was going to be. His worries are very quickly stifled by the way that Andres, movements now slow and deliberate, lifts him and places him gently onto his back on the bed, then kicks his own shoes off and slots himself between Bastian's legs.

"Hi," he says as he smooths back Bastian's wind-blown and tangled curls. The look in his eyes as he takes Bastian in is ardent and sincere, like he's looking at Bastian for the first time, and Bastian has never felt more seen.

"Hi," Bastian whispers back, his eyes slightly closing as Andres works his fingers through his hair again.

Andres's lips pull into a soft smile. "So, you love me, huh?"

Bastian laughs, the question surprising him. "So fucking much," he says, his eyes going wide as he looks up at Andres, who's propped up on his elbow, looking down at Bastian while he continues to run his fingers through Bastian's hair and loosening the tangles as he goes. "I'm sorry I didn't say it out loud sooner."

"I didn't think I needed you to."

"Well, I mean it. I love you, and I'm not messing this up again."

Andres narrows his eyes at Bastian, his smile becoming devilish. "Don't make promises you can't keep, babe," he teases, but it's warm.

Bastian's mouth shoots open wide in shock, and he quickly feigns innocence. "I guess you're going to have to save me from myself every now and then."

"I guess I am," Andres says and dips his head back down, bringing their lips to meet once again, kissing Bastian like he's the only thing that matters in this world. Like he's waited to taste Bastian for a lifetime, despite the fact that they've been here before.

It's different this time. After everything, there's a new intensity to the connection between them. A new level of devotion that makes Bastian's heart sing once his clothes are removed and Andres is nestled above him, slowly and carefully pressing himself inside of Bastian, locking his eyes with him as he begins to gently rock their bodies together.

"I love you," Bastian whispers again into Andres's ear as they sink into a steady rhythm.

"I love you too," Andres says back. "I always have."

It was good. It was really good. Repeated four more times between Sunday night and Tuesday morning good. Andres even handed the reins for Graze over to Simone for the night on Monday.

"I could get used to this," Andres says as he hands Bastian another cup of coffee to enjoy before he has to leave for work.

"I can't imagine you get that much joy out of serving me coffee," Bastian says as he takes the mug.

Andres shrugs, then sits to face Bastian on the couch's opposite side with his own mug of coffee. They immediately begin tangling their feet together. "You'd be surprised," he says. "But what I meant was having an actual weekend or night off together. You know this was the first time in our relationship that one of us didn't have to run out the door to go to work for a full two days."

Bastian checks his watch. "I gotta run out the door in like fifteen minutes."

"True." Andres laughs and grabs hold of one of Bastian's socked feet with his free hand. He gives it a squeeze. "Maybe we can adjust our schedules to fit with each other's a little more."

Bastian smiles and hides it behind a sip of his coffee. It's a nice thought, but it's not really possible. Neither of them has a job that makes things like "weekends" or "date nights" an actual thing. The best either of them can really hope for right now are fake clients booked at the end of the day to free up an evening or a kitchen fire that shuts down dinner service. Neither are good options since a kitchen fire is likely to cause more work for Andres, and Bastian's boss is watching him like a hawk, still pissed about him not coming to work that one Friday.

Not wanting to crush Andres's desire for something as wonderfully mundane as being able to have a day or two off together regularly, Bastian swallows his coffee and agrees. "It really would be nice."

"I'll look into it," Andres says and gives Bastian's foot another reassuring squeeze. "Maybe we can promote Simone to GM or something."

"I'll see if I can cut a day out of my schedule or start taking one night a week off or something similar," Bastian says, knowing full well that Mitchel will never allow for such a thing. Bastian's chair is almost always full.

Even as impossible of an idea as this is, Bastian finds himself really wanting to make it happen. His mind wanders all day as he works diligently behind the chair. What would it be like to cut his schedule back? To be able to take a day off when he chooses? To not have to plan vacations six months in advance to be able to give his boss and his clients, who have no respect for his time, enough warning that he'll be missing for a week? To lounge on the couch with Andres and drink coffee without one or both of them needing to run out the door?

Before he had left for work in the morning, he had promised Andres that he'd swing by Graze for dinner and a drink, then head back to Andres's place to wait for him to come home. As he makes the walk from Salon Azure Blue in River North to Graze in the West Loop, listening to "So Alive" by Love & Rockets, he doesn't even think about his studio in Boystown and his fabled walk-in closet. It's not only a few days or a night off he'd like to have with Andres every week. He craves and wants everything he can have with him. He wants to wake beside Andres and fall asleep next to him. He wants to bump shoulders in the kitchen as they cook. He wants to share showers as frequently as they share a pot of coffee. He wants to roll around naked in the sheets with Andres whenever possible and suck him off with the view of Chicago behind him through the floor-to-ceiling windows of Andres's luxury condo.

And because Chicago seems to have a certain type of magic to it that answers its inhabitants' dreams when they stick it out and stand behind the city with its shit winters, competitive job market, toxic dating scene, and horrendous traffic, Chicago takes this moment to present Bastian with a solution. He almost trips over the sandwich board containing a For Lease sign pointing at a propped-open door beside an art gallery on the corner of Randolph and Desplains. Curious and having his mind already playing with possible solutions to his plight for a life that resembles something close to normal, he turns and steps inside. He's met with a narrow staircase, similar to the one he's already accustomed to climbing each workday, and another sign directing him to the second floor.

What he finds when he arrives up there is perfect. It's a small space, large enough to house three salon stations and chairs, a place where two shampoo bowls would fit well, an exposed brick wall that would display products nicely, and two large windows to let in natural light and fresh air. He can see it all, plain as day—himself and Laura and Marny working side by side as they have been for these last ten years. Except here, there are no hassles from a boss expecting more from them. There are no sales quotas to reach when selling products. There's no having to take the Willows of the world who have insane requests to give them hair inspired by the phoenix or overindulged nepotists and their never-ending demands. It's a simple space they can make their own—a place where they can set their schedules and take the clients that they want and not have to give sixty percent of what they bring in to a boss who's never satisfied and always wants more.

Life has changed for Bastian, and obviously Laura as well, and Marny is always on the hunt for a new adventure. The three of them have collectively outgrown Salon Azure Blue, and for their lives to take off and move in the direction that they want to go, it's become clear that it is time for them to branch out.

Before Bastian can let his brain overthink this decision for him, he pulls out his phone and texts Laura and Marny the address with directions to meet him here tomorrow morning; then he grabs a pen and signs on the dotted line of the lease application that the real estate woman is holding and says a prayer to the hair gods that after a background check, his measly savings, and semi-decent credit history is enough to get him approved.

CHAPTER 18

A ndres hooks his chin over Bastian's shoulder as Bastian finishes cleaning up the breakfast dishes.

"What time are we meeting the girls?" His voice and his breath are comforting as they tickle Bastian's ear.

"Nine," Bastian says and takes a glance at his watch. They have fifteen minutes to get there.

"Leave those." Andres gives Bastian a firm and loud kiss on the cheek. "I'll finish them when I get back."

"Are you sure?"

"Yeah, I'm sure." Andres laughs. "I can handle the dishes. *You* starting your own business is more important."

"Me *maybe* starting my own business," Bastian corrects. For as excited as he was about the prospect of this last night and how equally ecstatic Andres was for the opportunity that presented itself to Bastian, upon waking this morning, he's feeling a bit unsure.

Andres spins Bastian around in his arms, and Bastian quickly grabs a dish towel as he's being turned to dry his hands. "It's a good plan," Andres assures. "You're gonna make it work."

"That's assuming I even get the lease. There have to be a thousand people better than me that could take that space."

"And if there are, then we'll find you a different space." He pauses, grabs onto Bastian's shoulders, and regards him thoughtfully. "This is the right path for you. I can feel it."

"Then why does it feel so terrifying this morning?"

"Isn't that how you felt about us a few months ago?"

"Yeah," Bastian says through a laugh.

Andres squeezes Bastian's shoulders and then rests his forehead against Bastian's. "And look how we turned out. Pretty good, right?"

"Pretty good after I nearly destroyed it."

"But you didn't. And you won't destroy this."

Bastian chews on his bottom lip, averting his eyes from Andres's. "I know nothing about running a business."

"You know everything there is to know about how a salon should be run. And I can help you with the rest if you need it."

"You have your own business to run."

"I do," Andres admits and brings his hands to cup Bastian's cheeks, tilting his head up to face him again. "But I talked to Justin, and we're going to promote Simone to GM at Graze. And I'm going to be taking on a less hands-on role at the restaurants. I'll still be busy, but the hours will be better, and helping you isn't a chore."

"You say that now." Bastian sighs. "But I'm a lot of work."

"Not to me, you're not," Andres says softly and punctuates it with a kiss to Bastian's lips. "Now go grab your coat. We gotta go."

"It's kind of small, don't you think?" Laura asks, looking around the space.

"In comparison to Salon Azure Blue, sure," Bastian admits, trying not to be crestfallen by her initial reaction. He was hoping for something a little more enthusiastic.

"Yeah, but I'm not leaving Salon Azure Blue to go to another salon just like it," Marny says from where she's standing and looking out onto Randolph Street from the window. She turns and glances at Bastian over her shoulder. "Can I call dibs on this spot?"

"Sure," Bastian says and gives her a grateful smile. "And you can have the other window spot if you want, Laura."

Laura looks at the empty space by the other window, then back at him. "But how would this work? There's no room for us to grow. No extra space for extra chairs. Where will we put the apprentices that we train once they're done? And I don't even think there's space for a receptionist."

"It'll be tight," Bastian admits, but Marny's words keep playing on a loop in his head. "But what Marny said was right. I'm not looking to open another Salon Azure Blue. We don't need an apprentice to assist us or a front desk person to make our schedules. This is to give us freedom."

"Freedom by having us do our own shampoos?" Laura questions.

"I will do all of our shampoos if it means I never have to do another children's cut," Marny says and claps Bastian on the shoulder. "I'm in, boss."

Bastian kisses Marny on the cheek. She always has been the easiest going of all of them.

Laura turns her attention to Andres. "You've been awfully quiet. What do you think of this?"

"Honestly," he says, his hand running across the exposed brick wall. "I think it's rather brilliant. At this size, with very little overhead, the three of you could run it like a co-op. Split the rent, the cost of product, anf minimal utilities and call it a day. Everything else you make is all profit that you can put into your pockets. That's a far better deal than the forty percent of what you bring into the house you're making at Salon Twice Blue. You can cut your client load in half and still come out on top with more free time and control over your life. Sounds like a win-win to me."

"But what if our clients don't follow?" Laura asks.

"Some won't," Bastian admits. "But a lot will. We're only a few blocks away from Salon Azure Blue, and the train lines all converge in the Loop two blocks east of here, so we're easy to get to."

"And you're still within walking distance of your condo," Marny points out, making Laura tilt her head in thought.

"Besides, Laura, do you really want to deal with Mitchel after you have the baby?"

"He's already giving me the cold shoulder," she admits and reflexively brings one hand to rest on her round belly that she can no longer hide.

"You can keep working at Salon Azure Blue all the way up until you go into labor, and then when you're ready to come back to work, you can start here at your pace. No pressure. No fifty-hour workweeks. Your schedule and your wants and needs for yourself," Bastian says.

Laura's lips pull into a hopeful grin, making her glow more than she already is. "I mean, I'm basically starting over when I come back from maternity leave anyway. I may as well do it on my own terms."

"That's the spirit," Andres says, coming to stand next to Bastian and putting his arm around him.

"So you're in?" Bastian asks her.

"Yeah. I'm in."

It turns out that the most challenging part of opening your own salon isn't getting your finances in order, weeding through paperwork and getting business licenses, or planning to set up the place to make it look like the salon of your dreams. It's keeping it quiet that proves to be the hardest.

Bastian wants to scream out loud and run straight to Marny and Laura the moment he hangs up with the real estate agent calling to inform him that he has been approved with Andres as a co-signer and that the space is now his. But he can't. He already looks suspicious enough, having gone out onto the fire escape to answer the call. Running across the salon from there would be a dead giveaway that something is up.

However, with giddy, shaking fingers, he can text Andres the excellent news.

> Got approved! The space is mine!

> Congratulations, babe! I'm so excited for you! When can we get in there to start working on setting it up?

> I'm picking up the keys after work tonight. Can I stay at your place?

> Definitely, I'll cut out of work early and meet you there if you'd like.

> That would be great.

> Celebratory drinks afterward?

> Yes, please.

> *Good. I'll see you in a bit.*

Andres sends, but the three tiny dots of someone still typing keep Bastian from putting his phone away.

> *And Bastian, I'm proud of you.*

Bastian glows from the praise. It's not the first time that Andres has told him that he's proud of him. But it is the first time Bastian has ever felt like he is truly deserving of the sentiment.

> *Thank you.*

Bastian's dad holds his hand out from where he's lying on his back, installing the two new shampoo bowls Bastian purchased for the salon's backbar. "Wrench, please!"

Bastian hands him a wrench and is thankful for his dad's presence here, making it so Bastian doesn't have to hire a plumber to do the installation. He, Andres, and Marny, with a little bit of help from Justin, who mostly spent his time trying to keep Laura from climbing ladders, painting walls, and carrying heavy boxes up the stairs, have managed to get a lot of the preliminary work done, but none of them are equipped or skilled when it comes to plumbing.

"Not much longer until this place is ready," Dominic says, his voice slightly muffled from inside where he is lying. "Are you giving your two-week notice soon?"

"Two-week notice," Bastian rolls his eyes, "that's a laugh."

"It's the right thing to do, Bastian. Even if your boss isn't a good person." A wrench appears in Bastian's eyeline again. He grabs it. "Towel, please."

"It's not even about Mitchel being a bad person," Bastian says and hands his dad one of the new shampoo towels he's been folding while his dad installs the bowls. "It's more that a two-week notice doesn't really exist in this industry. From the moment I tell him I'm leaving, it's game on. He'll tell me to leave immediately, and I'll be lucky even to be able to grab all of my things."

"He can't do that," Dominic says, grunting slightly from whatever plumbing effort he's exerting underneath the sink.

"Actually, he can." Bastian sighs. "And he has. I've seen him do it to other stylists. I have to have all of my ducks in a row before I say that I'm leaving. That includes having my station fully packed, my client files copied, and my game face on as I endure him chewing me out."

"Have you told your clients at least?"

"I can't do that either," Bastian says. "I can't trust them to keep their mouths shut. And I still need more time to get everyone's color formulas and contact information so I can begin calling them *after* I leave Salon Azure Blue for the last time. This is all a very time-sensitive matter. It takes planning and organization. All of which I am horrible at."

Dominic slides out from under the shampoo bowls and begins wiping his hands with the towel Bastian had handed him. "You look pretty organized to me," he says, his tone uncommonly gentle. He claps Bastian on the shoulder. "It's good to see you taking some control over your life."

"Thanks, Dad," Bastian says with another roll of his eyes that he keeps hidden from his father by looking down at the folded towels in his lap.

Dominic throws the towel over his shoulder and runs the water in both of the bowls. "All set," he says with a clap of his hands. "Is there anything else I can do around here?"

Bastian stops his folding and looks around. The place is starting to really come together. The mirrors—all propped up waiting to be hung in their respective spots—are large with a deep ebony frame that will stand out nicely against the warm, brown, exposed bricks of the walls they'll hang on. The station and shampoo cabinets, which are partially put together, are custom-made pieces that Andres and Justin commissioned from the guy who made the bar and barstools at Graze. They were admittedly expensive and way out of Bastian's budget, but Andres was right. They do make the place feel warm and cozy and add a bit more charm than some basic storage cabinets he could've found at IKEA, though that is where he purchased the shelving for the retail products. Costs did need to be cut somewhere. There's still plenty of work to be done, but once the rest of the products arrive—including the color line that they will be working with—and the stylist chairs, they, in theory, will be ready to open the doors.

"I think we're pretty good," Bastian says. "And thank you for doing this. I know this isn't exactly how you'd like to spend your Sunday."

"It's no problem. Bears are on a by-week anyway." He pauses and shuts the water off in the shampoo bowls, then wipes them dry with the towel he had used to dry his hands before he hands that towel back to Bastian. "You want to come back to the house for dinner? Your mom is making a lasagna."

"I wish I could," Bastian says as he tosses the towel into the salon laundry bag that he'll take home to wash. "I need to go up to Boystown and check on my apartment, do some laundry, then meet Andres back at his place when he's done for the night."

"I thought Andres was done with the late nights and week-ends?"

"He is," Bastian says. "Or, at least, he will be. He's still training his replacement."

"The two of you are happy?"

"Of course." Bastian shrugs. "I thought that was obvious."

"And isn't your lease up on your apartment soon, too?" Dominic asks.

"Yeah ..." Bastian says slowly. His father's sudden insightfulness is a little off-putting. He tries not to dwell on it. They've never really been the type of father and son to discuss each other's lives in detail. That's more something Bastian engages in with his mother. "And my landlord notified me last week that he's raising the rent. For some reason, he thinks I'm crazy enough to spend eighteen hundred dollars a month on that tiny place."

"You've been crazy enough to spend sixteen hundred dollars a month for all these years."

"It does have a nice closet," Bastian says, giving the retort he's grown accustomed to whenever anyone has anything bad to say about his apartment.

"Seems silly to pay rent all the way up there for just a closet."

"It's not *just* the closet. I love Boystown," Bastian says, though that doesn't necessarily ring true. Boystown is vibrant, and he has found unquestioned acceptance and community there for the last ten years, but he's finding himself feeling restless whenever he's at his place instead of with Andres at his. He has to admit that while Boystown is where he came into his own, Andres is where he feels the most at home and at ease with himself. Perhaps amidst all this change, he's outgrown Boystown, and it's time to move onto someplace else. It might be time to move in with Andres and live out those regular domestic desires he's been having permanently.

The only problem is, he can't simply say, "Hey, Andres, I know things have been crazy these past six months and we were together, and then we were not together, and we're both in a place of great change right now, but let me add another wrinkle and move into your space that you have laid out to suit all of your needs because my rent is being raised to an uncomfortable level and I miss you on the nights I spend away from you, and I miss you even more in the mornings, and I'm freaking out right now, even though it looks like I'm fine. I can give you unlimited blowjobs in lieu of rent if that works." In theory, that last part should be enough to make all of this work, except Andres really isn't someone who can be bought with sexual favors.

"You know, Bastian," Dominic says, breaking him of his thoughts about Boystown. "You and I aren't all that dissimilar."

"How so?" Bastian asks, for never, outside of sharing the same nose, has Bastian ever considered his father and him to be the same.

"I don't know if your mother ever told you, but I almost lost her once."

"Like what? In a mall or something?" Bastian jokes.

"No," Dominic says with a laugh, "though that is an option with her." He claps Bastian on the shoulder again and looks out the window onto Randolph Street. "I almost didn't ask your mother to marry me," he says solemnly. "She wanted it. Insisted on it. But for some reason, I couldn't believe that a woman like your mother could ever possibly be interested in a guy like me."

"That's ridiculous," Bastian says, even though he definitely knows the feeling. But to imagine his father experiencing the same doubt that Bastian did seems both absurd and also strangely right.

"It was ridiculous," Dominic agrees. "But I didn't realize it until after I almost let her go."

"But why would you do that?"

"I thought she could do better." He pauses, and Bastian looks at his profile in time to see a smile spread across his lips. "I still think that. Your mother deserves the world, and I knew then that there was no way I could provide that for her."

"But she insisted that you could," Bastian says, memories of his mother assuring his father that everything was going to be alright when he lost his job all those years ago. That they'd manage. That the love they had was enough. And she was right. They did manage, even when things were tight while Bastian's dad started over.

"And I did. For the most part," he says. "Maybe not in the way that I had expected, but in a way that worked for us."

"Yeah." Bastian nods his head, understanding dawning over him. Like Bastian, his father had to learn the lesson that in order to live the life you want, you have to stop dwelling on what you don't have. That you can't let your feelings of inadequacy be in control. That you have to accept the fact that the right person loves and chooses you for you and not what you can give them materially.

"Earth to Bastian," Dominic says, breaking Bastian's train of thought.

Bastian jolts. "Sorry. What were you saying?"

"I was saying I was gonna get going."

"Right. Of course." He takes a breath, turns to face his father, and extends his hand. "Thank you for helping with this."

"Not a problem, Bastian." He grabs Bastian's hand, shocking Bastian by not shaking it but pulling him into a hug instead. "I'll come out next Sunday as well to help you again. Maybe even bring your mother by. She's so proud of you, you know?" he asks with two hard thumps onto Bastian's back. The thumps say the quiet part of that last statement for him; he is proud of Bastian as well.

Bastian swallows thickly. "Yeah, that'd be nice."

The rest of the week goes smoothly. Well, as smoothly as it can go for Bastian while working ten-hour days at Salon Azure Blue, followed by another few hours spent organizing, cleaning, and polishing up his salon each night, preparing it to open in two weeks on November first, a little before Laura is due and well enough before Thanksgiving. He could open the place sooner if he forgoes sleeping, but his body clock refuses to let that happen. And as he crawls into Andres's bed after a Friday night spent checking in and stocking the backroom supply shelves with the salon's first color order, he feels like he could sleep for a year.

"This is new," Andres murmurs as he rolls onto his back and lays Bastian's head down on his chest.

"What's new?" Bastian asks as he rests his head and closes his eyes.

Andres sleepily runs a hand up and down Bastian's back. "Me already in bed, and you crawling in after a late night at work."

Bastian squeezes Andres a little tighter around his middle. "Yeah, sorry about that," he says around a yawn. "I was too tired to try and make it all the way back up north. I hope you don't mind. I should've texted you earlier."

"Bastian," Andres says seriously. "Of course, I don't mind. I'm always happy to be woken up by you. In fact ... I've been thinking."

"Yeah, what about?"

"I was thinking that you should move in here if you wanted."

Bastian's heart rate picks up. It's exactly what he wants, but he can't help making sure that Andres means it. That this is something he truly wants as well. He figures it's best to list the reasons why to help his case. "I mean, with the new salon only a few blocks away, it makes sense logistically. And we spend most nights together anyway, and it would be nice not to have to schlep our stuff back and forth. And with my rent going up, financially, it would be a big help—"

"You just can't say yes, can you?" Andres interrupts with a sleepy laugh but wraps both arms around Bastian, holding him tighter.

Bastian cranes his neck, lifting his head away from Andres's chest to scold him for his teasing, but all he's met with is a look of complete fondness that he feels from his head to his toes and everything in between. "Yes, Andres," he finally says. "I'd love to move in with you."

CHAPTER 19

"Good morning, Oliver! I brought breakfast for you!" Bastian greets as he stops at the front desk and places a bribe—an iced coffee with a triple chocolate and cherry donut from Brew—down onto the counter. It's a big day for Bastian, and he needs all the help he can get.

Oliver eyes the treats, then raises an eyebrow at Bastian, looking at him with skepticism. "Good morning, Bastian. What is it that you need?"

Bastian puts on his sweetest, most innocent-looking face. "Well, since you did ask, I do have a small favor you could do for me."

"Okay ..." Oliver says slowly. "You don't need me to book Martha Stewart with you again, do you?"

"Oh, no. Don't you worry about that. Martha is never coming back here."

"Doubt," Oliver says, with a set jaw and one raised eyebrow. "What is it that you want, and am I going to get fired for doing it?"

Bastian brings a hand to his chest. "After bringing you this lovely breakfast, you don't trust me?"

"It's exactly because of this lovely breakfast that I don't trust you." He grabs the coffee and takes a sip. "Now out with it."

Bastian drops the act. "Fine. I need a printout of all my clients and their contact information. Marny's too, and Laura's if you could."

"You're fucking kidding me, right?"

"No."

"When are you planning on telling Mitchel you're quitting?"

"Today, after my last client."

"By phone call?"

"It's not like he's gonna show up to work today. It's Saturday," Bastian says, causing Oliver to laugh. There's more chance that Mitchel is likely to wake up in a different country after a bender than make an appearance at the salon on a Saturday. It's why Bastian picked this day to tell him.

"Alright," Oliver says, then takes another sip of his coffee and starts typing on his keyboard. Within a few seconds, there's the telltale whirring of the printer cycling through all of the requested information. He hands Bastian the stack of papers but holds onto them and gives Bastian a warm but sad smile. "You're a pain in the ass, Bastian. But I'm going to miss you."

"I'm gonna miss you too, buddy," Bastian says, pulling the papers from Oliver's hand, then playfully ruffling his short-cropped hair.

Quitting his job goes exactly how Bastian expects it to. There's yelling, berating, threats to sue him, then begging, groveling, and then more threats to sue him. Marny's phone call goes similarly, and Laura's call, in a surprise twist, isn't even answered. She gets to leave Mitchel a voicemail. But it doesn't matter. They've quit, and on Tuesday, they will open the doors to Studio Collective together for the first time. It's exciting, and the three of them want to celebrate.

"What's the plan tonight?" Marny asks as she closes up the box containing everything that was in her station.

"We drink!" Bastian proclaims, causing Laura to tap her foot and cross her arms over her belly beside him. He shrugs, then amends, "Me and you drink," he gestures back and forth between him and Marny, then points at Laura with his thumb, "she gets apple juice."

"Thanks," Laura says. "That sounds really celebratory."

Bastian puts his arm around her. "We can celebrate again once you pop."

"I'm gonna hold you to that." She laughs and kisses him on the cheek. "Come on. Justin said he'd be outside waiting for us with his car."

"Oh, thank God! I did not want to have to carry this home," Marny says and picks her box up off the station counter.

"I can carry it for you," Lizzie's dreamy voice says as she steps into their workroom with Bethany right behind her. Both of their eyes are sad and watery, and though technically they were both promoted today, Bastian knows how they feel. He remembers clearly what it was like when his first mentor left Salon Azure Blue ten years ago. There's a special bond between assistant and stylist. A shared camaraderie and sense of *we survived this shit together*. But he did his job well, as did Laura and Marny. These two young women are ready for whatever the salon world throws at them next.

Marny puts her box down and immediately envelopes Lizzie into a hug, then grabs Bethany to join them as well. "I'm gonna miss you two," she says. "Best assistants I've had yet."

"Best assistants *we've* had yet," Bastian amends, joining the hug. "I'd take you both with us if we could. But this is your place now."

"Thank you for everything," Laura says, trying to join the hug around her baby bump. They end up having to put her in the middle, and she's a big mess of tears. Truthfully, they all are for myriad reasons, but all of them are happy just the same.

After bidding the rest of the salon farewell and getting one last eyeroll from Oliver, Bastian walks outside with a new spring to his step. It's a beautiful day for late October. And if they lived anywhere other than Chicago, where the weather is never predictable, he'd be surprised by the warmth that the sun blessed the city with today. It feels like a sign that they have made the right choice, that they are on the right path, and that their lives are starting anew.

"Get in! We're going celebrating," Justin says from the rolled-down window of his Range Rover. He pops the back hatch, and Bastian places his box of belongings inside, then helps Laura and Marny do the same.

"Where are we going?" Laura asks as she gets into the front seat.

"To a surprise," Justin says with a waggle of his eyebrows.

Laura turns in the front seat to look at Bastian. "Did you know about this?"

Bastian, just as surprised as she is, shakes his head no. He catches Justin's eyes in the rearview mirror. "Where's Andres?"

"He's meeting us there."

"And where is *there*?" Marny asks.

"Enough with the questions," Justin says as he puts the Range Rover into gear. "Trust us. We know what we're doing."

What they are doing becomes apparent relatively quickly when they pull up to Tribune Tower and stop in front of the valet.

"Justin!" Laura exclaims, understanding in her voice. "This was supposed to be our wedding day."

"It was," Justin confirms. "And I've never been so glad not to get a deposit back in my life."

"Did you usurp my big day by throwing yourself another wedding?" Bastian asks.

"No, you ass," Justin chides from the front seat. "Andres and I are throwing *you* a party! All of you, of course, but definitely you, Bastian. This new salon was your doing."

"Thanks, Justin," Bastian says, feeling truly touched and clapping Justin on the shoulder from the back seat before he gets out of the vehicle.

"You're welcome," Justin says, opening his door. "Now, let's get inside. Andres is waiting."

"Is it only Andres up there?" Laura asks, reaching for the door handle.

"No, it's not *only* Andres. How dumb do I look?"

"Honestly, you look pretty dumb," Marny teases him as she steps out of the car.

"Hey! That's my husband you're talking about!" Laura exclaims. "Also, I wish I'd dressed better."

"You look perfect," Justin says, helping her out of the car. She really does look beautiful in her long black maxi dress and faux-sleeved shawl.

Andres presenting Bastian with a brand-new Balmain blazer this morning for today makes a lot more sense. He said it was for luck, but Bastian should've known better. He's just relieved he'd had the good sense to hang it in the salon's coat closet instead of wearing it all day and risking getting color or hair clippings on it.

"You're biased," Laura says to Justin, then takes a deep breath and stills herself, rubbing at her belly.

"You okay?" Justin asks.

"I'm fine." Laura waves him off. "It was only a kick. This kid is running out of room."

"Yeah, they are," Bastian teases and strides past them to the front door, which is being held open for them by the doorman.

"Remind me again why I'm following you to this salon?" Laura asks from behind him.

"Because you love me, and I'm your work husband, and you wouldn't have it any other way."

"And because he finds and reads the best monster porn out there," Marny adds, and Bastian holds up his hand for a high five as they walk. She hits it.

"That's why you're my favorite employee," Bastian says at the crack of their hands.

"We haven't even opened up the doors, and there's already toxicity," Laura says, then struggles to wrap her arms around Bastian as the elevator doors close before it carries them up to the top floor.

The sight they are met with when the doors open at the top is breathtaking. The sun is beginning to go down, and it's lighting the sky in a beautiful array of pinks and oranges that blend nicely with the soft golden lights and rich fall colors that have been used to decorate the inner space from the linens to the small bouquets on the tables that the guests are mingling around. The balcony outside has an unobstructed view amongst the vast ornate pillars, and Bastian can see Andres standing out there talking with Bastian's mom and dad, both of whom are dressed in their best "formal" ensembles. His mom is in a simple black dress that she's worn for every wedding and black-tie event she's been invited to for the last decade, and his father his usual dark grey suit and likely light blue tie that he says he wears because it matches Bastian's mother's eyes. He's not wrong.

"Go say hi to your man out there," Justin says, giving Bastian a nudge with his shoulder.

Bastian looks at Justin quizzically.

"He doesn't bite," Justin's expression turns thoughtful, "unless you're into that sort of thing. Which, if you are, don't tell me. You know what, forget I was talking. Get your ass out there."

"Thanks, that wasn't foreboding at all," Bastian says, his stomach in knots.

Justin claps Bastian a tad too harshly on the shoulder and nudges him forward again as he steps away from him to move towards Laura and Marny and says, "I'm gonna get a drink. Laura, you want a mocktail?" He offers an arm to her that she takes, then turns and offers Marny his other arm. "How about you, Marny?"

"Yes, please! Full booze for me, though," Marny says, hooking her elbow inside of his and giving Bastian an excited smile as they walk away towards the bar.

Bastian takes a deep breath and has a look around. It's not a large party, but the people here are of some significance to Bastian. He can see Walter and Juanita talking to Justin's parents under the gothic archways, all of whom look very much like the aristocrats that they are—though Justin's parents look far more jovial and less haunted. That being said, they both wave kindly at Bastian when he walks past, even offering him smiles that somehow both carry the ghost of Julian on them. Laura's parents are also here, and if Marny wasn't originally from Michigan, it's a safe bet hers would've been as well. The rest of the guests are just above acquaintances; they'd be friends if Bastian had more time to build a solid relationship with them. Like Simone and Padma and Alex—thankfully no Haley—but a few other familiars from the restaurants, particularly ones who sit in Bastian's chair on occasion. It's intimate and guaranteed to be a drama-free evening, assuming that Andres isn't waiting on the terrace so he can drop some sort of a bomb onto Bastian's day that will have one or both of them fleeing this place. But the little shy smile that is generally reserved only for private moments between Bastian and Andres at home flits across Andres's lips when he catches sight of Bastian through the windows. He discreetly waves him over, and Bastian goes willingly, being drawn to Andres just as he was on that first day of school twenty-five years earlier.

"There he is," Andres says when Bastian steps through the glass doors onto the terrace, prompting Bastian's parents to look at him. "The guest of honor."

"You can't be talking about me," Bastian says, trying to play humble as he smooths down his blazer. He is feeling rather pleased with himself. This has been a big day, and the next three are going to be as significant. Not only is he opening the salon on Tuesday, but he's moving what's left of his stuff that he's keeping into Andres's place tomorrow and handing over his apartment keys to the new renter on Monday. It's a series of significant events that the Bastian of spring earlier this year would've been wholly freaked out about, but with Andres by his side, Bastian feels like he can conquer anything.

"Sorry, Bastian," Andres says and takes his hand. "But this is definitely about you."

"Hello, honey," Annemarie says and gives him a kiss on the cheek in greeting. Her eyes are a bit puffy as if she's already been crying.

"It's only a salon, Mom," Bastian says as he kisses her back. "There's no need to get so emotional."

"I know, Sebastian," she says, her voice catching. She wraps him awkwardly in her arms to hug him and proceeds to get even more emotional.

Dominic places an arm around her shoulder and guides her away from him. "Come on, dear," he says. "Let's give these boys a moment and grab something to eat."

She quickly wipes at her eyes and gives Bastian and then Andres each a kiss on the cheek.

Bastian curiously watches them walk away. "What the hell was that about?" he says, his eyes still on his parents stepping through the terrace doors.

"She's simply excited for you, is all," Andres says from beside Bastian, squeezing his hand.

"It's a small, three-chair salon. By the way she's blubbering, you'd think I was getting married or something."

"About that..." Andres says and gently spins Bastian around by grabbing onto his other hand as well. The look in Andres' eyes is nothing but sincere.

Bastian's own eyes open wide, and his breath hitches on the inhale. "Are you proposing to me? In front of all our family and friends?"

"Well, technically, yes. But the only ones who know what I'm doing right now are our parents and Justin. So there's still plenty of room for you to say no," Andres assures and squeezes both Bastian's hands. "But since I am as sure about you today as I was when I first met you when we were five, I'm confidently standing here asking you, Bastian Russo, to marry me?"

"You wanted to marry me when we were five?" Bastian teases, but heat is rising in his cheeks and his eyes are beginning to blur. He's been in love with Andres for ages. It's a shame it took him until this year to realize it.

"Maybe not marry," Andres admits. "But I did know when I first saw you that I wanted to be your friend."

"And now you want to be my husband?"

"I do." Andres shakes his head and laughs. "What do you say? Do you want to marry me up here on this terrace in front of all our family and friends?"

"I don't know." Bastian thinks back to when this all started in spring. "My mom warned me about boys like you."

"Lies, your mother loves me."

"Then it must have been my dad that said boys like you were trouble."

"Nope, not him either. I actually think he prefers me."

"Okay, you might be right about that." Bastian laughs, a tear sneaking down his cheek that Andres wipes away for him. "Then it must have been my girlfriends."

"For goodness sake, Bastian!" Laura's voice calls from somewhere behind him. "Say yes!"

"Shut it, you!" he yells over his shoulder.

Andres starts laughing harder and lets go of Bastian's hands to slide them up his body and cradle Bastian's face between his palms, tilting his head to look directly at him. "You just can't say yes, can you?"

"Of course I can," Bastian says, now laughing with Andres and not even caring that he has an audience. "What was the question again?"

"The question was, Bastian Russo, will you marry me?"

"Yes, Andres Wood. I will marry you," Bastian says around his joyous laughter, and Andres's lips colliding with his, kissing him like he is the only thing that matters. And right now, after all they've been through, not only this year but in all the years leading up to this moment, Bastian finally believes it to be true.

CHAPTER 20

Waking the next day with a brand new, gold Cartier band on his finger, Bastian knows exactly two things. One, Andres gave him that ring after he said yes to his proposal. And two, he's never been happier in his entire life.

It would be cliché for him to say that his happiness was found in a relationship, and really, that doesn't do Andres any justice. Andres didn't show up on some white horse and make Bastian's problems disappear simply by existing. He showed up on a motorcycle and proved to Bastian with his actions that Bastian was someone worth making space in his life for. He showed him how to take charge and grab hold of his own fate. He taught him how to breathe and trust someone with his heart. And jumping to conclusions was not an Olympic sport for him to be the best at.

He can't help but laugh at himself. It's meant to be a silent laugh, but it bubbles up through him and makes its way out, pulling his lips into the broadest smile he's worn yet as the sun shines down on them through the bay window of Bastian's Boystown apartment.

"What's so funny?" Andres sleepily asks from behind him. He pulls Bastian in even closer, holding his back flush to his chest.

"Just ... me ..." Bastian says through his laughter, cheeks aching and eyes getting a bit watery.

"You are quite funny," Andres agrees. "Care to fill me in on the joke?"

"Yeah, I'm the joke."

Andres playfully spanks the right side of Bastian's ass. "Don't call my fiancé a joke."

"Well, you have to admit at least that your fiancé is an idiot."

Andres playfully spanks him again. "And don't call my fiancé an idiot."

"Fine." Bastian huffs. "What can I call him?"

With a kiss placed across Bastian's shoulders for each point he makes, Andres lays it out for him. "You can call yourself intelligent, resourceful, charming, handsome, mischievous, and the love of my life."

Bastian's lips pull into a playful smirk. "You forgot humble."

"Did I?" Andres teases and spins Bastian around in his arms. He grabs Bastian's left hand and places a lingering kiss on the knuckle above his ring finger, letting his eyes lock on Bastian's and stilling him for a moment before Bastian begins laughing again. "Alright, what's so funny now?"

"It's us. This. If someone had told me years ago that this was where we would be, I'd never have believed them, and yet, it makes so much sense. How could I not see it? And why did I wait so long to grab what's been in front of me this entire time?"

"I'll argue that you grabbed it at the right time," Andres says thoughtfully.

"You confessed to me that you've loved me the whole time. You can't tell me you never wished I would get my head out of my ass."

"Oh, I wished that constantly, and I fully expect to continue to wish that regularly. Us spending the rest of our lives together isn't going to change how stubborn you can be."

"Hey," Bastian says, his lips turning down.

"Don't pout," Andres lightly scolds while giving Bastian's ass another playful swat. All these light spanks are starting to make Bastian's dick stir. "I love how stubborn you can be. You stick to your guns. That's admirable."

"Fine," Bastian says, still pouting, but now it's more for show. After all, he is getting quite excited, and his cock is hardening where it is situated beside Andres's.

Andres reaches around his waist and pulls him firmly against his body, a smirk on his face. "Did I say brat when I made your list?"

"No, I believe you left that one off, just like you did: humble," Bastian points out.

"Well, excuse me, my love. I surely meant to say brat."

"And humble?"

Andres's lips pull into a smile, and now it's his turn to laugh uncontrollably. "Yes, and humble. You are ... easily ... the most humble man in existence."

"Are you saying there's a woman more humble than me?"

"Oh, for fuck's sake." Andres laughs out loud. "You are *the* most humble, lovable person to ever walk the earth, and I am so lucky and honored to call you mine."

"Much better," Bastian says, his lips pulling out of their pout and into a mischievous smile as he slides his hand down between them. "What do you think, fiancé; should we celebrate with one more goodbye Boystown fuck in this apartment?"

"I'm way ahead of you, Bastian," he says and rolls Bastian onto his back, slotting himself between Bastian's parted legs and dipping his head down to kiss him.

And Bastian has never been more in love.

Bastian hands both sets of apartment keys to a young man who doesn't look a day over twenty. How he's going to afford this place, Bastian doesn't know. But he can tell by the look in his eyes that he is the perfect resident for it. He looks curious and excited, and given his slight accent, Bastian guesses he fled to Chicago from Wisconsin as soon as he could. He needs Boystown to help mold him into who he's meant to be, much like Bastian did all those years ago. To give him the confidence to grow and thrive and be comfortable in his own skin. To Bastian, handing these keys over feels like a rite of passage, the next step in his expanding life.

"How long did you live here?"

"Five years," Bastian says. "The best apartment I ever had."

"It's perfect. Why on earth would you leave it?"

A satisfied smile spreads across Bastian's lips. "I've simply out-grown it."

"Lucky me then."

"Lucky you indeed," Bastian says. He takes a moment to look around the tiny space and take one final glance at his old life that he's leaving behind. He'll never forget living in this apartment, this neighborhood, and adding his heartbreak and wisdom to the closet wall. He'll cherish his days spent here and look back at them fondly. Holding out his right hand to the new renter, he gives a bit of unsolicited advice as they shake hands and say goodbye. "Remember, in Boystown, everything you read on a closet wall is true."

The young man looks at him quizzically.

"Well, I'm off," Bastian says, letting go of his hand. He could give the new tenant more advice, but then again, part of living in Boystown is learning the lessons it has to offer you on your own. "My fiancé and I left you a bottle of housewarming champagne in the fridge and my old wine glasses in the cupboard. Good luck to you. This is a hell of a place to live."

"Thanks. You too."

Bastian spins on his heel and heads for the door, giving it all one last wistful look before he exits for the last time and walks to the Red Line.

Andres had offered to drive Bastian back and forth today, but handing over the keys and taking this final step into his new life felt like something Bastian needed to do on his own. Besides, the wind blowing in off the lake right now, carrying with it the first vestiges of another Chicago winter, is far too harsh for a ride on the back of a motorcycle. Andres will need to put it away for the coming months and go back to carting Bastian around in his BMW instead.

Once on the train to get to Studio Collective for opening day, he checks the time and answers messages from clients looking to book appointments with him. It's exciting to make his own schedule, choose when he wants to come home, and pick who's worth staying late to squeeze in.

The train stops at the platform at State and Lake Street, and Bastian steps off it to walk the rest of the way to the salon. Bastian's week is almost completely booked at work, but he's cut his hours back significantly to make space for his and Andres's life together. He no longer needs to work the constant hustle and daily grind that was beginning to burn him out. He's done the math. The new arrangement he's working under as his own boss has him making more money with less effort. He should have done this years ago.

Yet, like living in Boystown, working at Salon Azure Blue also served its purpose. It's where he honed his craft, built his clientele, and made a name for himself as a desired and sought-after stylist in Chicago. Studio Collective wouldn't be possible without Salon Azure Blue, even with its constant headaches. And for that, he will always be grateful.

"Good morning, boss," Marny says from where she is leaning against the building's brick facade at the salon door.

"I'm not your boss, and you could've let yourself in. You have keys." Bastian laughs. Sure, it's solely his name on the lease, but he, Marny, and Laura—once she decides to return from maternity leave—are all in this together.

"Maybe so." Marny shrugs and uses her foot to press herself away from the building. "But I like how you get embarrassed when I call you boss."

"I do not get embarrassed," Bastian denies as the telltale sign of heat creeping into his cheeks.

"Sure you don't," she says and presses a finger to his cheek as he holds the door open for her. "Besides, it didn't feel right to open the doors without you."

Sighing, he follows her up the stairs, then unlocks the second door leading into the salon itself. He flicks on all the lights and takes it all in, a serene smile playing across his lips at the tranquility he feels upon entering.

Pulling his phone out of his back pocket, he checks the time. His first client should be arriving soon. He opens Spotify and hits play on The Cure's album *Wish*, letting the beginning riff of the song "Open" fill the space to set the tone.

"Going back to your goth roots for the day, I see," Marny teases him as she sets up her station.

"I never left my goth roots. I just bought better clothes," Bastian says, catching her eyes through the mirrors with one eyebrow smartly raised.

She lets out a loud guffaw and says, "Touché," then returns to setting up for her day. "It's reminding me of late nights spent dancing at Neo."

"More like early mornings. Stepping out their doors with the sun coming up." Bastian sighs in remembrance of the legendary late-night hot spot. "Chicago will never be the same without that place." He pulls out his shears and places them down onto his station, then grabs a cutting cape out of the shampoo cabinets to use for his first client. He's almost ready when he hears the sound of footsteps climbing the stairs leading up to the salon. Turning, he sees Andres as he's walking through the door.

"How'd it go handing over the keys?" Andres asks and places a quick kiss on Bastian's lips.

"It went well," Bastian says and unfolds the cutting cape. He gestures for Andres to sit in his chair.

"You're not sad at all?"

"God, no." Bastian laughs. "It was high time for me to move out of that place."

"Plus, having a long-distance engagement isn't optimal."

"Our engagement likely wouldn't have survived regular commutes on the Red Line."

"Definitely not," Andres agrees, looking faux-serious. "Besides, I quite like our new arrangement."

"As do I," Bastian says and steps behind his chair. He pulls Andres's hair out of the knot, securing it to the back of his head, and begins running his fingers through the strands. Catching Andres's eyes in the mirror, he smiles serenely and asks, "Tell me, what do you want to do with your hair today?"

The End

Acknowledgements

The logical place to start is with my publishers who took a chance on an unknown, un-tested, and wholly inexperienced first-time author who has no idea where commas or apostrophes go. Alex and Tina at Rising Action Publishing, thank you for believing in me and this book and helping to bring Bastian and Andres to the rest of the world. I'm so honored to have found a home with the both of you and I can't wait to see where we go together. Somedays, it's still hard to believe this entire process was put into motion when Alex commented on my pinned tweet, saying this book sounded right up her alley.

The team at Rising Action made this dream come true, but to RJ and Sarah, without the two of you, this dream would have never been dreamt in the first place. Thank you for the endless encouragement and veracious reading of my roughest of drafts from start to finish.

Thank you to my beta readers and critique partners! Your binge reads of this book, sometimes in one sitting, helped give me the confidence I needed to push through the query process. Jess, I kept a copy of this manuscript in my docs that is covered in your emoji reactions as a trophy. It's modern art and Bastian would visit it at the Art Institute if he could.

Speaking of art, thank you to Lucy at Cover Ever After for bringing the boys to life with the cover! You nailed it and I'm still in awe every time I hold my book in my hands. I can't wait to work with you again.

A very special thanks needs to go to my boys RJ, Jacob, and Bradley. I feel like between the three of you, I've gotten an exclusive education and sneak peek that not everyone is privy to on the inner workings of being a gay man. Your honesty and openness with me about your lives is greatly appreciated. I hope this book has done your experience justice in the way I set out for it to from the start. I'm proud of it, almost as much as I'm proud of the three of you.

Now, this is a long one, so buckle in like you're stepping on the salon floor for a ten-hour shift with nothing but lion's mane heads of hair crammed into a day with no lunch. I dedicated this book to everyone who's ever worked a day behind the chair, but there are a few of you who get an extra honorable mention. To Laura, Crystal, Stephanie, and Courtney. Ashley, Angela, Tiffany, and Lesly. Natalie, Megan, Taylor, and Adrian. Lauren, Katherine, Jennifer, and Ivy. Kara, "Quinn", Gabriel and Timea. Matt, Erin, Kate, and Daniel. I couldn't ask for a better team to tackle high-end salon life with. To Becky, Kyle, Trent, Rasheeda, Alex, and Cory, for holding down the front desk. And to David and Jason for bringing us all together. To Jaci, Jessica, and, lastly, to Karen for providing me with a calm and quiet space to close out my career when the time was right for me to leave it all behind. Pieces of all of you are scattered throughout this entire book. I hope you felt seen as you read it. I hope you yelled out at least once, "OMG! THAT IS ME!" Or, "Yep. I know that mood."

There's magic in the air within a hair salon. While that magic is often visible in what we produce for our clients and the miracles we work on their hair, the true magic is in what binds us all together. We are creative, hardworking, dedicated, resilient, and the funniest people I know. And I'm not just saying that so you all continue to give me free haircuts and discounts on products. I'm saying it because I need you to tell your clients to purchase my book. ;)

Thank you to my mom and dad for being thrilled when I told you the news I was being published. Even after I had spent the previous two years telling you I was up to absolutely nothing. You took it in stride. Thanks to my sister and brother for not batting an eye as I change course yet again. It has to be exhausting watching your little sister repeatedly throw caution and convention to the wind, refusing to do anything the way she's supposed to.

To my friends, thank you to all of you for being nothing but encouraging and for shaking your heads and smiling at me, simply saying, "Of course you did," when I told you I wrote a book and that someone wants to publish it.

And finally, to my love, my partner, my other half. Without you, none of this would be possible. You've always encouraged and supported me whenever I have a new idea, and not once have you tried to tamp down my lofty and sometimes impossible dreams. Wherever this leads, it's for both of us because it was a team effort. Thank you for everything, but most of all, thank you for never asking to read the book.

About the Author

KC Carmichael is an American author of romantic comedies. She is an ex-hairstylist who spent her time behind the chair not only styling her clients' hair but also listening to their stories and sharing her observations about the beauty and hilarity of life and love. She lives in Chicago, where she holds two controversial opinions about her beloved city: winter is the superior season, and the actual Chicago-style pizza is pan pizza cut into squares for easy sharing.

Boystown Heartbreakers is her debut novel. Stay tuned for her forthcoming three-book series being released in winter 2025.